RED
★
MISTRESS

OTHER BOOKS BY ELIZABETH BLACKWELL

While Beauty Slept

In the Shadow of Lakecrest

On a Cold Dark Sea

RED ★ MISTRESS

A Novel

ELIZABETH BLACKWELL

LAKE UNION
PUBLISHING

Published by Lake Union Publishing, Seattle

www.apub.com

Amazon, the Amazon logo, and Lake Union Publishing are trademarks of Amazon.com, Inc., or its affiliates.

ISBN-13: 9781542006514
ISBN-10: 1542006511

Cover design by Shasti O'Leary Soudant

Printed in the United States of America

To Mike Bailey,
friend and comrade

London Evening Standard
May 18, 1938

Mysterious Death in Maida Vale

A woman was struck and killed by an automobile on Tetchly Road, W9, late yesterday evening. She has been identified as Marie Duvall of Toulouse, France, age 35. While there were no witnesses to the incident, residents reported hearing the sound of an impact at approximately 9:45 p.m. Officials at the French embassy are assisting the police in their inquiries. Anyone who is acquainted with Miss Duvall or who witnessed a vehicle driving recklessly on the evening in question is asked to contact the Westminster police station.

Mrs. George Weatherby, who discovered the victim and alerted the authorities, said she was shocked such a tragedy occurred in her quiet neighborhood. "Young people today drive far too fast, with no care for anyone else," she said. "You can't cross the street without being afraid for your life."

RUSSIA

1914

I've had many faces, many names. I've died and been born again. In prison, I was reduced to a number. But I began life as Nadia Shulkina, a name I was once proud of. A name that led to my death.

On every family tree, there are sturdy central branches and scrawny offshoots. The Shulkins were a grand old family—rich and well connected—but even as a girl, I knew that my brother and I hovered at the bottom of the hierarchy. Our father was the younger son of a younger son who inherited a midsized house in Saint Petersburg and a modest country estate, Priyalko, that was a fraction of his cousins' landholdings. Because we were surrounded by those who had more, our own position felt far from privileged. Papa—Count Shulkin to the world—was all his title implied: proud of his lineage, politically conservative, and rarely seen in public without the medals he'd earned for loyal service to the tsar. Beneath the pompous exterior, though, he was kindhearted and generous, always putting in a good word for friends or loaning them money. He had a similarly good-natured relationship with our staff, or so I thought. Did our servants secretly sneer at him behind his back? One of the revolution's many cruelties is the way it has corrupted my own past, tingeing even happy memories with retroactive doubt.

My father and mother were comically mismatched, a fact they both acknowledged with resigned acceptance. Mama's grandfather was a French wine exporter who married into an aristocratic but bankrupt Russian family; his son, Mama's father, was a businessman at ease in Paris as much as Saint Petersburg, and his children were raised accordingly. Mama played Debussy nocturnes on the piano, made sure her cooks produced flawless petits fours for her afternoon gatherings, was a loyal patron of the ballet, and hired a French nurse when my older brother, Vasily, was born. Mama often told us she had no tolerance for crying babies and only began spending time with us when we were able to talk. In French, of course.

Mama may not have been maternal in the traditional sense, but I didn't care. To me, she was something far better: a real-life romantic heroine. Artistic and emotional, with downward-tilting eyes that gave her face a naturally wistful expression, she was more beautiful and interesting than any other mother I knew. Flitting from enthusiasm to enthusiasm—the piano, painting, fine needlework, poetry—Mama was drawn to extremes, whether she was celebrating the completion of a sketch or lamenting the tragic ending of a novel. Whatever mood she touched on, it was soon replaced by another, and I adapted accordingly. I never doubted that Mama loved me, fiercely, even when she brushed me away. There was so much for her to do, so many new things to try, and never enough time.

Mama called Papa's extended family "boring old sticks-in-the-mud," preferring to socialize with artists and the adventurous members of society who funded them. The only time I saw my Shulkin cousins was at large family celebrations, most often a christening, since the Shulkin women reproduced at a staggering rate. Whenever the extended clan gathered, Mama was the object of pitying glances— *only two children!*—and it wasn't until years later that I suspected it wasn't bad luck that had kept my family so small. Vasily and I were more than enough for Mama.

If I tell you that my brother was handsome and effortlessly talented at everything from horse riding to dancing, you'll assume I resented him. Quite the opposite. I adored Vasily, with a devotion embedded in my bones. He was five years older, an age difference that kept us from being competitive, and he treated me like a pet our parents had brought home to entertain him. And like a puppy, I trailed after him, panting for attention. I had friends my own age, the daughters of families Mama approved of. But Vasily, like the sun, outshone anyone else.

In the spring of 1914, I had no premonitions of war, let alone revolution. Yet I remember it as a troubled time. Vasily would be leaving for military college in the fall, and I was already grieving. I tried to be my usual compliant self, the good daughter who never caused trouble. Inside, however, Vasily's departure weighed on me like a sickness. My entire life was oriented toward my brother; who would I be without him? When we received the invitation to Maria Shulkina's debut ball, it felt like another blow. The grandest party in years—even the royal family might come!—and seventeen-year-old Vasily was old enough to go. His twelve-year-old sister was not.

I was too well behaved to make a scene. But I'd also spent years observing Mama's histrionics, and I knew the effect that could be achieved with silent tears. I moped and sighed and shuffled through the house like a second-rate actress rehearsing a death scene. In the end, a compromise was arranged: I could come for the dinner and watch the first few dances. Like Cinderella, I was going to the ball.

Mama, delighted at this excuse to spend money, called in her favorite dressmaker and ordered my first proper evening gown. She bought me coordinating shoes and gloves soon after. But on the evening itself, Mama was too caught up in her own preparations to be much help, so I was dressed by my governess, Miss Fields. Papa had hired her the previous year through a London employment agency, in an attempt to improve my atrocious English. Mama and I had braced ourselves for a humorless battle-ax—"The British are so terribly *serious!*" Mama lamented—but Miss Fields turned out to be relatively young, with a pleasant demeanor and an easy, round-cheeked smile. She won Vasily over by re-creating the Battle of Waterloo on the sitting-room floor, using marbles and Mama's collection of tiny silver spoons, and spent hours patiently reading *The Secret Garden* aloud with me until I could sound out the words myself. It wasn't long before my English was almost as good as my French—and both were far better than my Russian.

As Miss Fields pinned up my hair, I chattered away, fidgety with anticipation.

"I wonder if the princesses will come," I said. "The youngest is the same age as me."

"Anastasia, is it?"

"Yes. Wouldn't it be marvelous if I met her? Though I'd be too nervous to say anything."

The tsar and his family largely kept to their palaces in those days, due to what Papa called "the trouble in 1905." He'd never explained what that trouble was, and I'd never been concerned enough to ask.

I waved my arm in front of the lamp on my dressing table, admiring the sparkle of the diamonds encircling my wrist.

"What do you think?" I fretted. "It's so beautiful, but what if the clasp breaks and I lose the bracelet? Mama will never forgive me."

"It's your first grown-up party. Enjoy yourself, and stop worrying."

I heard Papa call my name from downstairs and took one last look in the mirror. My body was swathed in a confection of forest-green silk and cream tulle, colors that set off the dark hair and eyes I'd inherited from Mama. My hair had been twisted into an elegant chignon that made me look years older. For the first time, I felt the shiver of pleasure that comes with self-transformation. All the powers of subterfuge I perfected in the years to come had their roots in this moment, when I stared into that mirror and saw someone else.

Another shout from Papa.

"Coming!" Miss Fields called back.

She nudged me away from the mirror and toward the door. "Time to go."

I descended the front staircase with Miss Fields close behind, feeling like a queen trailed by her lady-in-waiting. Below, my admiring audience awaited: Mama, Papa, Vasily, and—to my great delight—my uncle Sergei, Mama's younger brother. Slight and dark featured like Mama, he shared her love of art and literature but not her erratic moods. The fact that he was in his early thirties and not yet married subjected him to incessant teasing, but he never seemed to care. "When I crave domestic bliss, I come to your house," he once told Mama, to which she replied, "Oh yes, I'm a model wife."

That's when I learned adults sometimes say the opposite of what they mean.

Secretly, I was glad we didn't have to share Sergei with a wife and a horde of children. Though he was constantly dashing off to Paris or Vienna, he visited our house often, always making time to talk to me. Unlike most adults, he actually seemed interested in what I had to say.

I rushed toward Sergei, and we kissed each other's cheeks.

"I thought you were in Italy!" I exclaimed.

"And miss the party of the year? I wouldn't dare." He took hold of my arms and twirled me around. "What a vision." Then, looking over my shoulder, he called out, "Good evening, Miss Fields."

"Good evening, sir."

Sergei enjoyed practicing his English with Miss Fields, though his flowery language sometimes made her laugh. "Your uncle turns the simplest conversations into poetry," she once told me, and I couldn't tell if she was making fun of him.

"Do we have you to thank for Nadia's astonishing transformation?" Sergei asked her.

"I didn't make the dress, so I can't take all the credit."

Still, she smiled proudly, and their shared approval made me prickle with satisfaction. In their eyes, I was no longer a little girl.

Papa was done up in his full regalia, his medals shimmering in the lamplight. Mama looked breathtaking in her deep-blue ball gown, a sapphire necklace twinkling in the spot where her bodice plunged. Vasily already looked like a soldier, in his gleaming boots and scarlet jacket. Sergei wore a tuxedo rather than one of his usual rumpled suits. Everyone looked so polished, so elegant. Like true Shulkins.

Old Ivan, the butler who had kept the house running since my grandfather's time, stood at attention by the entrance and opened the front door at Papa's signal. The Mercedes was waiting outside; a trio of maids stood by with our coats. Encircled by my family, I said a hurried goodbye to Miss Fields; she had strict orders to bring me home from the ball at ten o'clock, and I didn't want to waste any time. She beamed as if she were seeing off her own daughter.

"You'll dazzle them all," she said, and her confidence enshrouded me like protective armor. I gazed out the car window as we sped off, mesmerized by the eerie glamor of Saint Petersburg at night. Buildings that were imposingly elegant by day looked mysterious by lamplight; the canals were inky black, streaked with wisps of fog. As we drove along the brightly lit, pulsing Nevsky Prospect, swerving around old-fashioned carriages and other, slower automobiles, I was convinced this would be the most wonderful evening of my life.

With such expectations, it was perhaps inevitable that I'd start off disappointed. My cousins' mansion—with its heavy silk draperies and vast, echoing rooms—felt more like a museum than a home, and the party was similarly stuffy. It took nearly half an hour to pay respects to all my relatives, bowing down to kiss the hands of great-aunts I barely knew. At dinner, I was seated with the grandmothers and elderly spinsters—the social nonentities banished to the back of the room. But once the tables were cleared and the music started, my gloomy mood lifted. Women swept by, their dresses moving in seductive whispers while swords tapped against the legs of their escorts. My feet shifted from side to side, tempted by the rhythmic lure of a waltz. Though I stayed close to Mama, she paid me no attention, and I hoped if I stayed quiet enough, she'd eventually forget I was there.

"May I?"

Sergei stepped up to Mama and held out his hand. She smiled and nodded, and they spun into the swirl of couples, moving in effortless harmony. I hadn't known he was such a good dancer, and I wished with a pang of jealousy that I was the one in his arms.

Things hadn't always been easy between Mama and Sergei and Papa, I'd been told. Sergei, the publisher of a literary magazine, and Papa, a government minister, disagreed about politics, economics, and nearly everything else, and in the early days of her marriage, poor Mama was forced to play peacemaker when her brother and husband's arguments escalated into shouting matches. Those fights were now remembered with rueful grins, anecdotes from a distant past. Though Papa still referred to Sergei as a raving radical, and Sergei joked about Papa being an old fossil, each respected the other's intransigence. For while Sergei might lecture about workers' rights and Papa might grumble about some people having no respect for tradition, they were both members of the same tribe. A tribe that kissed women's hands and bowed their heads to those with superior titles and knew how to make a Viennese waltz look effortless.

Vasily had taken advantage of Mama's inattention to sneak off with a few of our older male cousins, and I wondered if I could make a similar escape. Maybe to the dining room, where I'd seen servants laying out punch bowls and trays of desserts.

"Nadia Antonovna?"

A gangly boy who seemed to be all legs and arms had come up behind me. Though he was at least a head taller than me, his cheeks were still youthfully soft. I had no idea who he was.

He gave me a quick, practiced bow and announced, "Mikhail Nikolayevich."

The same few names had been used for generations in the Shulkin family; you had to use both your own and your father's for people to know where you fit in. Knowing this Mikhail was Nikolai's son, however, wasn't enough. I could think of half a dozen Nikolais who were part of the extended Shulkin family. When the boy explained further— and I realized he was the son of Prince Nikolai, the richest and most revered of all the Shulkins—I was mortified.

"I'm so sorry," I stammered. "It's only there are so many cousins, and I can hardly keep track of the ones in Saint Petersburg, let alone the ones in Moscow . . ."

"Please, don't worry," he said. "I think we've only met once. At my grandmother's funeral?"

I remembered the train ride, in a luxurious private carriage; it was the farthest I'd ever traveled from home. But I couldn't remember anything of the service itself.

"That was years ago," I said. "I'm surprised you recognized me."

"I didn't. But I saw you with your mother, and I knew who she was, right away."

That explained it. Everyone remembered Mama.

We exchanged a few minutes of family-related chitchat, sorting through our connections, determining that we were third cousins. Mikhail told me he was fifteen years old and the youngest of eight children, most of whom were already married. While a boy his age wouldn't usually be invited to a distant cousin's debut, his mother had decided to bring him along to keep her company, promising visits to the theater and ballet while they were in town.

"Moscow's all right for entertainment, but nothing like here," Mikhail said. Though I'd never been to the theater or the ballet, I nodded in agreement. I continued nodding as he told me about a production of *Giselle* he'd seen at the Bolshoi, then veered abruptly into his family's summer plans. "Mother wants to stay in the South of France, but I'm hoping to convince her to go to Paris. Have you been?"

I shook my head, wondering if Mikhail was already regretting talking to such a boring nobody, but he didn't seem bothered by my silence.

"I'd love to visit one of those painter's studios. Where they've got canvases everywhere, and you can watch them mix the colors . . . Would you like to dance?"

Laughing at my puzzled stare, he swayed his shoulders.

"I can tell you want to," he said cheerfully. "Why don't we try?"

I held out my hands. Mikhail pulled me into the whirl of bodies, and my feet clumsily tried to match his movements. Gradually, I fell into his rhythm, allowing my arms to soften. We danced carefully but competently, not quite in time, but close enough. Mikhail kept up a stream of chatter—the youngest child delighted to finally find himself the center of attention—and I was relieved not to have to carry the burden of conversation, because how could I possibly express all I was feeling? There I was, dancing, with Prince Shulkin's son! Twirling and gliding in the midst of all this beauty, my heart pulsing in time to the music.

Then I saw Mama, scowling from the edge of the dance floor. The spell was broken.

"I have to go," I said, pulling away from Mikhail's arms. Mama's face shifted from disapproval to interest when I introduced him, and they talked for a few minutes while I hoped for a reprieve. My hopes were quickly dashed. Mama excused us and led me firmly to an anteroom, where Miss Fields was waiting with my coat. Mama handed me off with a quick kiss, anxious to get back to the party.

"How was it?" Miss Fields asked.

"Wonderful! I even danced!"

"Oh, I wish I'd seen that."

"Come have a look—I'll introduce you to my cousin Mikhail . . ."

Miss Fields shook her head, quick and firm. "No. I mustn't."

Of course not, I thought, chiding myself for such foolishness. A governess in a plain wool coat couldn't go strolling around a formal ball. Her thick, wavy hair had come loose from its fastenings—as it so often did—and wispy tufts fell against her forehead and cheeks. I adored her, but I knew she'd stand out like a duck amid peacocks.

"I'll tell you all about it," I promised.

As we made our way toward the front door, Miss Fields slowed her steps and peered through an arched doorway. In the distance, dancers moved in a flurry of color, their movements in step with the orchestra's commands. There was something in her eyes as she watched them—a trace of longing—that made me wonder if Miss Fields had ever been to a ball. If she'd ever hovered at the edge of a dance floor, trying to catch a young man's eye. Before I could ask, she was ushering me away in her usual no-nonsense manner. The moment for confidences had passed. *When I make my debut, I'm inviting Miss Fields,* I decided.

I assumed, of course, that I'd have one.

A month later, we were off for our annual summer stay in the country. Those months at Priyalko usually sent me into a lethargic, dreamy state halfway between boredom and contentment. The summer of 1914 was different. From the very beginning, I felt on edge. Miss Fields had never been to the country with us, and I could tell when we arrived that she was disappointed, though she tried to hide it behind a stiff smile. I looked at the rutted, muddy front drive and the sagging chairs scattered across the front porch. Heard the squawk of chickens who'd wandered out from the back and the commotion as the servants swarmed forward to unload our things. I noticed the chipped gingerbread trim along the roofline and felt a disloyal surge of annoyance: *It's not as nice as I remembered.*

Elena, our housekeeper, and her husband, Yuri, the estate's overseer, were waiting at the front door. They had worked for us for years and were practically members of the family. Yuri took Papa off for an inspection of the newly repaired barn, and Mama began conferring with Elena on arrangements for the upcoming days: what was to be served for dinner; which houseguests would be arriving on which day. Though Priyalko was smaller and shabbier than our home in Saint Petersburg, we always had people to stay, since Mama and Papa preferred having company to spending time alone. In the country, entertaining was much less formal than in town. At Priyalko, I could wear light, loose dresses with no corsets and run around without shoes. It was the place I felt most free.

I led Miss Fields into the sitting room, which was filled with a hodgepodge of furniture collected by my grandparents.

"What's wrong?" I demanded.

"What do you mean?"

"You look sad."

"Hmph." I knew that noncommittal sound well. It was Miss Fields's way of delaying a conversation until she could muster an appropriate response.

"You don't like it here."

"Of course I do. It's not what I was expecting, that's all."

"How?"

"Oh . . ." More stalling. "Country houses in England, for a family like yours, look rather different."

"What do they look like?"

"More open, I suppose. More windows. Set in a garden, rather than hidden in the trees. But it doesn't matter, not at all. This is perfectly lovely. Very cozy."

"Cozy," I understood, was another word for "small," and "lovely" was an all-purpose word for when you wanted to be polite. When I showed Miss Fields to her bedroom in the back—a tiny, airless space with all the charm of a storage cupboard—I felt even more ashamed.

"It's only for sleeping," I said, apologetic. "You'll see. We spend all our time outside."

"Then I shall be very happy."

And indeed, almost everything I remember from that summer is set against a backdrop of trees and sunlight. Gatherings on the porch and picnics in the clearing Mama called *"mon petit paradis."* People were always coming and going: friends and relatives of Papa's, friends and relatives of Mama's, with occasional overnight visits from other Saint Petersburg families who were traveling to their own, more distant estates. They couldn't have all been there at the same time, but in my mind the visitors meld into a single mass, as if the events of dozens of different days have been condensed into a single afternoon. My uncle Sergei was always organizing meetings and salons in town and wouldn't have left Saint Petersburg for more than a week at a time. Yet he seemed to play a part in almost everything I remember. Either in a leading role or catching my eye from the background.

Sergei collected friends the way a child gathers shells at the beach: indiscriminately, delighting in their novelty, indifferent to their flaws. His social circle included everyone from respected novelists to barely literate rabble-rousers, though he knew better than to invite the most unsavory of his companions to my parents'. That summer, he brought along two men: a poet named Boris—who was either so aloof or so shy that he avoided eye contact even when spoken to directly—and a political writer named Alek. Alek was tall and self-contained, a person who always seemed to be listening but only spoke when he wanted to make a point. Though he was younger than Sergei, his seriousness made him appear older. Unlike Sergei, he showed no interest in children, which was a relief. Alek was the sort of man who intimidated me into silence.

"We're an embarrassment," Alek pronounced the first night, at dinner. "Compared to the rest of Europe, Russians are backward and superstitious—"

"Because we worship God while atheist Socialists take over everywhere else?" Papa objected. Any swipe at Mother Russia provoked him into a furious defense.

"I'm not talking about God." Despite Papa's indignation, Alek remained calm. "I'm talking about our people. We are oppressed by an archaic class structure that keeps us chained to the past. Like prisoners."

The word felt like an attack, a sudden burst of flame. We all knew, from Sergei, that Alek had actually been a prisoner, serving a two-year sentence for writing antigovernment pamphlets.

Papa changed the subject by praising Russia's railroads—"The envy of the world!"—as Alek smirked and asked whose labor had made them such a wonder. Vasily glanced at me across the table, his eyes wide: *This is the best dinner we've had in years!* Then Mama's voice broke through the bickering.

"The one thing I can't stand about revolutionaries is that they have no sense of humor. Really, Alek, must you all be so deadly serious? Don't you ever enjoy yourself?"

In a stage whisper, Sergei told Alek, "My sister doesn't tolerate political talk during the summer."

Alek nodded sheepishly at Mama.

"My apologies, Madame Shulkina."

Mama smiled brightly, and I felt the tension ease.

As if to reinforce Mama's command, a carriage arrived the next day, overflowing with guests intent on enjoying themselves. Princess Nemerova—the second wife of an ancient, invalid nobleman—was doing her best to spend his fortune on self-described artists who all happened to be young and male and handsome. Two of her latest protégés accompanied her, both dancers named Piotr (quickly dubbed "Piotr the Blond and Piotr the Brown" by Mama). Mr. and Mrs. Volodnov were painters, she of landscapes and he of portraits, most notoriously a full-length study of his wife, naked, in the bath. Both cultivated an image of bohemian dishevelment: Mrs. Volodnova's auburn hair was pinned haphazardly, so that locks cascaded down her neck, and Mr. Volodnov wore his paint-spattered tunics open at the chest. With their dramatic expressions and loud voices, it seemed like they were always performing for an audience, even if it was only each other.

I was old enough to know when adults were up to something, but too young to interpret their coded signals. Those weeks in the country were filled with strange interactions I wouldn't understand until years later. People were always splitting into pairs or small groups, then regathering in new combinations, making it impossible to keep track of everything that was going on. I puzzled over each incident, but most remained inscrutable, like the jumble of colors in the abstract paintings Mama loved and Papa dismissed as an assault on his senses.

Mama, who'd lately discovered photography, spent hours posing one person or another by picturesque tree trunks and sunlit meadows. The Volodnovs set up easels behind the house and made a show of preparing their paints each morning, though they spent so much time socializing that they made little progress by the end of each day. Princess Nemerova coaxed Boris into reciting some of his poetry, while Piotr the Blond and Piotr the Brown sat beside her with the self-conscious poise of statues. *If I was as rich as the princess,* I thought, *I might pay good-looking young men to follow me around, too.*

During my wanderings around the estate, I often heard Mama's voice.

"Alek! What was that story you told me earlier, about the tsarina?"

Or, "I'm sure Alek has something to say about that . . ."

Another time, teasing: "Oh, Alek, you are terrible!"

Mama often seemed to be making fun of Alek, widening her eyes in exaggerated astonishment at something he said, and then shaking her head. I never heard him flatter her or try to win her over, yet she clearly enjoyed his company. "I never know what you're thinking," she once told him. That, I suppose, was at the heart of his appeal, though I didn't understand why at the time. To me, he seemed cold and vaguely threatening. And therefore, best avoided.

Often, Miss Fields would tear me away right as things got interesting. Papa would start in on Mama, asking how long the Volodnovs were going to stay, and Miss Fields would appear with a brisk "Time for your lesson." Sergei and Alek would be reading a letter from a friend in Moscow, muttering over some scandal, and Miss Fields would come up behind me, demanding we pick wildflowers for a botany study. Miss Fields even suggested, once, that we walk to the village, an excursion I suspected Mama had encouraged to get me out of the way.

I knew the village where our estate laborers lived was close by, but I'd never had a reason to visit. In my mind, it was like New York or the moon: a place I knew existed but that had no connection to my daily life. Miss Fields and I walked ten minutes or so along a dirt path worn solid by generations of servants traipsing back and forth. Only the most generous definition of the word "village" could describe the settlement we eventually reached. Rows of wooden shacks lined a single, dung-spattered cart path. No building appeared to be larger than a single room, and chickens and pigs roamed in and out, alongside muddy children. Miss Fields looked from left to right, as if searching for some other, more appealing place. A group of sullen men were gathered in front of the largest dwelling, and the oldest of them pulled away and approached us.

"Do you need help, miss?"

I shook my head but couldn't think of anything to say that would explain our presence. I spent an agonizing moment being stared at by both the man and Miss Fields, then dropped my head. Miss Fields nodded to the man and turned away, motioning for me to follow. Once we'd gotten out of earshot, Miss Fields exclaimed, "Well!"

I knew what that meant. "It was not what you were expecting."

"No."

"It's different from English villages."

"Yes."

Miss Fields didn't explain why, and I was too embarrassed to ask. She was clearly following one of her favorite precepts: *If you haven't got anything nice to say, don't say anything at all.* I remembered an illustration in one of Miss Fields's books, *Emma*, by Jane Austen. The engraving showed two characters walking in town; behind them were shops, carriages, and an oval of grass with grazing sheep. If that was what Miss Fields expected to see, it was no wonder she was disappointed. My face and body prickled with shame. Here, steps from my own house, was vivid proof that Alek was right: compared to England, Russia was poor and backward. But I wasn't moved to pity on behalf of my family's miserable tenants. I was angry because the village's squalidness reflected badly on Papa.

Though Miss Fields did her best to keep me occupied, she couldn't be everywhere at once. There were times I was able to sneak off and witness scenes that remain etched in my memory all these years later, like films I've replayed countless times. Scenes such as the Volodnovs and Papa, walking through the alley of fruit trees behind the house. Mr. Volodnov trudged ahead, looking for a ripe pear to eat, and Papa offered an arm to Mrs. Volodnova. She stepped closer, tilting her head, whispering so that her lips nearly touched Papa's ear. I knew there was something odd about the way they were standing, with her body twisting like a vine around his. Papa looked flattered and sad at the same time—how was that possible?—and Mrs. Volodnova dipped her mouth closer to his neck, and then Mr. Volodnov called out from close by. Papa and Mrs. Volodnova pulled apart, suddenly and silently, and by the time Mr. Volodnov joined them, it was as if I'd imagined the whole thing.

Another day, I saw Mama and Alek sitting on a log by the river, their feet in the water. Mama had pulled her skirt up to her knees and taken off her stockings; I remember the shock of her white legs and girlish pose. I crouched behind a tree and watched as Mama burbled and laughed; I wasn't close enough to understand what she was saying. Alek watched her and listened, his mouth curved in the barest suggestion of a smile. When my legs began to cramp, I crept away, feeling as if I'd witnessed a scene from a play that I'd arrived at late and been forced to leave early.

Other moments I remember as images frozen in time. Miss Fields watching Sergei and Alek as they conferred at a window, while Mama watched Miss Fields. The two Piotrs, holding hands in the woods and talking in close-up whispers. Piotr the Brown cornered by Princess Nemerova after supper, her fingers dancing at the edge of his sleeve; Piotr the Blond sulking at the other side of the room. Mr. Volodnov placing his hand on his wife's backside and giving it a decisive, possessive squeeze.

For the most part, I found such incidents amusing—adults acting like children. Other things I saw were more disturbing, for they underscored how much I still didn't know. Sergei pacing the garden and turning away when I waved. It was the first time he'd ever shunned me, and the rejection stung like a slap. Mama crying, not in her usual dramatic, self-pitying fashion, but quietly by a tree at the side of the house, mouth pressed shut, her emotions channeled into the tears that trickled down her face. I was always the first to hug and comfort Mama when she got in one of her moods, but that day, I knew instinctively to stay away.

Worst of all was the day I spied on Vasily. My brother loved the country, and he was always off riding or hunting, manly activities I was never invited to share. When I saw his horse sauntering by the rye fields one afternoon, I was pleasantly surprised. Maybe I could convince Vasily to take a walk with me. As I drew closer, I heard a pained, grunting noise coming from behind a cluster of bushes. Was Vasily hurt? I began walking faster, until I could see around the edge of the branches. Vasily was on the ground, lying on top of a peasant girl I'd never seen before. Her face, turned upward, was slack and uninterested. Their clothes obscured the actual specifics of the act, but I could see Vasily pumping his hips up and down, and I knew—in the most general terms—what they were doing. As Vasily's breaths grew more frenzied, I turned away, embarrassed for him and myself. If I took the path back to the house, he might see me, so I snuck into the rye instead. A short while later, Vasily pulled himself onto his horse and rode off. The girl stood and straightened her dress. She had broad cheeks and a flat nose; she wasn't ugly, exactly, but none of her features were in any way noteworthy. There was nothing to explain why my brother would have chosen her.

The girl passed directly in front of me, walking toward the village. She held a piece of cake with pink icing, the same cake we'd had at the end of our midday dinner. It must have been a gift—or payment?—from Vasily. The girl thrust the cake into her mouth and devoured it in a few ravenous bites, as if she feared it would be snatched away. It was disgusting—*she* was disgusting—and my feelings about what happened in those bushes became indelibly entwined with my feelings for the village as a whole. My perfect brother couldn't be blamed; he'd been tricked into sinning.

I never told Vasily what I'd witnessed, and so it became just another of the secrets that simmered that summer. None of which had anything to do with me, I thought, until late July, when Miss Fields told me she was leaving. The news was so unexpected that I couldn't believe it, even when I saw the packed bag in her room.

"Why?" I demanded.

"You're getting too old for a governess. There are some very good finishing schools in Saint Petersburg, I hear."

"I don't want to go to school!" I protested, but Miss Fields cut me off with an abrupt shake of her head.

"It's what your parents want. I wish I could stay, but it's not possible."

Though I'd never seen Miss Fields and my parents so much as disagree, I understood what her words implied: she'd been dismissed. Why? I tried to take Miss Fields's hand, but she turned deftly aside and reached for her hat. Pushing down her emotions as she pinned it in place.

"Can I write to you?" I asked.

Miss Fields gave me a wan smile, the kind adults give children when they talk about imaginary friends.

"I don't know where I'll be living, just yet."

A tremor of worry flashed across her face, and I was bewildered again by the suddenness of her departure. What was the rush? Why wasn't Miss Fields at least given time to find a new position?

"I'll tell you what," Miss Fields said. "I'll write you first, when I've gotten settled."

I remembered the illustration from *Emma* and pictured the two of us walking together through a country town. Someday, I told myself, I would find a way to visit Miss Fields. This wouldn't be our final goodbye.

When the carriage was ready to take Miss Fields to the train station, I obeyed her final command and didn't cry. The sobs came later, when I flung myself down on her lumpy bed, in the back room that was so much gloomier than she deserved. Mama tried to comfort me, with tentative pats on the back, but ignored my pleas that she tell me why Miss Fields had gone. Grief moved through my body in waves of pain, leaving me hollow.

Priyalko felt desolate without Miss Fields, and other losses were soon to come. On August 1, Germany declared war on Russia, and Papa and Vasily left for Saint Petersburg soon after. Vasily was exhilarated by the prospect of being a real soldier at last; Papa was more wary, yet resolute about doing his duty. Sergei dashed off letters to

European correspondents, telling Mama it was all such a waste and gloomily setting off on walks by himself. As our guests packed up and left, Yuri grumbled to Mama that the army had better not call up any of Priyalko's men before the harvest was in. With fewer meals to prepare and more time on her hands, Elena baked elaborate treats for my afternoon tea, treats I was too dispirited to enjoy. Sergei gave me only a perfunctory goodbye when he left a few days later. Once, I would have been hurt by his lack of interest in me. But I'd been hardened by the loss of Miss Fields, and I didn't cry.

During all the suffering to come, I hardly ever cried.

LONDON

1938

Confidential

To: Roger Ballantry, Secret Intelligence Service (SIS)

From: Inspector Hugh Thornton, Metropolitan Police

Enclosed are the requested documents regarding the death of the woman identified as Marie Duvall. For your convenience, I will summarize them here:

1. **Telegrams exchanged with the Toulouse Police Department:** As is standard procedure for the death of a foreign national, the appropriate authorities were notified in the woman's city of origin. They informed us that the address on the woman's passport did not exist and were unable to locate any friends or relatives of a woman with that name.

2. **Coroner's report:** Death was caused by multiple internal injuries and broken bones, consistent with the force delivered by a moving vehicle.

3. **Witness statements:** While all residents of the immediate area were questioned, most did not see or hear anything unusual on the night in question. Mrs. George Weatherby was the first to come to the victim's aid and confirms the victim was not breathing.

Shortly after receiving the enclosed telegrams from the Toulouse police, I was contacted by the Office of the Prime Minister and ordered to close our inquiry and forward the relevant documents to you. Please be assured that I am at your disposal should you require any further assistance, and I hope to one day be informed of the resolution of this most curious case.

RUSSIA

1917

Ask a historian, and they'll tell you the Russian Revolution began on February 23, 1917, when throngs of angry women marched through the streets of my hometown. Saint Petersburg had been renamed Petrograd, in a burst of Slavic pride, but three years of war had dimmed the city's sparkle. The shops were more than half-empty, and everywhere you saw lines of people, slumped inside their coats and stomping their numb feet, waiting for their rations of bread. A simmering frustration seemed to have infected us all: Mama moped that no one ever had parties anymore; Papa muttered about the army's incompetence; and I was weighed down by worry for Vasily. He'd been in Galicia for more than a year, trying to push the Germans out of Poland, and his letters were infrequent and maddeningly short. I was fifteen years old, yet there were still no plans for my debut into society, let alone the new wardrobe that was supposed to come with it. Some days, it seemed like all I did was wait—for an end to the war, for my brother's return.

And then it all changed, almost overnight.

I didn't witness the beginning. When the factory workers made their way to the Winter Palace, demanding bread and peace, I was at school, doing sums and reading Shakespeare's sonnets. The first I heard of any trouble was when the chauffeur took a roundabout way home, telling me the Nevsky Prospect was too crowded with protestors. Papa mentioned the commotion at supper, but there'd been similar, short-lived uprisings before. There was no reason to think this one would be any different. Papa was hardly a Socialist, but even he sympathized with the marchers' demands: What woman wasn't worried about feeding her children? Even our previously lavish dinners had been reduced to a single course, sometimes no better than soup and bread. Mama complained the Germans were trying to starve us into surrender.

The next morning, Papa told me I wasn't going to school. Anna, one of our housemaids, had gone out early to buy coffee and said there were still crowds gathered around the palace.

"Best not to leave the house until it dies down," Papa said.

And so, those first stirrings of revolution brought my own, more personal liberation. With no school or social obligations, I spent most of the day in my room, reading and sketching. I'd always enjoyed the meditative nature of drawing, the way it made time slow down. Now and then I heard gunshots, but assumed it was just soldiers, showing off. Downstairs, Papa paced and Mama fretted and Old Ivan made occasional forays outside to find out what was happening. When I came down for tea, he reported that the streets were crowded with people—factory workers, soldiers, students—all demanding an end to the war.

"Isn't that what everyone wants?" Mama asked. She'd been telephoning friends who were similarly homebound, but the situation was so muddled that even rumors were hard to come by.

"I'll go to the ministry tomorrow," Papa said. "Find out what's going on."

All of us, still, assumed it was only a matter of time until everything went back to normal.

Later that night, I heard the distant thud of our front door knocker. I slid out of bed and into my robe, then ran to the top of the stairs, drawn by the sound of agitated voices. My uncle Sergei was standing in the front hall, flanked by Papa and Mama, who was hurling questions at her brother.

"Give him a moment," Papa chided.

Sergei shrugged off his coat into Anna's waiting arms. She laid the coat on a chair, pulled a cloth from her apron, and knelt to wipe the mud from Sergei's boots. When she finished, Sergei followed Papa and Mama into the sitting room, and I crept down the steps to eavesdrop. Anna, just as curious, lingered in the hallway. I put one finger to my lips and gave her a complicit look: *I won't tell on you if you don't tell on me.*

Sergei was talking quickly, invigorated.

"It's incredible," he said. "The excitement—you can feel it. Strangers are hugging each other in the street. You see people smiling like they haven't in years."

"I don't see what there is to smile about," Papa said. "Anarchy?"

"Hope."

Mama snorted dismissively, as if the concept was ridiculous. "Hope for what?"

"For an end to this blasted war, for one thing," Sergei said. "What has it done for our country but reduce us to misery?"

"Now there," Papa warned, and I didn't have to see him to picture his face: the indignant frown, the red unfurling across his cheeks. "There are brave men out there, fighting for our country."

"Yes, men like Vasily. And even he has given up pretending that there's anything honorable about what he's doing."

There was a long, weighted silence, and I remembered my brother's last visit. Vasily never questioned his mission—he was a soldier, through and through—but it was the first time he'd been honest about the conditions on the front lines. The men in his company were peasants who'd marched off to war in boots made of bark. Vasily and his fellow officers made repeated, desperate requests for supplies that never came and in the end were told to strip the bodies of their slaughtered comrades for ammunition. Mama said his coat was a disgrace—it was dull with ingrained mud and coming apart at the seams—but Vasily refused to have a new one made. He wouldn't go back to his men in a fresh uniform when so many of them were wearing rags. The night before he left, Mama repaired his coat herself, weaving her love into every stitch.

"It's been two and a half years," Sergei said quietly. "And we're no closer to winning than we were at the start."

According to Papa and Vasily, Russia was the greatest empire on earth, with the greatest army. Everyone complained about the war, but I'd never heard anyone admit that we might lose.

"Sergei," Papa said, in the expansive tone of one surrendering his sword, "we could debate this for hours. As we have in the past. But even you must agree that nothing can be accomplished until order is restored. What's being done to get these rabble-rousers off the streets?"

"An excellent question." I could tell by the way he said it that Sergei was smiling. "The tsar and his ministers have left the palace. There are calls for him to abdicate. That would leave the Duma in charge, I suppose, but the leaders of the workers' groups want their soviets to have a say. There's talk of a constitutional assembly, elections—don't you see? The people will finally be heard. Just like in your beloved England."

Papa harrumphed. "'The people.' That's an awfully vague term."

"Like it or not, things are changing. Speaking of which, I'd put a red banner or cockade on the front door."

"What for?" Mama asked.

"It's the symbol of revolution, and whatever your private leanings, it won't hurt to make a show of support."

"You'll be telling me to walk around in a peasant's tunic next!" Papa said.

Sergei laughed. "I wouldn't dream of it. You'll be wearing a jacket and tie till the day you die."

In the days after Sergei's visit, we learned to be wary of knocks at the door. Sergei had told my parents that bands of army deserters were roaming the city, men with weapons and no clear loyalty. Until the police got things under control, it would be wiser to stay indoors. Papa instructed Old Ivan not to admit any strangers, but we had no visitors for days, other than a few servants from neighboring houses who came to the kitchen door to ask for news. We didn't have any to share. It wasn't until a week later that we heard fists slamming violently against the front door.

Papa and I threw down the cards we'd been playing after supper and rushed to the front hall. From a hubbub of indistinguishable shouts, a voice called out, "Open up!"

Mama ran out from her sitting room, and Papa thrust me into her arms.

"Go," Papa urged.

Old Ivan came shuffling forward, but Papa waved him away. As Mama pressed against my back, pushing me up the stairs, I heard the bark of male voices and the clatter of boots across the floor. In the upstairs hallway, I began to make the turn to my room, but Mama grabbed my arm and pulled me into her bedroom, then the adjoining bathroom.

"Stay here," Mama ordered before closing the door.

My hands and legs felt shaky, and I was conscious of each ragged breath. I heard the creak of drawers as Mama moved around the bedroom. Then came the thunder of footsteps on the stairs. Papa was speaking, then Mama, and then the bathroom door opened. Papa stood in the doorway, smiling ruefully, giving me a look that said, *I know there's nothing funny about this, but play along.*

"The house is being searched for weapons," he told me. "I said we have none, but these soldiers are intent on making sure." He put his arm around my waist, and his fingers pressed into my stomach, holding fast. "As you can see, my friends, there's nothing here but a bathroom and my daughter, Nadia."

Half a dozen men in filthy military uniforms milled around my parents' room, pawing at the bedsheets and rummaging through the bureaus. Their smell felt like an assault, the earthy bitterness making me want to cover my face. I knew better than to do so. Mama was standing at the end of the bed, her arms crossed tightly across her chest, looking quietly defiant. The soldier who appeared to be in charge stepped closer when he saw me look at him, tilting his face so I could see the scar that ran from his cheekbone to his chin. I'd never had anyone look at me with such contempt. *What have I done?* I thought, panicked. Papa squeezed me closer, just enough to remind me I was a Shulkin. I mustn't look scared.

One of the men pulled out a knife and began slicing into the mattress. Others kicked clothes into piles on the floor and ripped open pillows, releasing clouds of feathers. Watching them caper around like rowdy children, I realized most of the soldiers weren't much older than me.

"Have you satisfied yourselves with a look at my underclothes?" Papa asked with an indulgent smile. "Perhaps I can offer you a drink in honor of our brave fighting men. I have a son in the army, you know. The Fourth Cavalry."

"Good for him," the scarred man sneered, but Papa was already urging the rest on with waves of his hands.

"To the dining room. I have some excellent bottles of champagne I've been saving for a special occasion. We will toast the revolution. Something to eat as well, what do you say?"

The promise of food was enough to lure them out, even the man with the scar. When they'd gone, Mama threw herself against me and held on tight, murmuring prayers of thanks. There was something odd about the embrace—Mama felt all lumpy—but it was only after she let go that I realized why. Flashing a self-satisfied smile, Mama pulled out the top of her bodice to show me the necklaces and rings she'd hidden inside.

We waited in that ruined room for two hours, until Papa called out for us. Through a combination of charm and bribery, he'd convinced the men to leave.

"They were only boys," he told us. "Young soldiers crave discipline, whether they admit it or not, and once I'd proved I had nothing to hide, they fell in line." Even their leader had softened in the end, when Papa took him aside and slipped him a fistful of money.

Papa said we shouldn't have any more trouble, but he hired armed guards, just to be sure. Gradually, we drifted back into our old routines. Mama returned to her weekly round of social calls, and my school reopened in mid-March. There, I heard about what happened while I'd been hidden away at home. Policemen, imperial guards—anyone who could be denounced as a "tsar's man"—had been shot on sight, their bodies lying in the streets for days. One old prince who resisted a search by self-declared revolutionaries had been murdered in his home, but no one I knew had been killed or even injured. The violence had been terrifying, but short-lived.

As the snow softened to slush and sunlight began to pierce the stubborn Petrograd haze, it seemed the worst had passed. Even Papa approved of the tsar's abdication and agreed it was time for a fresh start. But with so many different groups elbowing for power, it was impossible for any one faction to get anything done, and I soon grew tired of my father and uncle's political debates. As the chauffeur drove me to and from school in our Mercedes, we passed a few buildings that had been damaged by gunfire. Other than that, the city looked much the same.

In late May, the servants began packing for our move to the country. I'd heard stories about trouble on large estates; according to the biggest gossip in my school, crazed peasants were marching across the land with pitchforks, killing their masters and putting heads on pikes.

When I brought the story up at dinner—not really believing it, but wanting to be reassured—Papa scoffed.

"Ridiculous! The Socialists spread stories like that to scare us away."

"It's not all rumors," Mama said. "The Goletskys?"

"He got what was coming to him." Turning to me, Papa said, "Prince Goletsky was a boor and a tyrant. He took pride in whipping his servants himself. I'm not at all surprised that one of them used this unrest as an excuse to kill him."

"It was more than one," Mama said. "They stabbed him in the chest and burned the house down around him."

Papa's glare made Mama flush.

"Stop frightening Nadia," he said. "Yes, there have been a few incidents. But that's no different from here or Moscow. At least in the country, we'll be away from all the radicals." Papa turned to me. "I received a letter from Yuri yesterday, and he's seen no signs of trouble."

On the afternoon we arrived, Elena was waiting at the door with a plate of gingerbread. I pounced on it immediately, while Mama supervised the unpacking. Papa went off to tour the estate with Yuri, and when he returned, Mama and I were reading in the front room, curled on opposite ends of the sofa.

"Everything's as it should be," Papa said. "There's no need to worry."

Mama nodded slowly, out of politeness rather than agreement. She looked paler than usual, and she hadn't bothered to change out of her traveling clothes. Perhaps, like me, she'd been affected by the melancholy of the near-empty house. How different it was from the summer of 1914, when every room hummed with laughter and whispered confessions. I thought of Miss Fields and felt a pang of remembered loss. She'd never written, never told me why she left.

"Yuri did ask about the land reforms," Papa said.

I didn't know what he was talking about, but Mama suddenly looked more alert.

"I told him I didn't know any more than he did. That we'd have to wait until the assembly meets in the fall. But I have no doubt things will change." Papa's voice softened into the tone he used when Mama got one of her headaches. "I expect we'll have to break up the estate."

"But we have so little land as it is!" Mama protested. "Compared to your cousins', it's nothing!"

"Compared to most people, we have far more than we need. I don't know what will happen. But I want you to be prepared."

"You're as bad as Sergei," Mama said. "Do you really believe we're no better than peasants?"

"The tsar abdicated because Sergei was right. People want an end to the war and a chance to make an honest living. Our duty, now, is to concede graciously. Why shouldn't I give a good man like Yuri a plot of land to call his own? Isn't that a fair price for his years of service?"

Mama looked down at her skirt as one hand smoothed the fabric over her knees. "Of course. That's not what I meant."

Normally, I wouldn't have interrupted a grown-up conversation. But Mama looked so sad, and Papa looked so serious, and Priyalko— my refuge, my escape—was being threatened by the same uncertainty that haunted us in Petrograd. It wasn't fair.

"Doesn't Mama always say no political talk during the summer?" I asked. "Let's do a play reading instead. We can pull out the dress-up clothes from that trunk in the yellow bedroom . . ."

Mama shook her head. "I haven't the heart for it. I'm sorry."

"Ah, Katenka," Papa said.

How strange, to hear that girlish nickname coming from my formal father. He'd never used it in front of me. Mama didn't look up from her lap, and Papa didn't move from his seat, but I still remember exactly how they looked, more clearly than I remember their far more frequent fights. I've clung to that image as proof that, deep down, they loved each other.

Mama was determinedly cheerful at dinner that night as we discussed our plans for the rest of the summer. Vasily would be on leave in June, the first time he'd been home in nearly a year. Without him, our family never felt quite right; we were a wobbly circle of three rather than a solidly balanced foursome. Vasily's return, I believed, would shake us out of our melancholy.

Until then, I had a few weeks to fill, for the most part on my own. I read and played endless rounds of solitaire; I hung around the kitchen and pestered Elena until she gave me a scrap of leftover dough or apple slices dusted with cinnamon. Most afternoons, I wandered the woods and fields of the estate. There were a few small incidents that struck me as strange, though I didn't realize their significance at the time. Once, when I was at the river skipping stones, I saw two peasant girls downstream, washing clothes. Normally, the girls would have hurried through their work, anxious to be finished and out of my sight. This time, though, they didn't sink into respectful bows when they saw me. They stared right back, direct and unafraid, and their upright bodies sent a message I was quick to understand: *We have as much right to be here as you.*

Another afternoon, I was picking wildflowers when I noticed that the fields were strangely empty. No men stomping through the dirt; no oxen trudging alongside them. All I heard were the rippling calls of songbirds. Was it a religious holiday I'd forgotten? Country people were more pious than my parents, and I assumed everyone must be at church. By the time I returned to the house, carrying enough flowers to fill three vases, I didn't even think to ask.

While the unsettled political situation had kept a few families in Petrograd, most owners of the estates surrounding ours had proceeded with their usual summer plans. But there were no parties or picnics; people kept to themselves. When Mama received a letter from the Niederhoffs, our closest neighbors, informing her of their impending arrival, she waved it in front of me, smiling with her old exuberance.

"It feels like forever since we've seen anyone, doesn't it? Let's surprise them. We'll go over tomorrow afternoon. I'll have Elena make a treat for the children."

When we arrived the next day, I was surprised to see Mrs. Niederhoff herself open the door.

"Ekaterina, Nadia—thank God you're here!"

Mrs. Niederhoff was high-strung at the best of times, with a voice that mirrored her agitation. That day, she sounded particularly shaky.

"The servants are on strike!" she announced. "Can you believe it? All the nonsense in those pamphlets has gone to their heads."

"What pamphlets?" Mama asked.

"Haven't you seen them? Those anarchist troublemakers have been handing them out everywhere, telling the peasants to rise up against their oppressors. Oppressors!"

Mrs. Niederhoff's daughters, ten and eight years old, sat in the front room in matching sailor dresses, their ponytails tied with navy-blue ribbons. I could hear their two younger brothers running in a nearby room, taking advantage of their mother's distraction. The girls usually would have rushed up to me and asked me to play, but today they only gave me woeful looks.

"They're all refusing to work," Mrs. Niederhoff went on. "Here and at the farm. Even my housekeeper, who I thought was as loyal as an old dog! They're preparing a list of demands, and they'll present it to Mr. Niederhoff when he arrives on Friday. In the meantime, what am I to do? Prepare all the food myself? With what? They're picking everything in the garden and keeping it for themselves! I need to tell my husband, but I can't go to town to send a telegram—I've got no driver—and I'm afraid he'll accuse me of being hysterical and not understand how dreadful things are . . ."

"Hush," Mama said, patting Mrs. Niederhoff on the arm. "I'll go home and tell Anton. He can come over and sort it all out."

"I would be so grateful. You haven't had any trouble at your place?"

Mama shook her head. "It's all as usual."

Mrs. Niederhoff pushed her hair back from her face in a dramatic gesture of defiance. "I know why they're doing it. A German family—who will stand up for us?"

Mama managed a weak murmur of disagreement, but Mrs. Niederhoff shook her head. "No matter what we do, we're the enemy."

The war had made things difficult for families like the Niederhoffs, whose names proclaimed their foreign ancestry. I knew Mrs. Niederhoff had been born in Moscow—she made a point of telling everyone—but her parents had emigrated from Germany, as had her husband's. Given the terrible things we'd heard about Germans since war was declared, was it any wonder people questioned the Niederhoffs' loyalty? Mrs. Niederhoff once told Mama, weeping, that she wished her boys were old enough to fight, so they could clear the family's name.

I smiled at the Niederhoff girls, but they remained stone-faced.

"You can't stay here, with all this going on," Mama declared. "Why don't you come back with us?"

"Oh, you're so kind," said Mrs. Niederhoff. "Are you sure?"

"Of course. Fetch what you need, and we'll go right now."

After Mrs. Niederhoff bustled off with her daughters, I muttered to Mama that we couldn't possibly take them all. The car was useless on the muddy country roads, so we'd driven over in our smallest carriage, designed to seat four people. With all the Niederhoffs, we'd have a total of seven passengers.

"The little ones can sit on our laps," Mama said. "We can't leave her here—she's close to hysterics."

On the drive back to the house, I remembered the empty fields I'd walked past a few days before. The eerie silence. Had our farmers gone on strike? Did Papa know? I tried to ask him when we arrived home, but he was too distracted by Mama and Mrs. Niederhoff. Soon after, he left to talk to the Niederhoffs' overseer, and Mama instructed

Elena to double that night's dinner and get rooms prepared for our guests.

Papa returned while Mama and I were helping settle the children upstairs. When we came down, he escorted Mama and Mrs. Niederhoff to the sitting room. I followed shortly after and sat at a card table near the window, half-heartedly working on a sketch I'd started earlier. It was obvious I'd come to eavesdrop, but Papa didn't object. Perhaps he'd decided I was old enough to hear the truth.

Papa's face sagged in surrender as he addressed Mrs. Niederhoff. "I'm afraid I wasn't able to settle anything. A man came from Petrograd—a workers' activist—and convinced everyone the estate belongs to them."

"An activist!" Mrs. Niederhoff scoffed. "A criminal, more like it, if he's encouraging others to steal! We must find him and have him arrested. That will put an end to it."

"Who will arrest him?" Papa asked. "The tsar's police force? There are no policemen, practically speaking. Not in Petrograd, and certainly not out here. If you object to the will of the people, you're asking for trouble."

"The will of the people? Which people?"

"Not us, I'm afraid. I've arranged to send my driver for the rest of your bags, tomorrow morning. Then you can catch the late train back to the city."

"I'll go with him," said Mrs. Niederhoff. "Your driver won't know what needs to be packed—"

Papa interrupted. "No. It wouldn't be safe."

I watched as Mrs. Niederhoff's anger wilted into resignation. There was a painful pause, and then she stood. "Thank you. Please excuse me—it's been a long day."

Mama rose, too, asking if there was any way she could help, but Mrs. Niederhoff brushed her off. Afterward, Mama sank down on the sofa next to Papa and gently asked, "Was it terrible?"

"Their demands were quite clear. They'd been told the land belonged to whoever worked it. I tried to tell the overseer there was no such law, but you can imagine how far that got me. He wasn't rude, exactly— more uninterested. As if nothing I said was of the slightest importance. It came out that he had a son who'd died at the front, and a nephew, and that led to the usual idiotic conspiracy theories about German spies. The Niederhoffs have lost their workers' loyalty, and there's nothing to be done about it."

Mama tsk-tsked, but without her usual indignation.

"Nadia!" Papa called out.

Gingerly, I approached the sofa, expecting to be sent away. Instead, Papa reached out for my hand and pulled me closer, until I was sitting between him and Mama.

"I don't want you to worry," Papa told me. "We will work things out with our people calmly and fairly. But as long as these agitators are stirring up trouble, I don't want you going off on your own anymore. Especially not in the woods. Yuri has spotted smoke from fires; they may be camping out there."

I felt Mama stiffen, but she squeezed my hand and managed a grim smile. At first, it was soothing to feel my parents so close. Guarding me from the dangers that hovered outside our windows. I thought of the paths and clearings I was no longer allowed to roam. The dull, droning hours I'd have to spend under my parents' oppressive protection. I felt their arms against mine, holding me in place. The heat glowing from their skin. My blouse was stuck flat against my sweat-speckled chest, and I suddenly felt nauseous.

I pulled myself free and stood up. "I'm going to bed."

I stomped up the stairs, my feet proclaiming the frustration I couldn't put into words. Mama believed tantrums should be ignored, so it was Papa who knocked on my door a few minutes later and asked if we could talk.

"Why?" I called out.

"Everything will turn out all right. Don't worry."

The same thing he always said, ever since the war had started. Did he even believe it? I didn't respond, and after a long, weighted silence, Papa walked away.

The Niederhoffs left the next afternoon in a cacophony of shrieks and overstuffed bags. Papa escorted them on the train back to Petrograd and wasn't expected home until evening. The house felt even quieter than usual after they'd gone. Mama pulled out her watercolors and set up an easel on the front porch, and I joined her there soon after, laying an oversized piece of paper on the floor and sitting cross-legged with my pens. I waited for Mama to criticize my posture—"That's not appropriate for a young lady" was a particular favorite—but she was lost in the distractions of creation. I began drawing a map of an imaginary land; if I couldn't explore our forest, I'd invent one. Swirling lines became branches and trunks, then roads and mountains and streams. An entire world, conjured from ink.

Papa was home in time for a late supper. Petrograd, he told us, was awash in revolutionary posters. He'd even brought back a souvenir, a red star overlaid with the word "Peace" that he wore pinned to his jacket. Mama harrumphed in disapproval, but I thought it was funny. Who'd have believed it: Count Shulkin, a revolutionary!

"I dropped in on Sergei," Papa said to Mama. "Looks like he hasn't slept in days. The magazine is selling double what it used to."

"At least the revolution has benefitted someone in this family," Mama said dryly.

"He promised to visit when Vasily's here." Papa swept his palm across my cheek. "We'll have a grand time then, won't we?"

Papa's cheerful voice and touch restored my hope. Only one more week. With Vasily as a chaperone, I'd be free to roam around the estate, and Sergei's outrageous stories would jolt us out of our gloom. I saw Mama brighten with the same anticipation, and soon the three of us were chatting eagerly about our future plans and taking second helpings of braised lamb. Unaware of the throng that was marching toward our door.

The soldiers in Petrograd had knocked first. This time, the front door slammed open without warning and crashed against the opposite wall. Papa sprang up, still holding his wineglass. A crowd of men wearing peasant tunics stomped into the house, their voices the roar of an approaching storm. Mama half ran, half stumbled from her seat and wrapped her arms around my shoulders.

The vanguard of the horde crammed into the doorway of the dining room, then spilled inside. A dozen men, their glares like weapons. I recognized some of them from the farm but didn't know their names. I'd never had a reason to learn.

"Gregor," Papa said, addressing the man closest to him. "What's all this?"

Papa looked no different than he would in a Petrograd salon, smoothing over a disagreement between friends. *It will be all right,* I told myself as Mama's hands trembled against my chest.

Gregor was compact but burly, someone the others looked to as a leader. His mouth was barely visible under his bushy black beard. "We've come to take what's ours."

I heard thumps and heavy footfalls in the front room. It was impossible to tell how many people had invaded the house. Through the doorway, I glimpsed the swish of a skirt. Women, too?

"I've gone over all this with Yuri," Papa said. "Where is he?"

"Yuri is no longer in charge," Gregor said. "If the land is ours, why do we need an overseer?"

"He's a worker, just as you are . . ."

"*Your* worker. He's no better than the rest of us."

Papa's face didn't change, but his silence worried me. He glanced over at Mama, and Gregor barked, "Get them out of here!"

A trio of men pulled me and Mama out into the hall. We huddled against the banister at the foot of the stairs, Mama shielding my body with hers. All around us, invaders swaggered like an army of monstrous ants, scavenging whatever was in their path. A young woman came traipsing down the stairs, and I recognized her broad, plain face. It was the peasant I'd seen in the fields with Vasily, three years before. She was holding a bundle of rolled-up fabric. My clothes. A ripple of green silk trailed out from one edge, and my chest seized with fury. I'd outgrown the gown I wore to Maria Shulkina's coming-out ball, but I'd kept it in our trunk of theatrical costumes; it was the most beautiful dress I'd ever owned. I wanted to rip it out of that girl's filthy hands, but Mama's arms clung too tightly, forcing me to be still. When the woman made her way out the door, I saw she was wearing my new boots.

From the dining room, Gregor's voice rang out above the din. "Where are your guns?"

"I have only a few hunting rifles," Papa said. "They're in the storeroom by the kitchen."

One of the men rushed past me and Mama, toward the back of the house. In less than a minute, he was back, carrying three rifles. He handed one to Gregor and one to another of the men.

"Where are the rest?" Gregor demanded.

"That's all I have," Papa said.

"I've been told you people all carry guns," Gregor said. "For protection."

"I never needed protection, before tonight."

Mama moaned, the usual warning sign before she burst into tears. With a terrified "Shush!" I begged her to keep quiet. If Mama got hysterical, it would only make things worse. We had to follow Papa's example and stay strong while the storm raged around us. Eventually, it would pass.

"Have you been to the wine cellar?" Papa asked. Playing the gracious host, just as he had with the soldiers in Petrograd. "There are some very fine vintages. Go ahead—help yourselves."

A gaggle of peasants rushed past me in a flurry of shouts and stomps. Everywhere I looked were scenes that didn't seem possible: strangers pawing through Papa's papers; muddy footprints trailing across the Persian carpets; children racing past, laughing, as one swatted at the other with Papa's walking stick. I watched a pair of women carry away stacks of our family's china, and all I could think about was breakfast the next morning: *What will we use to eat?* Even Mama's fear didn't seem quite real. With her laborious breaths and quivering body, she looked like an actress overplaying a role, trying to sway a disinterested audience.

The peasants were getting louder, more festive. They passed around bottles, tipping the necks toward their mouths, laughing when the wine dribbled down their chins. At the top of the stairs, two middle-aged women were posing for each other in Mama's hats, like girls let loose in their mother's wardrobe. The front doorway was a bustle of movement, with furniture and linens being moved out while empty-handed newcomers arrived to claim their share. Papa was still standing at the head of the table in the dining room, and he gave me a cautious nod. Assuring me that despite everything, he wasn't afraid. I smiled back.

Gregor appeared in front of Mama, breathing heavily.

"Where are the jewels?"

Mama shook her head, seemingly incapable of speech. The day after our Petrograd house was invaded, we'd sewn her most valuable pieces into corsets and petticoat hems. But those garments were hidden beneath a loose floorboard in town. Gregor grabbed Mama's arm, roughly, and she let out a tiny yelp.

"We don't bring our jewels to the country," I blurted out. Anything to distract him, to make him stop.

In a withering imitation of my educated accent, Gregor drawled, "We don't bring our jewels to the country."

Suddenly, Papa was standing beside me.

"It's true," Papa told Gregor. "Search our rooms—if you haven't already."

"Anton . . . ," Mama pleaded.

I squeezed her hands, hoping she'd understand. *Please be quiet. Papa knows what to do.*

"Get back!" Gregor barked.

He shoved Papa aside. Papa stumbled into the huddle of men standing behind him, men who were twitchy with alcohol and resentment and fear. One of them wobbled, and the others lunged forward toward Papa, the force of the onslaught heaving him to the floor. Papa cradled his face with his arms as the men's boots pounded his body in a nauseating rhythm of thuds and grunts. Mama, openly sobbing, buried her head against my neck. But I couldn't look away.

An outburst of laughter from the front room diverted the men's attention, and they turned to see what was going on. Papa's hands and arms sagged; his face was so blood-spattered that I couldn't tell his nose from his mouth. But his chest was moving—hesitantly, painfully. He was breathing. He would be all right. I believed it right up to the moment Gregor raised his rifle, steadied it, and shot Papa in the head.

Mama screamed, and the sound jolted me into action. I grabbed Mama's arm and ran down the service hall. I had no plan, no destination. Only one thought propelling me forward: *Get away.*

From the kitchen, an urgent whisper called out, "Here!"

I dashed inside, clutching Mama like a rag doll. Elena gestured frantically for us to follow her. I caught only disjointed images of the kitchen's near destruction: cabinet doors torn off, drawers emptied, the larder picked bare. Chicken bones, apple cores, and other bits and pieces were scattered across the floor, as if whoever had done this wanted to defile every surface.

Elena led us out the back door, across the kitchen garden, toward a wooden door that lay flush with the ground. The root cellar. Mama was burbling incoherently, but I didn't even try to understand what she was saying. Elena pulled up the door, and all I could see was the top of a narrow wooden staircase. It looked like the entrance to a tomb.

Elena nudged me forward. "I'll come back for you when I can."

There'd been no time to fetch a lantern or candle. When we climbed inside and Elena shut the door over us, the darkness was impenetrable. My legs shook as I felt my way down, extending one arm behind me to support Mama. I could tell I'd reached the bottom only when the wobbly boards gave way to packed-down dirt. I shuffled ahead, trying to get my bearings, but everywhere I turned, my legs collided with barrels of stored food. Eventually, I sank to the floor, exhausted and despairing. Mama collapsed next to me.

"What are we to do?" she mumbled. "What are we to do?"

God help me, I nearly slapped her. I was only fifteen—how could I possibly answer such a question? She was the adult; she was the one who was supposed to take care of me. But like a freshly lit matchstick, my anger surged hot and bright for only a few seconds. Mama had always been delicate, bred for beauty and charm. I was the one who'd known, instinctively, to run.

An image of Papa flashed before me—the shot, the blood. My mind felt as numb as my body, entirely drained of the fervor that had propelled me out of the house. I'd seen it happen, yet it didn't seem real. Just one more impossible image to add to all the rest.

"Elena will get help," I told Mama. In the dark, it was easier to fake a confidence I didn't feel. "All we can do is wait until she comes back."

We must have been down there for hours, though time had no meaning in such a place. At some point, we lay down, pressed up against each other like kittens. I don't know if Mama slept; I certainly didn't. I thought of Papa, of what was happening at Priyalko, unable to stop the remembered unfolding of each horror. When Elena finally lifted the door, the sky was reddening into dawn. Mama and I climbed out, into the silent kitchen yard. I looked at Mama's dirt-streaked dress and tangled hair and wanted to cry.

"You're safe for now," Elena said. "The troublemakers are sleeping off the effects of last night. But you have to go, right away. Yuri will drive you to the station. There's a train in an hour."

"We need to fetch our things . . ."

Elena gave a quick shake of her head, her expression making clear what she wasn't prepared to say out loud: *You have no things. Everything's gone.*

"Count Shulkin," Mama whimpered. "I can't leave him."

"Yuri will take care of him, I promise." As if Papa needed help dressing, or a boot polish. I thought of Papa's body, lying alone in the hall, and felt weak with grief.

Elena ushered us to her quarters, off the kitchen. She brought a basin of water so we could wash up and urged us to eat some bread, though neither of us was hungry. From underneath her bed, Elena pulled out the box where she kept the household accounts and gave Mama the bag of money she'd hidden inside. We heard horses approaching from the stables, and Elena checked to see that the way was clear before leading us outside. Yuri was seated on top of the carriage, his face gray with exhaustion. Mama pressed a handful of bills into Elena's hand.

"We owe you our lives," Mama said. "Thank God for you and Yuri. I can't believe everyone else, all the rest of our people . . ." Her voice shook. "I can't believe they hate us so much."

"Gregor's always been trouble, but the others were tricked. Fed lies by that man."

"What man?"

"The one who was here before. He's been spreading lies all over, turning everyone's heads with false promises . . ."

"I don't understand. The one who was here before?"

"That friend of your brother's. The one called Alek."

The faces of our many houseguests had faded with time, into a mostly indistinguishable mass. But Alek I remembered clearly. Alek, who'd always been listening, always been watching. That summer,

Mama had been surrounded by flamboyant friends, yet she'd always seemed to be looking for Alek.

"He's been visiting all the estates in this area," Elena continued. "Telling people to take the revolution into their own hands and that any nobleman's property could be confiscated. I only heard about it from Gregor's wife last night, otherwise I would have warned you."

Mama's face had gone slack with horror. "Alek was here?"

Elena shook her head. "He left before the trouble started. That kind never takes the blame."

Mama's composure, already fragile, shattered completely once we entered the carriage. She sagged against me, too appalled to even cry. Scenes I'd found bewildering at twelve years old became clearer now that I was fifteen. Mama had openly flirted with Alek. She'd acted half-besotted with him. He'd basked in her attention, even encouraged it, and all the while he'd been sneering at our card games and picnics and five-course dinners. We had welcomed Alek into our family, and he repaid us in blood.

Hate surged through me like a scorching summer wind. Papa was gone; Priyalko was gone. But I was too tired and heartsick for the anger to take root. For Mama's sake, I'd have to take on all the miserable duties that lay ahead. There were telegrams to send, and a funeral to be arranged. The green silk party dress had marked my transition from child to young woman, but it was the ride away from Priyalko that carried me, unwillingly, into adulthood. With Papa gone and Vasily off fighting, I was the only one who could take care of Mama. Present a brave face to the world. *You're a Shulkin,* I could imagine Papa chiding me. *Act like one.*

And so began my next act of transformation.

LONDON

1938

To: Director, SIS

My sources in France have confirmed the suspicions we discussed last week in the matter of "Marie Duvall." After our stationery expert stated the passport was likely a Soviet forgery, I made inquiries to my contacts in the French Security Services, two of whom verified "Marie Duvall" was an alias used by a known Soviet agent, code-named "Red Mistress." She was involved in a notorious murder (see attached documents) and is considered extremely dangerous.

It goes without saying that this information must remain strictly confidential. One can imagine the outcry that would ensue were it known that this woman was able to travel to England undetected.

I suggest the body be cremated and buried as soon as possible. No doubt you know of someone who can handle such a matter discreetly.

—Roger

PETROGRAD

1917

A family can be obliterated suddenly, by fire or flood. For us, the end came in a series of humiliations and losses. There was enough time in between to adapt, to believe the worst had passed. Then another cataclysm would descend. I learned to inoculate myself against hope, growing sturdier with each new blow. Softness and innocence were stripped away, leaving only the primal impulse to stay alive. Like my country, I was both destroyed and reborn through revolution.

In the summer of 1917, I thought Papa's death was the most terrible thing that would ever happen to me. It was only in the years to come, when churches were raided and robbed, and priests murdered, that I realized we'd been lucky to have a proper funeral service. That we'd had time to mourn. Yuri and Elena drove Papa's body to the city, in a coffin Yuri built from a tree he'd chopped down at Priyalko. Mama offered them a place with us in Petrograd, but Elena politely declined.

"We're not city folk. Too many people, not enough fresh air. Besides, who else will keep an eye on the house?"

She genuinely believed we would come back one day. The peasants at Priyalko had organized a "Farmers' Collective"—whatever that meant—but Elena said there'd been no further trouble, and no one had objected to her and Yuri remaining in their quarters. All the usual routines continued: the early planting had begun; the chickens were producing more eggs than ever. Only a week had passed since Papa's murder, and it seemed impossible—immoral—that life continued there largely unchanged. Knowing Elena, who took such pride in the house, she'd been the one to scrub away Papa's blood, though I didn't want to ask. Imagining it was hard enough.

Vasily was able to push up his leave to attend Papa's service, and he was Mama's main source of support in the following days. It was Vasily's death she'd been preparing for, ever since the war started, and there were times she seemed unable to believe that her son was alive and her husband was gone. "Who would have thought?" she'd say, her voice drifting off with a shake of her head.

Vasily did his best to live up to his role as head of the family. He'd gotten a promotion and new uniform and looked every inch the resolute Russian officer as he greeted guests at the funeral reception. He'd cut his hair very short—they were all doing it, he said, to cut down on lice—and his face looked thinner, but no less striking. He made time to speak with every guest, seemingly with ease. Only someone who knew him as well as I did would have noticed the signs of strain. The way his eyes dulled whenever he had a moment to himself, or the catch in his voice when he talked about Papa. His hands were chapped and weathered, glaring evidence of the hardships of army life, and he usually kept them clasped behind his back or sunk into his pockets.

Mama had given Vasily only the vaguest description of what happened at Priyalko, and he'd told her not to upset herself by talking about it. But I wanted him to know the truth, craving his absolution for surviving when Papa did not. On the night of the funeral, after I'd seen Mama to bed, I came back downstairs and saw Vasily sitting by the fireplace in our front parlor, in the armchair that had always been Papa's. With his shirtsleeves rolled up and legs stretched out, he looked like the brother I remembered from years before, the one whose confidence deflected all troubles.

I stood in the doorway, wondering if he wanted to be left alone. "I thought you'd gone to bed."

"Is Mama all right?" he asked.

I shrugged. The doctor had given her something to help her sleep, and I'd convinced her to take it. She'd refused to get into bed until Anna was sitting on a chair by the door, guarding it.

"She's afraid to be alone," I said. "After that night."

Vasily tilted his head, beckoning me forward. "You can tell me, if you want."

I walked to the fireplace and sank onto the carpet at Vasily's feet, curling my legs underneath my skirt. The same way I used to sit with Papa.

"They shot him, right in front of us. I watched him die."

Once the first words were spoken, the rest came easier. I told Vasily what it had been like to have our home invaded. To witness the defilement of a place we both loved.

"There was a girl who pushed right past me carrying a handful of my clothes. No shame at all." *The girl I saw you on top of,* I was thinking, not that I ever would have said it. "I don't even know her name, but I recognized her. Big-boned, with one of those faces that always looks like she's frowning."

Vasily didn't show any particular interest, but he'd always been good at keeping secrets. How many times had he met with that girl? I'd seen no signs of seduction between them, let alone love. With a queasiness I preferred not to examine, I remembered sneering at her shameless behavior. But how much choice did she have?

"Don't tell Mama," Vasily said, "but all these Socialists and Bolsheviks are stirring up trouble in the army, too. Forming committees—soviets—and telling soldiers they don't have to salute officers. Are we supposed to hold meetings and vote before each attack? It's madness! Some officers have even been killed by their own men. Not in my division, but you hear stories."

"The war has to end soon. How much longer can it go on?"

"As if I could answer that!" Vasily attempted a laugh. "We've had successes. If you asked me a few months ago, I'd have told you things were looking better than they have in a long time. But with all this political uncertainty, who knows? It's impossible to run an army without order and discipline."

The mighty Russian Army was the pride of our country. Wasn't it strong enough to withstand a few rabble-rousers?

"I'm counting on you to look out for Mama," Vasily said. "I can't count on Uncle Sergei. You know what he's like."

"He's doing his best. The magazine takes up so much time . . ."

"Exactly. He's always put work over family. You're the one who's here with Mama every day. Keep her busy. Make sure she doesn't brood too much. Encourage some of her artist friends to visit."

Our house hadn't hosted salons or poetry readings for years, but I nodded anyway.

"I know it's not fair to ask this of you, at your age. You should have nothing on your mind but dresses and boys."

I'd be turning sixteen in a few months; this was the summer I was supposed to be planning my debut. The loss of a party was nothing compared to the loss of Papa. But it still stung, the smaller hurt compounding the larger one.

"We'll be fine," I said. Vasily would be back on the front lines soon, and I wouldn't add to his worries. "Everyone says Petrograd is much safer now."

"Tell Mama that." I noted that Vasily didn't confirm it was actually true. "Elena told me you were very brave, at Priyalko. I'm proud of you."

I'd been trained to modestly decline compliments, but I couldn't help flushing with pride. Vasily didn't hand out praise lightly.

We passed the rest of my brother's visit quietly, accepting condolence calls but largely keeping to ourselves. When Vasily left, the house sank into gloomy silence, Mama and I moving wordlessly through the cavernous rooms like ghosts. My birthday in September passed like any other day: school, a quiet supper, in bed by nine. Although a few of my school friends had been given small coming-out parties by their parents, Mama didn't offer to host one for me, and I didn't ask her to. Those gatherings, with their forced cheerfulness and nostalgic reminiscing, seemed more depressing than no party at all.

Outside our home the provisional government lived up to its name. It was a temporary stopgap, incapable of inspiring loyalty or trust. For the most part law and order had been restored in Petrograd, though occasional riots by disgruntled soldiers or factory workers kept us on edge. Nothing ever felt resolved; we lived with our breaths half-held. When the Bolsheviks took advantage of the unsettled political situation to seize power in October, it seemed like yet another twist in an ongoing drama, rather than a definitive end. The country was already a mess, divided and ungovernable. As Sergei told me, repeating the conventional wisdom, it was only a matter of time until Lenin and his friends were pushed aside by someone else.

"Alek's a Bolshevik, isn't he?" I asked caustically. To Mama's horror, Sergei still saw Alek socially, believing his friend shouldn't be blamed for my father's death. "He must be delighted."

Sergei shrugged. "It's one thing to preach revolution. Running a country is another matter. Who knows how long the Bolsheviks can hold on?"

We soon learned that the truly ruthless are not easily displaced.

Within a few days, proclamations from Lenin were posted all over the city, declaring that those who lived off the work of others were parasites with no place in the new Communist state. The usual class-warfare slogans, I assumed, but we soon learned that they were more than political posturing. Sergei had spent months organizing the paperwork for

Papa's estate; now, he told us in blank-eyed shock, there was no estate. We couldn't withdraw money from the bank, because the government had confiscated all of our accounts. A few weeks later, near the end of the year, we received a notice that our house was being turned into a dormitory for nurses who would be working in the city's new health clinics. All our possessions were now considered property of the state.

"Everything?" Mama asked in horrified wonder, and I could only shrug. The following day, we watched as our family's treasures, collected over generations, were taken away. Paintings and candlesticks and crystal and blankets—all gathered in heaps and carried out the front door. Mama's tiaras and Papa's fur hat. Vasily's toy soldiers and the dolls Sergei had bought me in Paris. Mama and I were told we could each pack one small bag of personal items, though the dour man in charge didn't explain what that meant, and we were too cowed to ask. Under the watchful eye of a guard with a gun, I crammed what I could into the satchel I usually used for my schoolbooks: two dresses, some undergarments, a brush, and my drawing pencils. My sketchbook was too big to fit, and when I struggled to cram it in partway, the man grabbed it from my hands, flipped through it, and carelessly ripped up the pages. He stared at me as the tattered pieces fell around our shoes, daring me to cry. I stared back, dry-eyed.

I convinced Mama to pack only her most practical housedresses, made of the heaviest, most durable fabrics. She followed my instructions sluggishly, her muscles slowed by misery. The guard laughed when she pulled open a drawer bursting with creamy, lace-trimmed nightclothes and brassieres, and Mama's face crumpled with shame. I was the one who pulled out what she needed and rolled the pieces tight, as if it were perfectly normal for an unshaven stranger to stare at my mother's most intimate possessions. I also convinced Mama to change her silk shoes for boots.

The guard motioned toward the stairs. "Go on."

Go where? The guard either didn't know or didn't care; we were no longer his problem. Mama and I hovered at the top landing, watching the hollowing-out of our home. Unlike the terrible night at Priyalko, there was no aura of violence or vengeance. It was an efficient looting, men passing in and out in brisk, organized formation. Everyone knew their place, except us.

"What do we do?" Mama asked me, as if I'd planned for such a calamity. The notice of confiscation had only arrived the day before, and neither of us had imagined we'd be turned out so quickly.

Mentally, I ran through the names of people who'd take us in. Sergei would, of course, but he lived in a single room over his office. My cousin Maria's family, the only other Shulkins who lived in Petrograd, had gone south, to the Black Sea resort of Yalta, where the Moscow Shulkins were planning to join them. Mama had friends and I had friends, but they were probably losing their homes, too. With growing unease, I realized everyone we knew fit the Bolsheviks' definition of a parasite.

It was a late afternoon in January, bitingly cold and already dark. The thought of being quite literally turned out onto the street, with no money and no food, gave me the courage to approach the man in charge.

"Excuse me, sir."

The man turned, his face twisted into a scowl. Immediately, I realized my error. "Comrade."

He gave me a slight nod, allowing me to continue. Not a cruel man, just overworked and distracted.

"Please allow us to stay a day or two more. We'll go as soon as we find another place to live."

"Only workers are entitled to housing."

"Then we'll work."

The man stared at me, assessing my sincerity. I stared back, determined to prove I wasn't as spoiled as he might assume.

"Wait in the kitchen with the others," he ordered.

The "others," Mama and I discovered, were what remained of our staff: Olga, the cook, and Old Ivan, the butler. We'd lost servants in a steady trickle through the late summer and fall, as the old order gradually crumbled. But I'd never expected nearly all of them to desert us. Olga made tea, and Mama persuaded Old Ivan to sit down with us: "Why stand on ceremony now?" *At least these two are loyal,* I thought, before wondering if they were simply too old to be tempted by the promise of change. We drank from plain staff cups; all Mama's fine porcelain had been packed up and taken away.

It was well into the evening when we finally were informed of our fate. Mama and I could stay in one of the servants' rooms on the top floor, in exchange for cleaning the house and preparing it for the nurses' arrival. Once the dormitory was open, Olga and Old Ivan would stay on to help run it, and Mama and I would be left to fend for ourselves.

Mama didn't say anything as we shuffled upstairs and into what had once been Anna's room. There were two iron-framed beds topped with thin blankets. It was so cold that I kept my coat on as I unpacked our bags. Our possessions only half filled the small dresser. Mama sat and watched my meager attempt to look busy.

"Nadia . . ."

Her voice faded, as if she didn't have the strength to produce another sound. She looked almost weightless, a feather at the mercy of the wind. I would have to be her shelter. Protect her from the forces threatening to blow her away.

"I'll find us a place to live," I told her. "I promise."

Mama's head dipped in the barest suggestion of a nod.

"For now, we'll work hard and keep quiet. We mustn't give them any reason to distrust us."

Mama did her best the following morning. She wrapped her hair in a kerchief, like a peasant wife, and filled bucket after bucket with water at the kitchen sink. Though it must have shattered her heart to scrub the same floors she'd once flitted across in a rustle of silk, she kept to her task with grim-faced concentration. We moved the mops clumsily at first, quickly drenching the hems of our skirts, but within a few hours we'd developed a method. Wipe in a thick, straight line across one edge of the room, then work our way back on a parallel path underneath. Look down at the streaks of water rather than up at the empty walls.

At midday, Olga shrugged when I asked what there was to eat. "All the food is gone. Ivan and I got ration cards, to eat at a canteen."

I sought out the man who'd allowed us to stay and approached him as obsequiously as a serf appealing to the tsar.

"Comrade, my mother and I did not receive food ration cards."

"Rations are for workers."

"My mother and I are working," I protested. "You've seen us cleaning the floors, all morning."

"No rations for former people."

It was the first time I'd heard the term that soon defined my life. The new Communist state not only wanted to strip families like mine of our privileges and wealth, it wanted us to disappear completely. Once you were deemed a "former person"—as anyone with a noble name was—you became a living ghost. But I didn't know that yet.

"How are we supposed eat?" I asked the commander.

He threw up his hands, the classic gesture of a helpless bureaucrat. "That's not my problem!"

Fear overpowered my hunger. With a bashful apology, I backed away.

In the late afternoon, when the grumbling in my stomach had progressed into a painful ache, I heard Sergei calling my name from the front hall. I ran out of the downstairs bathroom, where I'd been cleaning up the mess left by the dozens of men who'd emptied our house.

"The kitchen," I whispered, pulling my uncle along before the commander could see him.

Mama was on her knees in the butlers' pantry, scrubbing empty shelves that used to be stacked with serving platters. She bounded up to hug Sergei, and I caught only a quick glimpse of his shocked face before she'd clutched his head to her shoulder.

"Thank God you've come! You heard what happened?"

Sergei nodded. "It's going on all over town."

We huddled in a corner as Sergei told us which other families had already been pushed out of their homes. So many names. The Shulkins who'd gathered at the Black Sea resorts were all planning to leave the country.

"That's all well and good for Prince Shulkin," Mama said. "He's got houses in Italy *and* France! We've got nothing."

"Not quite nothing," I murmured, pointing discreetly to my waist. Mama and I still had the jewels sewn into our corsets, which she said we'd save for an emergency. Wasn't that exactly the situation we were in?

"I couldn't leave without Vasily," Mama said. "How would he find us?"

We hadn't received a letter from the front for months; we didn't even know if my brother was still alive. Mama said he had to be, because we'd have been informed of his death by telegram otherwise. I wasn't so sure, given the chaos in the Russian Army, but tried not to think about it. Imagining Vasily dead felt like a betrayal.

"Even if we could afford the train or boat fare, we'd be as poor in Europe as we are here," Sergei said. "Let's not rush into anything. The Bolsheviks are serious about getting out of the war, at least, so Vasily should be coming home soon. We can decide what to do then."

"How are we supposed to eat?" Mama's voice quivered, which was usually the precursor to dramatic tears.

Sergei seemed surprised that we'd been denied ration cards; he'd gotten one yesterday, when a representative of the new Commissariat of Culture had come to the magazine office to tell them it had been nationalized.

"I know some people in the new government," Sergei said. Alek, I assumed, though I didn't want to say his name in front of Mama. "Things are so unsettled that I'm not sure who to approach right now, but I promise I'll sort things out. Find you a place to live—or you can move in with me. In the meantime, I'll share my rations."

"So will I."

I turned and saw Olga, the woman who was as much a part of this kitchen as the stove and the sink. Ever since I was a little girl, she'd loved feeding me. I couldn't walk into the room without her putting together a plate of snacks or insisting I take a bite of whatever she was cooking. Now that the pantry was bare, this was all she could offer. A gesture of love, from someone I'd always taken for granted. I couldn't find the right words to thank her, but I could tell by the way she reached for my hand and squeezed it that she understood.

Every morning, I wondered if this would be the last day we'd be allowed to stay in the house. But once the cleaning was done, workmen arrived with new furniture, and Mama and I kept busy setting up the dormitories. Then the nurses moved in, and we were given a constantly rotating, never-ending list of chores. With half a dozen women in each bedroom, sharing the same three bathrooms, there was always something to clean. Mama and I bathed in our room with a bucket of cold water.

When we weren't mopping or folding or polishing, we were in the kitchen, helping Olga make breakfast and dinner for fifty women, on rotating shifts throughout the day. Officially, Mama and I weren't allowed to eat those meals, but Olga found ways to sneak us food. A small loaf of bread hidden in a pile of towels. Roasted potatoes tucked in the bottom of a cleaning bucket. She made sure Mama and I cleaned the pots every evening, so we could eat whatever we scraped off the bottom. It was never enough to make me feel full, which is why I remember

1918 as the beginning of the hungry years. But it was enough to keep us going.

Sergei kept saying he'd find us something better, but eventually we all realized there wasn't anything better. Compared to some of Mama's old friends, we were actually fortunate: we had a room to ourselves and indoor plumbing. Gradually, imperceptibly, Mama and I adjusted. My hands reddened and hardened as my arms thickened. In time, I could carry two full buckets of water without any of it sloshing over the side. Mama's voice, which used to ring through the house, grew softer and more deliberate, used only when necessary: "Pass the soap" or "I'll take up the sheets." She nibbled at her food and grew steadily thinner, but insisted she felt fine whenever I asked. She'd always been one to make a fuss over the smallest inconvenience, but when she faced true suffering, she mustered a strength I hadn't known she had.

When the Bolsheviks made their peace settlement with Germany, delivering on their promise to end the war, Mama was ecstatic. "I could kiss Lenin himself," she gushed, and I caught a glimpse of her old sparkle, hidden beneath her drab washerwoman's veneer. Soon, Vasily would be back, and we could put this sad, diminished life behind us. I'd always wanted to visit Paris, a place I pictured in eternal twilight, lit by the glow of streetlights and the Eiffel Tower. Vasily would take care of Mama, and our Shulkin cousins would help us get settled. The weight of my family's future would no longer rest on my exhausted shoulders.

Then we received a letter from Vasily, written in a rushed scrawl. He wasn't coming back to Petrograd—he was doing his duty and fighting for his country. No further information, no forwarding address. Mama cried with a tightly wound misery that worried me far more than her old histrionics, and I rushed through my afternoon chores so that Mama and I could sneak out and see Sergei before we had to start making supper.

Though Sergei's literary magazine was now an official Communist publication, little else at the office had changed. The front room, crammed with desks and disheveled-looking writers, had the same smell of fresh ink and stale coffee. At a long table in the back, Sergei and a group of editors were huddled over a page layout. The only people who seemed to notice that we'd entered were the two men in Red Army uniforms who were leaning against one wall, smoking. I waved at Sergei, ignoring the soldiers. They made me nervous.

When Sergei heard we'd gotten a letter from Vasily, he murmured, "Upstairs."

I'd never been to what Sergei called his apartment, though I assumed from Mama's teasing that it was small and unimpressive. My uncle prided himself on having simple tastes. Even so, I was taken aback by the room's starkness. A bed and wooden chair sat side by side near the lone window; a table with a basin and kettle was tucked into a corner. There was no other furniture, only stacks of books lined up like pillars and a small iron stove. The bare wood floor creaked as I walked forward, and I saw the telltale scrapes left by hastily moved furniture. It hadn't always been so empty, I realized. Just like at our house, everything of value had been stripped away.

Sergei read through the letter, then folded it tight. "It sounds like Vasily has gone off with Kerensky."

I knew the name, of course—at one point, General Kerensky had been the commander of the entire Imperial Army. But that great fighting force no longer existed, and most of the soldiers Kerensky once led had been absorbed into the Communist Red Army. Now Sergei told Mama and me the news we'd never see in an official paper: troops were gathering under Kerensky in what they called the Volunteer Army. Loyal to Russia, not Communism, they were determined to drive out the Bolsheviks.

"Do you think they can?" Mama asked. She looked more hopeful than she had in months.

"If they get enough foreign support," Sergei said. "The British and the French invested millions in Russia, before the war. They'll never get that money back as long as Lenin's around. I'd say that gives them a very good reason to support Kerensky."

"Do you have any idea where Vasily might be? We could visit him, maybe—"

Sergei abruptly cut her off. "You can't have anything to do with Vasily. Our position is bad enough as it is."

He walked over to the washbasin and dropped the letter inside. Then he pulled a matchbox out from his pocket.

"What are you doing?" Mama protested.

Sergei ignored her. He lit a match and touched it to the paper, conjuring a streak of flame. When Mama cried out and rushed over, Sergei held her back.

"You can't keep anything that makes you look suspicious. If Vasily writes again, you must do the same thing. Burn the letter immediately."

"I'll hide it. You're not a mother—you don't understand. Just holding a paper he touched makes me feel like I'm with him."

"From now on, you're a loyal comrade." I'd never heard Sergei speak with such cutting precision. "Your room could be searched at any time. They might already be doing it, without you knowing."

It can't take long, I thought. *We have hardly anything left to search.*

"I've worked very hard, cultivating friends in the new government," Sergei continued. "I'd prefer they not know that my own nephew is fighting against the Red Army."

"Friends," Mama scoffed. "The same friends who were going to get us ration cards? A place to live?"

"There is no place for someone like you!"

Mama took a quick, hurt breath, but Sergei made no attempt to soothe her. "There are hundreds of people pouring into the city each day—young peasants fresh off the farm—and not nearly enough apartments for them all. I've heard of families of ten living in a single room! Why do you think you've been allowed to stay in your house this long? Because you're such a good worker? No, you're there because I groveled to the new commissar of worker housing, telling him how convenient it would be for my sister and niece to take care of the dormitory because they know the building so well and want to see it cared for. The job you think you're too good for is a blessing!"

We all have moments where the world as we know it shifts on its axis, shaking our certainties and forcing us to face our assumptions in a new, harsh light. I'd thought Sergei survived the revolution relatively unscathed. It had never occurred to me that he'd been walking a treacherous tightrope, currying favor with the new government while trying to protect his ostracized family. Mama was wrong. Sergei might not have a child of his own, but he understood what it meant to love one.

"It makes me sick to think of you cozying up to Bolshevik thugs," Mama lamented.

"They're not all thugs. Alek, for example."

Mama's face twisted, as if the very mention of his name made her feel sick.

"You found him quite charming, didn't you?" Sergei asked. "That summer at Priyalko?"

The air seemed to harden around us, forcing our bodies still. Sergei and Mama glared at each other, their faces mirror images, danger crackling in the air between them.

"As I've tried to tell you many times, Alek genuinely regrets what happened to Anton." Sergei's voice was steely but calm. "Yes, he talked to some workers at Priyalko, but only about forming a collective farm. He swears he never encouraged violence."

"I don't believe him," Mama snapped. "In my eyes, he's a murderer."

"He's a Bolshevik, an important one. Put your feelings aside."

"Don't you have any regrets?" Mama asked sadly. "All those articles you published, for years, about reforming Russia. This is where your Socialist dreams brought us. We're considered traitors in our own country. Trapped, like animals!"

The Bolsheviks had taken over all the ports and border crossings shortly after our Shulkin relatives fled, and former people were no longer allowed to leave. Even in our pitiful, malnourished state, it seemed we were too dangerous to be let loose in the world.

"We have nothing left, and I must deny my own son. Is that what you wanted?"

"Of course not. It breaks my heart to see you suffering. But you mustn't give up hope. I truly believe these trials will lead us to a better place. One where all men—and all women—are equal."

"There is no such place," Mama muttered.

I couldn't help wondering, *Why not?* I'd grown up hearing my uncle talk about freedom and fairness, ideals that were particularly appealing to a teenage girl. Now that the shock of my family's humiliation had dulled, I no longer resented each chore I was forced to perform. I got to my work dutifully and went to bed each night exhausted but accepting. I thought of all the hours I'd spent reading French novels and learning to waltz, while other girls my age had been scrubbing out my toilet and mending my underwear. With each mirror I polished and each floor I mopped, it felt like I was leveling out the tallies between what I'd earned and what I owed. No matter what the revolution had cost me, I wanted to believe that my suffering had a purpose, that it was a necessary stage in the rebirth of Russia. Most of all, I wanted to believe in Sergei.

And so, as 1918 began, I looked cautiously forward. I was prepared to work—I *wanted* to work—and felt there must be some place in the new Communist state where my education and perseverance could be put to better use than scrubbing toilets. When the winter cold eased and we were no longer dependent on the slivers of coal Olga snuck us, even Mama showed signs of her old self, humming Mozart sonatas as she swept and staying up late to rehem my dress so it wouldn't look ragged. "We must keep up our standards," she'd say with a wry smile.

I looked away from the former noblemen haggling at impromptu street markets, offering up their treasures in exchange for food. *We still have our jewels,* I told myself. *We're not that desperate yet.* The city I walked through looked like a reproduction of the place I'd grown up: the buildings in their proper places, intersected by an orderly pattern of bridges and canals. But it didn't feel right. So many of the people I'd known had left, leaving only their empty houses as proof they'd ever existed. All the shops were closed, their window displays empty or coated in dust. The streets stretched out in expectant, poignant silence, waiting for carriages and automobiles that never came. Even in sunlight, Petrograd was shadowed by the ghosts of its past.

When winter returned, Mama developed a hacking cough, right as the dormitory's coal rations started to be more closely monitored. Olga wasn't able to give us even the meager amounts she'd managed the previous winter, and Mama and I huddled against each other each night in the same bed. Even with our coats stretched across our blankets, we shivered. As Mama's breath grew steadily raspier, I grew obsessed with keeping her warm. Assessing the few possessions we had left, I wondered: *Is this worth Mama's life?* The answer was obvious. In December, I trudged to one of the black-market sites and traded a dress for enough coal to see us through January. When that was gone, I chopped up the dresser in our room and burned the pieces. Who needs a dresser when you have hardly any clothes? I traded Mama's silver-handled hairbrush and comb—a wedding present from her mother—for a precious ham-bone and a sack of vegetables, which Olga transformed into a stew so delicious that it made me cry. Mama's illness gave each day a crystalline intensity: *She must get better. It's the only thing that matters.*

Mama's cough eventually eased. But she never fully recovered; the sickness had obliterated her final reserves of strength. Though only in her early forties, she moved like an old woman, puffing up the stairs and hunching over the laundry. I did as much of her work as I could, but eventually I was taken aside by the head nurse, a brisk woman who walked through the dormitory like a mother hen in a barnyard, her eyes on the lookout for wayward chicks.

"Your mother isn't doing her share," she said tersely.

"She's been sick, but she's getting better, I promise."

"We've got new cleaners coming tomorrow. I'll need you both out by the morning."

"No, please—there must be a mistake. Let me talk to my uncle. He has friends in the Party."

"It's already been decided." She gave me a look that was pointed but not unkind. "You can't stay."

It was only then that I understood what she was really telling me. It didn't matter whether or not I was a good worker, or who Sergei's friends were. Someone higher up had decided the Shulkin women must go, and that order would be followed. Righteous anger rippled through me in a scorching wave, but I kept silent. I realized the head nurse had no more power to save my job than I did. For both of us, survival depended on obedience to the system.

There was only one place for Mama and me to go. We left our house for the last time the following morning, our sense of mourning only slightly lessened by the extra food Olga had snuck to us. The sun peeked out from the April gloom, its rays illuminating a strange mound in the middle of the street. Stepping closer, I saw it was a dead horse, ribs protruding from its emaciated flesh. My memories of the once-bustling avenue fought against this jarring new reality. The streetcar tracks were still there—unused for more than a year—as was the butcher shop where Olga placed her weekly orders. But the windows were boarded up, and the doorway was barred by a pile of rotting garbage. Belatedly sickened by the smell, I urged Mama on to Sergei's.

He welcomed us with embraces that took the place of words none of us could or wanted to say. Though the walk had taken less than ten minutes, Mama looked noticeably tired, and Sergei insisted she sit down while he made tea. He set the kettle on the stove, bustling around and making small talk. Sergei had never been comfortable with silence.

"I only have one cup, so we'll have to share," he said. "There's plenty to go around, though."

The tea was strong and hot; drinking it made me feel like I'd been revived by a magic elixir. "Thank God for your rations. Olga had to reuse the same leaves over and over—we called it tea, but it was mostly warm water."

I handed the cup to Mama, who took a few small sips before handing it to Sergei.

"Look at us," she said mournfully. "Three people sharing one cup. One room. How has it come to this?"

"We'll manage. You and Nadia can have the bed, and I'll sleep on the floor. Nothing I haven't done before, in my student days."

Mama liked to tease Sergei about what she called his "years of debauchery," when he darted between the major universities of Europe, making countless friends but doing very little actual work. This time, she didn't rise to the bait. Her face remained tilted to the floor, her shoulders slumped. Sergei shot me a pleading look.

"There's one thing to be grateful for, at least," I said cheerily. "We don't have to clean those bathrooms anymore!"

Mama managed a small smile, acknowledging my effort and doing her best to go along.

"You wouldn't believe the mess those nurses made," I told Sergei. "I always assumed women were neater than men, but that's clearly not true."

I described the head nurse's various tangles with Old Ivan and the ongoing feud between the nurses from Petrograd and the nurses who'd grown up in the country. After more water had boiled and we had our fill of tea, we moved the few pieces of furniture into a cozy arrangement in the corner, where Sergei could sit in the chair and Mama and I on the bed, facing him. Mama talked about the first time she visited our old house, when Papa was courting her, and I worried, at first, that such nostalgia would pull her back into grief. But on that afternoon, as the sun brightened her still-lovely face, talking about old times seemed to restore her. She told a story I'd never heard before, about a party during her first season, when she'd promised the same dance to three different young men and set off melodramatic threats of a duel. I caught glimpses of her former self in her eyes and her voice, proof she hadn't yet been fully defeated. And I felt the weight of all I'd have to do to keep that spirit alive.

There were no jobs available for someone with my name and background, despite Sergei's efforts. So I made myself useful in the only way I could: by waiting in line for bread. There was never enough to go around, even for those with ration cards, and after Sergei came home a few times empty-handed, I offered to take his place. The first day, I set out at sunrise, only to find hundreds of people already lined up, their bleary eyes lighting on me with no more than vague interest. After that, I began rising in the dark, standing outside for hours in the wind or the rain. Though I saw the same faces day after day, we rarely spoke. We were an indistinguishable, impersonal mass, reduced to a single need. Sergei smuggled what he could from the canteen where he ate lunch and dinner—a dried fish or handful of kasha wrapped in a handkerchief—but Mama and I subsisted mainly on those coarse, dry, precious loaves of bread.

One day, I took a bite and felt a sharp stab of pain. I reached into my mouth and pulled out a splinter that had stabbed my inner cheek. Sergei took the bread from my hands and held it up to his face.

"No wonder it's so terrible. They're stretching it with sawdust."

After that, I learned to pick through each piece before eating it. Mama was always insisting she wasn't hungry and that I should take hers, but I forced her to match me, bite for bite.

By the fall of 1919, we hadn't heard from Vasily in more than a year. We knew the Red Army was fighting the so-called Whites, on various fronts far from Petrograd, but there was no way to know who was actually winning. Then Sergei came bounding up the stairs one evening, and I knew as soon as I saw his strained expression that he was about to deliver bad news.

"The Whites are retreating, and Vasily's been captured."

I'd been so sure he was going to tell us Vasily was dead that I could only stare at Sergei in baffled silence. Behind me, Mama moaned.

"From what I've been told, he's with a group of former tsarist officers who are being held at the Peter and Paul Fortress."

"He's in prison?" Mama gasped.

"He's considered a traitor, Katenka. We're lucky he wasn't shot."

Vasily was alive and here in Petrograd. It felt like the best news I'd gotten in a very long time. "Can we see him?"

Uncle Sergei sighed. "I hope so. I'm trying."

Mama was crying, tears flooding down her cheeks and speckling her bodice. I leaned into her, grabbing her tight, relief surging through us like a jolt of life. She would take care of herself now, knowing she might see Vasily. I no longer felt quite so alone.

We cut the jewels out of our corsets and gave them to Sergei to use as bribes. Rubies and emeralds had little value in black-market food haggling, but they were still in demand with Party officials who had wives and mistresses to impress. After a few weeks of negotiation, flattery, and late-night drinking sessions, we were given permission for a visit with Prisoner Shulkin.

The prison commander met us at the front entry, a grim enclosure of damp stone. Jangling a key ring with ostentatious enthusiasm, he led us down a series of gloomy corridors, a procession designed for intimidation. Mama walked arm in arm with Sergei, looking more determined than I'd seen in years. The commander finally ushered us into a small anteroom, with benches flush against the wall. Sergei and I sat, but Mama paced, her fluttering fingers unable to rest.

"Wait here," the commander said.

Mama held herself together during the long, silent minutes that followed, but her self-possession crumbled when Vasily was finally brought in. My brother, who'd always swaggered more than walked, shuffled like an old man, off-balance. His prized army uniform hung around his shrunken frame in tatters. His shaved head made his haggard face look even more skeletal, and his hands shook as they reached out for Mama. She collapsed into his arms, sobbing, and I watched his teeth clench with the effort of remaining silent, refusing to burden her with his own pain. Sergei was crying, too, but silently, and after turning his head to wipe away the tears, he kept one hand pressed over his eyes. Unwilling to face what his nephew had become.

Vasily looked at me over Mama's shoulder and let out a sigh. He kissed my cheeks with cracked lips that scraped my skin, and I hugged him tight. I felt the ridge of each rib along his back.

"I'm so glad to see you," I murmured.

"Not half as glad as I am to see you. My beautiful sister."

I laughed, as I always did when Vasily teased me. Of course I wasn't beautiful; I was skinny and grubby, with stringy hair and chapped skin. Then I realized Vasily wasn't joking. His eyes were tearing up, as if I really was the loveliest girl he'd seen in ages, and it made me want to cry, too. But that wouldn't help my broken brother. I slapped him lightly on the shoulder and told him he should save his lies for someone who'd believe them. It was enough to elicit smile from Vasily and distract Mama from her weeping. To pull us all back from collapse.

Sergei kissed Vasily and urged him to sit down. Vasily clenched his teeth when he bent his knees, each movement belabored. Had he been injured in battle? Or beaten by his guards? Mama sat beside him, her hand drifting from his sleeve to his shoulder, seeking constant reassurance that her son was still there.

I'd imagined this reunion as a cacophony of voices, all of us competing to share our stories. But the years we'd been separated contained horrors we'd rather not revisit, and the conversation soon faltered. Vasily said he was being treated well—an obvious lie—and I reassured him that we had plenty to eat. Sergei prodded Vasily to tell us about the battles he'd fought in, but my brother, who'd wanted to be a soldier for as long as I could remember, refused to talk about the war.

"There's no point. We lost."

Every topic seemed to end in the same dispiriting silence.

"Uncle Sergei was lucky enough to get us a few dried herring the other day," I said, "and it made me think of that day Papa tried to teach you how to fish."

It was one of our classic family stories, one that each person recounted differently, from their own perspective. For Vasily, it was a parable about fathers and sons: Papa convinced he was right—despite his own inexperience—and Vasily showing him up by catching a bigger fish. To Mama, it was an example of men's stubborn foolishness: all that bragging about the big feast they'd bring home for supper, and after three hours, they caught two measly carp. I remembered hovering near the riverbank, conscious that I shouldn't break Papa's concentration, but too curious to stay away. It was one of the dozens of memories I had of Priyalko, each incident blurring into a generalized whole. Sunlight dancing on the water; the cushion of crushed leaves beneath my feet.

"Remember Elena's fish rolls?" Sergei asked. "I begged her to make them, every time I visited."

"Her honey cake," Vasily added. "I have dreams about that cake."

In shared disbelief, we went through all the dishes Elena would prepare for a typical Priyalko picnic, most of which we'd leave half-eaten. That led to a lively discussion of Mama's most memorable houseguests and eccentric protégés. We talked about all the people we'd known, including the neighbors whose eldest daughter Vasily had always tried to impress.

"Do you still see them?" he asked.

I shook my head. "They left when their house was taken, soon after ours." Like so many others, they had simply disappeared.

"Oh well, she had no interest in me anyway," he said. "She was a mature woman of twenty, and I was only seventeen. Practically a baby."

He pretended it didn't matter, but Vasily had always used jokes to shield his feelings. Had he really been in love with her? Wanted to prove himself as a soldier in part for her benefit? If so, her absence would feel like yet another blow. I'd grown so accustomed to the hollowed-out city that I hadn't realized what it would be like for Vasily, to hear that nearly everyone else was gone.

We couldn't have been talking more than ten minutes when the prison commander returned, flanked by two guards. Mama clutched Vasily's arm, while Sergei protested that we'd been promised more time. The men ignored him. The burliest guard wrapped a beefy hand around Vasily's shoulder and dug in his thumb, making Vasily crumple with a gasp of pain. The guard shoved Vasily forward, into the hands of his partner, who dragged my brother's limp body away. There were no goodbyes, no final embrace. Only howls from Mama, and Sergei's feeble attempts to comfort her. I was too shocked to say anything.

The prison commander stood in the doorway, making a show of impatience. Sergei managed to get Mama moving, and I wrapped my arm around hers. We trudged along behind Sergei and the commander as I did my best to console her, wiping her tears with the hem of my sleeve. We'd long since traded away our handkerchiefs. If the prison had seemed bleak when we first walked in, it was even worse on the way out. I'd gotten through the darkest days because I'd always believed my suffering was temporary, that Vasily would one day come back and take charge. That belief had now crumbled, along with my brother's strength. Instead of surrendering responsibility, I'd have to carry my brother as well.

"When can we see him again?" Mama begged Sergei.

"I don't know." Sergei looked as exhausted as I felt.

"What were you talking to that horrible guard about?"

"I asked if there'd be a trial."

Mama looked terrified, and I glared at Sergei. The last thing we needed was Mama having a fit on the prison doorstep.

"Nothing's been decided. The commander did say we could send food."

As if we have any to spare, I thought bitterly. Then I remembered Vasily's sunken cheeks; he was even closer to starvation than we were. "We will. We have to."

Sergei looked doubtful, but Mama gave me a grateful, heartrending smile. I'd be doing this as much for her sake as Vasily's. "I'll trade my coat," I said.

Sergei shook his head—"Nonsense!"—but I ignored him.

"I can wrap myself in a blanket when I go out. It will be just as warm. Coats always fetch a good price. I can get potatoes, some vegetables—maybe even a chicken."

Mama leaned against me. She was so frail, I barely felt the shift of weight. "Take my coat," she offered. "You're the one who's out all day, waiting in those bread lines. I don't need mine."

Mama's coat had been extravagantly expensive, back in the days when Papa used to grumble over the dressmaker's bills. Cut to perfectly flatter her figure, it was made of thick blue wool with fur trim, and the skirt swished elegantly around her heels as she walked. It was the only remnant of her past elegance.

"For Vasily," she said, and I nodded. I'd wear rags, if it helped my brother.

I've heard, in the years since, that Petrograd had lost half its population by the year 1920. Those of us left became foragers, stripping the city of anything edible, food our greatest treasure. I no longer flinched when I saw dead animals in the street, though it was rare to see a whole carcass; horses and dogs were quickly stripped for meat. In those early, desperate months, our survival depended on the so-called bagmen who traded in shadowy corners. Mama's coat bought us a few weeks of food—enough to send a package to Vasily—but after that I had nothing of value to barter. Using whatever charm I could muster, I arranged to wash and mend clothes in exchange for a bag of barley or a few herring. I received less savory proposals, too, which I quickly turned down. Yet every time I wondered, *At what point will I say yes?*

As the weather got warmer, I began going barefoot, to save wear on my cracked boots. I joined other mangy survivors in the gardens of formerly great homes, scrounging among the pots and urns for edible herbs. When those were picked clean, I grabbed weeds and gnawed on the leaves. I hunted the avenues for pine cones, which we ground into a bitter tea. I even suggested we go to Priyalko, my hunger for fresh produce overpowering the memories of Papa's murder. It was Sergei who explained why we couldn't: there were barely any trains running between Petrograd and Moscow, let alone on the smaller branch lines. Even if we could find a way to get to our old estate, we couldn't risk going there without travel passes, which were never approved for former people.

Once, Mama would have angrily protested such an injustice, but deprivation had softened her. She spent most of her time on Sergei's bed, reading or napping, rarely going outside. "What is there to see?" she'd say.

Sergei still talked optimistically of better times, but he was struggling, too. His magazine had been renamed *New Voices*—a rebuke, presumably, to old voices like Sergei's—and he'd been pushed aside as editor, in favor of a young Communist would-be poet. They kept him on as a contributor, but he was no longer a man of influence. The really important people—including almost all the Bolsheviks—had moved to Moscow, the new capital of the Russian Soviet Republic. Sergei didn't even know Vasily had been sent to a work camp until months afterward, when my brother sent a short, impersonal letter that had obviously been approved by a censor. I mailed him small packages of food, when I could, but had no way of knowing if they ever reached him.

Summer brought not only sticky, sleepless nights, but an infestation of lice. No matter how many times I scrubbed our clothes or

Mama combed out my hair, we itched and scratched, made miserable by this new form of torture. In a fit of frustration, I marched down to the magazine's offices, picked up a pair of scissors, and began cutting. I didn't stop until my hair hung to the length of my earlobes, and I felt an unaccustomed but welcome lightness at the back of my neck.

Mama teared up when she saw me. "What have you done? You look like a boy!"

"Short hair for women is all the rage in France, I hear," said Sergei. He gave me an approving nod. "You're the height of fashion."

I thought he was only saying it to make me feel better. No one could really admire a woman with short hair.

It wasn't long afterward that I began feeling sluggish and flushed. When even the lure of bread wasn't enough to rouse me from bed, Mama realized I had a fever. She insisted on taking care of me, even though she, too, was looking unwell. By the end of the day, she was lying beside me in bed, heat emanating from her skin. The next morning, Sergei barely had the strength to get us fresh water before collapsing back onto the blanket he used as an improvised bed. Exhausted and semi-delirious, we lingered on the edge of sleep, tormented by prickly rashes that overran our arms and chests. For days, we subsisted on the remains of a bag of kasha and the water I managed to stumblingly retrieve from the magazine's bathroom, downstairs. The pitcher shook in my weakened hands, and only the knowledge that we couldn't afford to buy another one gave me the strength to hold on.

Finally, one morning, I woke up and realized the mental fog had cleared. I could lift my head without feeling nauseous, and my arms no longer felt like they were weighted with lead. I saw Sergei standing by the window, combing his hair. The first hints of sunlight illuminated his wan cheeks.

He heard the creak of the mattress and turned. "Feeling better?" he asked.

I nodded.

"Me, too." Sergei held up his ration card. "I might be in time for a loaf. Are you hungry?"

Surprisingly, I was.

"There's fresh water in the basin. I'll be back as soon as I can."

Mama was still asleep, and I pressed the back of my hand against her forehead. Warm, but the fever seemed to have eased. After Sergei left, I slid out of bed and pulled off the grimy, sweat-stained slip and underpants I'd been sleeping in. There was no soap, but rinsing my skin and clothes in clean water felt like a rebirth. I hung the pieces up to dry and pulled on my dress. It felt strange with nothing underneath.

Trying to keep as quiet as I could so Mama would keep sleeping, I looked through Sergei's piles of books. Since most were English and French novels—useless on the black market, where they'd mark you as a class traitor—they were the one indulgence left to me. I flipped open one I'd never read, *Jane Eyre*. Inside the front cover was a bookplate, engraved simply *Fields*. With a hurt pang, I thought of my governess, who'd brushed aside questions as she packed her bags. Had she left this book behind by mistake? Or was it a gift to Sergei, for his kindness? I skimmed the first pages, then found myself caught up in the story, Jane's losses and frustrations resonating with my own. I started out with my back against the wall and my legs stretched out, then lay on my stomach. When my arms began to throb, I moved to the chair by the window. It was there that I first began to worry.

Mama's breathing was so slow and shallow that her chest barely moved. I perched on the edge of the bed and looked more closely at her flushed face, the slackness of her mouth. Was she only sleeping, or had she gotten sicker? I gently shook her arm. She opened her eyes halfway and gave me a groggy stare.

"How do you feel?" I asked.

She muttered something that sounded like "Devil!" and batted me away.

"Are you thirsty?"

She gave me a furious glare, as if I were an unwanted stranger. Then she turned away and closed her eyes, muttering angrily but incoherently. When Sergei returned not long after, I was fidgety with worry. My uncle wasn't the picture of health himself—his eyes were ringed with sunken shadows—but he agreed that Mama was getting worse.

"We have to find a doctor," I fretted.

"She doesn't have the right papers."

Denying former people medical care, I assumed, was Lenin's way of assuring we died off all the faster.

Then I had an idea. Ordering Sergei to look after Mama, I rushed out of our room and down the stairs. The route to our old house was so implanted in my memory that I could have followed it blindfolded. I almost wished I had, to prevent me seeing the grubby decline of my once-great city. From the outside, at least, the house looked the same. I pounded on the door and sagged with relief when Olga opened it. She'd always been soothingly even-tempered, so her shocked expression told me instantly how far I'd fallen. Belatedly, I remembered my chopped-off hair, the dress sagging off my shriveled frame, my lack of undergarments. I folded my hands across my chest to cover my bosom.

"Mama's sick. I need to see the head nurse."

"She's at the hospital."

I could see Olga's lips quivering, but I didn't have time for her pity. It would only slow me down.

"Where?"

"The old French Exchange Bank. Is it serious?"

Rage swelled up inside me, demanding to be let loose. "Yes, it's serious! She'll die if she doesn't get help!"

Olga dipped her head, visibly cowed. "I will pray for her."

What good will that do? I seethed. Then I remembered all the times Olga had hid scraps of food so Mama and I could eat. Pious women like Olga truly believed in the power of prayer, and shouldn't I take any help I could get?

I squeezed her hands. "Thank you. I'm grateful."

The bank's grand façade was lined with thick stone columns, a design meant to proclaim power and strength. Now, this financial fortress had been transformed into a monument of human suffering. The grand, high-ceilinged lobby was an overcrowded waiting room, its once-gleaming marble floors covered with ragged groups of women and children. The tellers' windows had been turned into nurses' stations, each with a line dozens of people long. Babies' shrieks and angry voices echoed throughout the vast space. It was chaos.

A soldier with a rifle slung across his back was stationed just inside the doorway. "Papers!" he demanded.

"I need to see Nurse Vasetsky."

"Why?"

He sounded bored, more eager to get rid of me than help. I noticed the crimson pimples on his cheeks and remembered Papa saying that young soldiers craved discipline. Doing my best imitation of Mama ordering around the servants, I snapped, "Inform her Nadia Antonovna Shulkina is here."

The soldier looked me over, considering his options. Unlike Olga, he didn't seem disturbed by my shabbiness; he'd no doubt seen worse.

"Wait here."

He ambled off along a side corridor, infuriatingly slow. The minutes ticked away as my frustration notched up. Finally, when my head had started throbbing from the constant din, I saw Nurse Vasetsky walking toward me in her familiar brusque way.

"Comrade Shulkina." Her voice was crisp, but her eyes were puffy with fatigue. "What do you want?"

"My mother's had a fever for days." I pulled up a sleeve and showed her the faint pink bumps sprinkled on my inner arm. "And a rash, like this."

Nurse Vasetsky examined my skin, lips pursed. "Typhus."

"What should I do? Is there some medicine I can give her?"

She shook her head. "Half my nurses are down with either typhus or cholera. The older you are, the worse it hits. There's no way to treat it, and even if there were, we've run out of supplies. We can't even do surgeries, because there are no more needles or bandages." She gave me the same stern look she used to keep young nurses in line. "My best advice is to get out of here before you catch something else."

"There must be some way I can help her."

Nurse Vasetsky was too good a Communist to suggest praying. So she said nothing, which was an answer in itself. Mama was dying, and there was nothing I could do about it.

It took two days. I sat and lay with Mama, washing her face, brushing back her hair. I read aloud from one of Sergei's poetry books, the same way she used to read me fairy tales when I was little. When she twitched and mumbled, delirious, I held her hand and told her I loved her.

The end, when it came, was peaceful. She slipped into a calm deeper than sleep, then simply stopped breathing. I told myself to be grateful her suffering was over, though I was too numb to feel anything at all. I went downstairs to tell Sergei, the words coming out with unnatural coldness: "Mama's dead." Sergei hugged me and started to cry, but I could only listen and dumbly nod, as stiff and fragile as a porcelain doll. It was Sergei who wrapped Mama's body in her blanket, Sergei who bribed the cemetery caretaker with her boots and stockings so she could be buried next to Papa. Sergei honored Mama by talking about his older sister who'd dazzled all of Saint Petersburg. That woman had died years ago, and the devastating truth was that it had been easier to love the quieter, smaller person she'd become. During the three years since Papa's death, we'd grown closer, and taking care of her had become the focus of my life. Who was I without her?

Sergei, in typical fashion, wasn't one to dwell. After the burial, he turned away from grief and back to his writing, though *New Voices* was publishing fewer and fewer of his pieces. He was always on his way to or from somewhere, making the effort to stay connected with the few friends he still had in town. The room was tolerable when he was there, chattering away, undeterred by my limited responses. But I spent most days alone, trying to read or sew, the silence sinking into my bones. The part of me that still had hope had died alongside Mama. There was nothing to look forward to, nothing but pain in looking back. I was simply existing, in an eternal, dismal present.

By the end of 1920, I was nineteen years old and barely human. I had no friends, no connections to the larger world. The usual distractions for a woman my age—romance, proposals of marriage—were so out of reach that they seemed inconceivable. A few days after the first winter storm, I saw an old woman lying in a snowdrift and wondered why she'd been foolish enough to rest there. Then I got close enough to see her blank-eyed stare and frozen skin. Bare, gnarled feet stuck out from the hem of her dress, and I wondered if her shoes had been stolen before or after she died. I walked away hurriedly, telling myself she wasn't my problem. I noted my lack of compassion as if from a distance, further proof of how much I'd changed. The following week, a stooped, elderly man slumped to the ground in front of me, as if his will to live had seeped away midstride. I cut right around him, my heart as frozen as the Neva River. Once, I passed a bundle that might have been a dead child, but I turned my head away. I didn't want to know.

It was Sergei who led me out from the shadows, when they threatened to become my permanent retreat. One evening, as we were sipping tiny portions of porridge to make it last as long as possible, he began describing the latest outrages of the *New Voices* editor, whom Sergei believed was barely literate.

"He wants to add illustrations to all the stories, not just the cover. The whole point of a literary magazine is the *words*, don't you think?"

I nodded, glad he was off on a tirade. It was so much easier when I didn't have to speak.

"He's making all the articles shorter and filling half the space with pictures. Like a children's book."

Suddenly, Sergei stopped and pointed his spoon at me. "They're looking for new artists. 'Loyal young comrades to create visions of the future'—his words, not mine. You should apply."

I still had my box of colored pencils, one of the only personal possessions remaining from my past life. From time to time, I'd slide them out and run them between my fingers, the smoothness soothing me. But it had been a very long time since I'd used them. I wondered if I was still capable of creating anything worthwhile.

"I'm not a member of the Party," I said. "Do you think they'd accept me?"

"You're young, at least." Sergei stood up, his eyes meeting mine, sparks of possibility crackling between us. "I'm going downstairs to get you something. I'll be right back."

We only had one small lamp, which Sergei usually used to read. That night, he placed it by my side at the table, next to the stack of paper he'd taken from the office. I ran my fingers over the smooth white expanse. All that empty, intimidating space. I picked up the black pencil, then the green. The first few strokes were awkward and self-conscious, but abruptly I saw it: the outline of a leaf. A line down, some outward, and I had the vague suggestion of a tree. My hand started moving on its own, independent of my thoughts, filling in the space with swirls and shading. The landscape I was drawing wasn't Petrograd or even Priyalko. It was a wild place, a place to disappear. I added browns and grays for depth and perspective. The unruly world I'd created came alive—and so did I.

Sergei brought up drafts of current magazine stories and urged me to keep working. The editor rejected my first set of illustrations, as well as the second. By my third try, I knew what he wanted: bold, strong images created with bold, strong lines. I drew a woman with legs as thick as a tree trunk, her mighty arms lifting a red-starred flag. With forceful strokes, I sketched farmers and factory workers, figures who stood tall and proud. This time, the editor nodded approvingly as he flipped through them.

"That's it, exactly. How would you like to expand this one for the cover?"

The *New Voices* office was filled with Communist true believers, but none seemed to know or care about my aristocratic past. They came from all over Russia, the sons and daughters of peasants and professors, brought together by their belief in a new start. Their enthusiasm gradually tempted me out from isolation, even when it took all my strength to make a few minutes of small talk. I began spending more time there, a willing audience for writers who wanted to read out their first drafts. In shocked wonder, I realized one of the young typesetters was flirting with me, though I was still too guarded to reciprocate. The editor paid me—unofficially—in packages of food, which nourished both my body and my confidence. There were moments I felt happy. How astonishing, to know it was still possible.

Russia was experiencing its own tentative rebirth, along with my own. The year 1921 began as cold and gloomy as ever, yet day-to-day life became gradually less miserable. The government, facing the mass starvation of its people, eased its policy of forced collectivization, and farmers were allowed to sell parts of their harvests. A few shops and cafés reopened. In late summer, food began arriving from the Americans. Some of the *New Voices* writers muttered that this so-called charity was a plot to infiltrate and bring down the government, but that didn't stop them from taking their share. I thought of Americans in only the vaguest stereotypes—loud and unrefined—but whatever their faults, they had done for us what Lenin had not. When Sergei and I shared a chocolate bar he'd gotten from one of his mysterious "connections," I nearly cried.

From time to time, I would see girls in hats or shoes that weren't ragged from overuse and wonder if I, too, might someday have new clothes. I'd worn the same two dresses for years, and though I'd cut a few inches off the hems to make them more fashionable, there was only so much I could do to rework them. My boots were so cracked I had to stuff them with newspaper to keep my feet from frostbite.

The tentative resumption of trade meant I could now be paid as a *New Voices* contributor, and I spent hours deciding what I'd buy with each ruble. It was always food, because imagining each taste was almost as enjoyable as the actual eating. One day in September, I saw a farmer selling late-summer produce from his cart and walked over. I pulled a coin from my pocket and asked how many cherries it would buy.

"You can have them all," the farmer said. He began folding a cone out of paper so I could carry them. "It's the end of the season—they won't last long."

He handed me the cherries, along with a bouquet of wildflowers. "Soldiers buy these sometimes, for their girls. But I've gotten no takers today."

I almost giggled. Who'd have thought the first man to give me flowers would be twice my age and missing half his teeth?

Though I planned to save the cherries as a surprise for Sergei, I couldn't help sampling one as I walked. The tartness was invigorating, and I sucked on the pit to prolong the sensation. I was only a few steps from the *New Voices* office when a voice called out, "Comrade Shulkina?"

A man was leaning against the stone façade, his hands plunged in his pockets. Tall, sharp-featured, with round glasses perched halfway down his nose. Though it had been seven years since I'd seen Alek Semelkov, I recognized him instantly. And just as instantly, my carefree mood vanished.

"I came to see your uncle, but he's gone out for a bit," Alek said. "It's such a nice day, I thought I'd wait for him outside."

He was around Sergei's age, somewhere in his mid- or late thirties. He'd been spared the premature aging that accompanies near starvation: His hair and moustache were still dark brown, his posture straight and assured. His pristine gray suit and freshly shined shoes made him look like a visitor from another, more civilized world. His eyes scanned my body, the same way the bagmen used to examine the items I brought to trade. A look that said: *What's this worth?*

He extended a hand toward me—long fingers, impeccable nails— but I twisted my own callused hands tighter around my bundles, out of sight.

"Aleksandr Semelkov. Perhaps you don't remember me?"

How could I forget him? Here was the man responsible for Papa's death, talking to me like an old friend. I wanted to keep walking, to snub him completely. But I knew I mustn't offend him.

"Uncle Sergei's friend," I said.

"I stayed at your family's summer house once. Though you've changed since then—you're all grown up." A smile to show he approved of the changes.

"You look exactly the same."

"It's kind of you to say so. How is your mother?"

"She died last year. Typhus."

"I'm very sorry to hear that. She was an enchanting woman."

His smug expression taunted me into provoking him. "Mama was never the same after my father's death."

Alek's face didn't change; we might have been discussing a stranger. "A terrible loss for your family."

"He was shot right in front of me. I watched him die."

For a moment, we were poised on a precipice, the air between us dense with tension. Had I gone too far?

Alek spoke slowly, in French. "We must be terrible so the people don't have to be." Then, switching back to Russian, "A quote from Danton, during the French Revolution. The lust for freedom leads mobs to violence. The state must channel those impulses, to prevent such bloodshed."

He'd always been a good speaker, quick with a clever argument. It was one of the qualities Mama had admired.

"I didn't plan or encourage the attack on your father," Alek continued. "I bear your family no ill will. I've done my best to help you, when I could. Your brother Vasily, for example . . ."

A familiar nervous panic thudded in my chest. "Is he all right?"

Alek nodded. "When Vasily's regiment surrendered, most of the officers were executed. I was the one who saw his name on a list and recommended rehabilitation instead. It was the right decision. He's been a model worker at the camp. I came here today to tell Sergei that Vasily has been approved for reassignment."

"What does that mean?"

"The Red Army is fierce but undisciplined. We're surrounded by enemies who refuse to recognize the new Soviet state—enemies like Germany and England who could send in troops any time. We can't fight back a foreign invasion with peasants who can barely aim a rifle, let alone march in formation. A decision was made at the highest levels to give amnesty to certain former officers in the Imperial Army, the ones young enough to be relatively uncorrupted. Vasily was offered a commission, and he accepted."

I was slow to understand that this was good news, since I always braced myself for bad. Not only was Vasily leaving prison, he'd be a soldier again. It was the only thing he'd ever wanted.

"Thank you," I said, the words inadequate to express my relief. My suspicion of Alek was easing into wary gratitude. "Would you like to come up for tea? I need to take these things in, and I'm sure Sergei will be back soon."

Alek's imposing presence felt too big for Sergei's cramped room, but I did my best to act at ease. My latest drawings were spread out on the table, and Alek bent down to look closer.

"These are very good. Did you do them?"

When I nodded, he murmured appreciatively. "I know some people at the Commissariat of Culture. They're always looking for artists to do posters and that kind of thing. I could put in a word for you."

I had no idea if it was a serious offer or simply Alek's way of showing off.

"That would be very kind."

I began pouring water in the kettle, and Alek waved his hand to stop me.

"I'm hungry, and who knows how long Sergei will be. Why don't we go have lunch? There must be a canteen nearby."

"There is, around the corner, but I don't have a ration card."

"I'll take care of it."

If I'd been told the day before that I'd willingly spend time with Alek Semelkov, of all people, I wouldn't have believed it. Yet I didn't just accept his offer, I found myself eager to go. Hearing what he'd done for Vasily had softened my reflexive dislike, and his imperious manner was strangely appealing. After so many years of doing everything for myself, being taken out to lunch felt like a luxury.

At the canteen, Alek took the manager aside and showed him a card that had an immediate effect. The manager ushered us to the front of the serving line and hovered behind us, making sure we got large portions. Then he led us to an alcove in the back of the room, where a table and four chairs were set aside.

"For favored visitors," he said, catching himself midbow. I guessed he'd been a servant in his previous life.

"Thank you, comrade," Alek said, curtly dismissive.

I sat down and dipped a spoon into my bowl of stew, amazed at its thickness. The meat was cut in generous chunks, and there was sausage, too, and potatoes and mushrooms. I hadn't eaten anything this rich in years.

"I moved to Moscow back in '18," Alek said. "It's a shame to come back and see the city looking so shabby."

"It was worse before. At least now we're not starving."

I'd meant it as a simple statement of fact, but I regretted the comment immediately. Complaining about the revolution could get you reported as a class enemy. Alek didn't seem bothered, but it would be safer to let him do the talking.

"Do you like living in Moscow?" I asked.

"Very much. It's where everything important is happening. Any young person with ambition goes to Moscow these days, not Petrograd. How old are you, anyway?"

"Nineteen."

"So young! I must seem like a grandfather."

"Not at all."

He smiled, clearly flattered, and his clear blue eyes no longer looked so aloof. Uneasily, I realized Alek would be considered handsome, by the kind of woman who's attracted to inscrutable men. Women like my mother.

"You have a sweetheart?" he asked offhandedly.

I shook my head. "I lead a very quiet life."

"That's a shame. At your age, I was carousing with my friends till all hours."

At my age, you hadn't lost most of your family. "All my friends left the country," I said lightly. "I have no one to carouse with."

"Well, there's no denying things have changed. The sorts of things I got away with then wouldn't be tolerated now, and rightly so. But there's still fun to be had in Moscow, if you know the right people. I went to a party not long ago where they played records smuggled in from France. Jazz."

"I don't know what that is."

"American Negro music."

Was he trying to impress me? Or trick me into admitting that I, too, wanted to break the rules by listening to decadent capitalist music?

"Most Shulkins went abroad, I hear. Why didn't you?"

This whole meal was a test, I realized, one I couldn't afford to fail. I couldn't simply lie—Alek was too clever for that—but I'd have to tell him the right version of the truth.

"We are Russians, loyal to our country. This is where we belong."

"Ah, but are you loyal to the revolution? You have to understand that anyone with your background will always be under suspicion. There are some people who say it's impossible for a person with noble blood to be a true Communist."

Some people? Or Alek himself?

"My uncle Sergei grew up in a rich family. He's a true Communist, isn't he?"

"Sergei's a different story. He's been preaching revolution since before you were born."

"I've scrubbed toilets and sewed until my fingers bled, without complaint. I've learned the satisfaction of a full day's work, and I want to contribute, the same as everyone else. Haven't I earned the right to be called comrade?"

My voice had risen; I was talking too fast. But it was all true, and I was caught up in the fervor of confession. I did believe in the best of the revolution's promises: that every person deserved to be treated equally. That we all should work, rather than live off the labor of others. I wanted, more than anything else, to prove myself worthy.

Alek took a sip of coffee, keeping me waiting. "You could still be sent to prison, on the basis on your name alone."

Despite the numbness that crept along my skin, I kept my gaze level. I knew, instinctively, that Alek would pounce on any sign of weakness. Through sheer will, I took a bite of bread crust and slowly chewed, though it grated like sandpaper.

Alek gave me a sly smile. "Personally, I've never believed sons should be punished for the sins of their fathers. If we say all men and women should be equal, shouldn't every person be judged by their work, instead of their family? You're living proof that a former noble can be rehabilitated into a good Communist."

My muscles eased; the danger had passed.

"Do you like working at the magazine?" Alek asked.

"More than cleaning bathrooms. Though I'd go back to that, if it's where I was needed."

"It would be a terrible waste of your talent. You're an artist. If you were in Moscow, you'd have many more opportunities."

As I scraped up the last of my stew, Alek talked about the Commissariat of Culture, dropping names while I nodded encouragingly, even though I didn't know who he was talking about. I went through one cup of tea as he described his travels abroad, then drank a second cup while he told me what he'd seen in the immediate aftermath of the revolution. Starvation, mass executions, the complete breakdown of society—to Alek, it had all been tragic but unpreventable, the dying throes of an old regime. The important thing was that order had been restored. It was time to put those troubles behind us and look toward the future. There was something reassuring about his certainty, his belief that good had triumphed over evil. The dregs of my final cup had gone cold when Alek finally rose from the table and said we should go find Sergei. He waved his arm, beckoning me forward, and pressed his hand against my back as I passed. Only a momentary contact, but the touch jolted through my clothes to my skin.

The man who'd instigated my father's murder had sent a clear signal. Should I pretend to ignore it and shy away? Or would I smile at the person who held my brother's life in his hands and encourage his attention?

It didn't feel like I had a choice.

LONDON

1938

To: Director, SIS

On further study of the "Red Mistress" documents, I agree that her death warrants further investigation. The woman who traveled to Britain as "Marie Duvall" was not only a known Soviet agent, but the wife of a high-ranking Communist Party member, Aleksandr Semelkov (a rather nasty piece of work—see attached file). It is of the greatest importance that we discover the reason she was here, as it was almost certainly approved by Stalin et al.

I have assembled a small team to see what we can discover of her movements in Britain. I request this inquiry be kept confidential, even within SIS. We must take all necessary precautions to ensure that this matter does not come to the public's attention.

I will keep you informed of my progress.

—Roger

MOSCOW

1922

It was marriage that made me a spy, long before my first mission. From the very beginning, I was keeping secrets, creating a character. Hiding my true self from my husband, and suspecting he did the same with me.

Sergei was shocked when I told him Alek had asked me to marry him, only three days after our lunch at the canteen.

"You hardly know him!" my uncle protested.

"You do. He's your friend, isn't he?"

"It's too sudden. You should wait, think it over."

"I'll marry someone eventually, so why not Alek? After what he did for Vasily . . ."

"So you're doing this out of gratitude? Obligation?"

Though I'd been afraid Alek might take his anger out on Vasily if I turned him down, that wasn't the only reason I'd agreed to marry him. "I love you," I told Sergei, "and I'll miss you terribly. But I need a fresh start, in Moscow. Alek can get me a good job, and I'll meet a lot of interesting people. I won't be constantly reminded of everything I've lost."

Sergei listened to my explanation, looking dismayed. As a man who loved grand gestures, he was disappointed that I'd made no mention of love or even affection, but how could I describe my feelings for Alek, when I didn't even understand them myself? Yes, he could be intimidating and arrogant, but I also found his self-confidence unexpectedly appealing. His ambition emboldened my own.

"You're just like your father," Sergei said at last.

All my life, people had compared me to Mama, telling me we looked like sisters, or that we had the same talent for art. It was moving to hear that a part of Papa lived on in me, too.

"You do what needs to be done," Sergei explained. "No complaining, no hand-wringing—you just get on with it. That's the sort of wife Alek needs. I hope you'll both be very happy."

I could tell by his strained smile that he had his doubts.

There was no wedding ceremony. Like all Bolsheviks, Alek was an atheist, and in any case, the churches had been shut down and stripped of their treasures. Alek and I filled out a form at the registry office, and with the thud of an official stamp, we were husband and wife. Sergei arranged a small party at the *New Voices* office, where Vasily made a surprise appearance. It was a shock, at first, to see my brother in his dour Red Army uniform, but he looked healthy and well-fed. I hugged him fiercely, reassured by the heft of his chest. It was the first time we'd seen each other since I visited him in prison—when Mama was still alive.

"How are you?" I asked as a dozen other questions burbled up. "Are you moving back to Petrograd?"

"No, I'm only here for the day. Comrade Semelkov arranged a few meetings so I'd have an excuse to come."

"That was good of him."

Silently, we acknowledged the even greater debt we owed Alek, for saving Vasily's life. Prison had worn away my brother's lighthearted gallantry, and as we caught up on each other's lives, he spoke like a hardened soldier: blunt and to the point. Once, he would have joked about me marrying someone almost twice my age, but unlike Sergei, Vasily didn't seem to find my decision surprising. Perhaps he thought of the match in military terms: I was simply doing my duty.

"I hope you'll be settling down soon," I told him. "Maybe in Moscow?" With the fighting over, the Red Army was undergoing a semi-chaotic reorganization; Vasily already had been assigned to four different regiments.

Vasily shook his head. "I've got orders for Tashkent."

I had only a vague idea where it was, but I knew it was far. Seeing my disappointment, Vasily gave me an encouraging smile. "I asked for the assignment. They're starting a new military academy, and I like the idea of training young soldiers. I think I'll be good at it. Besides . . ." He lowered his voice. "I have no interest in power struggles. I'd rather be somewhere safe."

I couldn't blame him.

Turning from me to the rest of the room, Vasily announced, "I've brought enough vodka to get us all thoroughly drunk. The first glass is for Comrade Semelkov and his new wife, Nadia!"

The toasts continued, and I gulped mouthfuls of vodka with each one. I had no idea how I'd get through the wedding night otherwise; I'd never done more than kiss Alek, and then only chastely.

Sergei trailed me like a shadow, reluctant to relinquish his role as protector. He teased Alek about robbing the cradle and needing a cane to chase after his future children, but the jokes were forced, as were Alek's laughs. My new husband sipped at his drink, rarely refilling the glass, an observer rather than a guest of honor. Sergei, by contrast, never stopped drinking or talking, growing increasingly sentimental as the night wore on. Near midnight, he put his arm around my shoulders and leaned his head against mine. He smelled of ink and sweat and an underlying scent I could only describe as home.

"Be careful," he whispered into my hair.

"Of Alek?" I glanced across the room, where Alek stood in the center of an admiring huddle. He looked like a teacher lecturing students. A stranger.

"He won't hurt you physically." Sergei's words were slurred, and his weight was pushing me off-balance. "Alek has always supported women's rights. Believes wives and husbands should be equal. I was speaking of your heart, dear girl. He is exactly the type to break your heart."

Not if I don't love him. The thought sprang so clearly to mind that I nearly said it aloud.

"I call Alek my friend, but I don't really know him. No one does. He can be so cold. Shutting everyone out."

I can be cold, too, I thought. *It's easier.*

"I wished better for you. I wanted you to have a grand love story, with a man who adored you."

"I don't need a grand love story. I'll be all right."

Sergei sniffled and wiped his eyes. "Perhaps it's for the best. You'll save yourself the pain."

Cautiously, I asked, "Was there someone who hurt you?" I'd grown up thinking of my uncle as a playboy, but as far as I knew, he'd had no affairs since the start of the revolution. Was there something I'd missed?

Sergei twisted away, his legs wobbly.

"I am the last person who should be lecturing on love. Come on. Let's have another drink."

It felt like a door had been opened a crack, then slammed in my face before I could get a look inside. Sergei had been about to tell me something personal, yet he'd shied away at the last minute. Maybe he was more like Alek than he thought.

In the end, my worries about the wedding night came to nothing. Alek had borrowed a friend's apartment so we could be alone, and he laughed at my stumbling, tipsy steps as he led me to the building's third floor. With a father's practical ease, he told me I needed to sleep and turned down the sheets while I stripped down to my slip. The bed seemed to sway beneath me as I lay down.

Alek tucked me in. "Good night."

His lips gently touched my forehead. Peaceful, not passionate. I closed my eyes and listened to Alek shuffle around the room. I kept my body still, waiting passively for whatever came next. The mattress sagged when Alek climbed in next to me, and his upper arm brushed against mine. But he made no other attempt to touch me. I heard his breathing lengthen, and reassured by the sound, I fell asleep.

The following day, Alek and I took the train to Moscow and our new life together.

We spent our first nights at a hotel near the train station, and every day, a bottle of vodka or wine would be delivered to our room, accompanied by a congratulatory note. Some of the wine was French, which was nearly impossible to get, since France was among the many countries that hadn't officially recognized the new Soviet Union. Smuggling it in must have cost a fortune.

Which meant my new husband was more important than I'd realized.

Unlike Petrograd, which felt haunted by its past glory, Moscow was focused on the future. There were signs of the revolution's toll—dilapidated storefronts, empty churches—but the damage was overshadowed by the new city being constructed on the ashes of the old. Everywhere I walked, I saw signs of activity: new factories, dams, and monuments; posters for lectures and plays. Unlike in my cosmopolitan hometown, many people wore traditional tunics and dresses, what I'd always considered peasant clothing. Moscow was remaking itself as a Communist utopia, but an emphatically Russian one.

Alek's status was soon confirmed by our housing assignment. Within a week of our arrival, we moved into an apartment in a building reserved for Party officials. At a time when I knew of extended families sharing a single room, we had a sitting room and bedroom all to ourselves and shared a communal kitchen and bathroom with only two other apartments. True to his egalitarian beliefs, Alek assured me I didn't have to cook; we could eat in the canteens. Even my more intimate wifely duties turned out to be less of a burden than I'd feared. Alek told me what to do, and I obliged. In bed, as in everything else, Alek didn't like to waste time.

Alek was similarly upfront on the subject of children. There was no question I'd get pregnant eventually—it was my duty to produce the next generation of revolutionaries—but when I suggested we wait a year or two, he readily agreed.

"I understand your reluctance. Motherhood may seem like a burden, when you've only recently attained your own freedom."

I didn't feel particularly free, but I nodded anyway.

"It will all be different soon. There are plans for communal nurseries, so mothers can work where they're most needed. There's no reason an intelligent woman like you should spend her days washing out diapers."

I pictured rows of cribs in a vast warehouse, the babies raised with industrial efficiency.

"The Commissariat for Health has a pamphlet on measures you can take to avoid a pregnancy. I'll get you a copy. In a few years, when the nurseries are up and running, we can revisit the matter."

It was a relief to know Alek wouldn't push me into having children before I was ready. Perhaps we both knew, deep down, that our marriage was too precarious to take on any extra weight.

During those first weeks, I studied Alek's rhythms and habits, adapting myself accordingly. Each new piece of information helped build the new persona I was creating: a supportive, unquestioning wife. I learned how he liked his coffee, when to talk and when to leave him alone. He worked long hours at the State Political Directorate, at a job he described as mostly paperwork. When he came home tired and preoccupied, I didn't ask questions; I simply went about distracting him with food, a radio program, or my latest drawings.

Soon, I hoped, Alek's connections at the Commissariat of Culture would lead to a job, and I'd no longer feel so isolated. The only people I'd met so far in Moscow were Alek's friends—like him, all Party members—and their wives, who had become my de facto social circle. But I had yet to feel that mutual tug of interest that establishes true friendships. The older wives were longtime Bolsheviks who'd been imprisoned or exiled before the revolution, true believers who'd railed against families like mine since before I was born. The other women I met were either boringly domestic or too self-absorbed. They'd all known each other for years and spoke in a shorthand of past experiences that I could never completely decipher. And as I nodded dumbly and smiled, I'd catch mystified glances: *That woman is Alek's wife?*

Why *had* Alek married me? It was a question that persisted like a chronic headache. I was young and obedient and pretty enough, but so were dozens of other women in Moscow. Women with much better political credentials than me. Why would a rising star in the Party marry a former person?

One evening, after a series of later-than-usual nights, Alek invited a few of his coworkers to our apartment for drinks. I welcomed them in, set out a bottle of vodka and glasses, then withdrew to the bedroom with a book. I'd borrowed a collection of George Bernard Shaw's plays in English from the library; as a proud Socialist, he was one of the few foreign authors I wouldn't get in trouble for reading.

I'd gotten halfway through *Heartbreak House* when someone knocked. Alek, I assumed, and I told him to come in. A petite, sharp-featured woman poked her head around the door. Tanya Grilinova was married to one of Alek's fellow political agents, and she was the kind of woman who always managed to have both the first and last word.

True to form, she started talking immediately.

"Dear comrade, so sorry to disturb you! I was visiting my sister—
she lives right around the corner—and Timofei said he'd get me on his
way home, and I waited and waited, and finally I realized it was just
like him to forget the time, and I'd have to come drag him out of here
myself. How are you? Reading?"

She took a swift, disinterested glance at my book and sat down
beside me on the bed.

"My sister's all in a rage because my other sister—Masha, she lives
in Odessa—was supposed to give her our mother's shawl when she died,
but Masha's held on to it, because she says Mother left it to her, and
really, it's the stupidest argument of all time, because the shawl isn't even
that nice. It's because none of us will ever admit the other one's right."

Tanya sighed with dramatic exaggeration. "You know how it is in
families. You have brothers and sisters?"

Though I assumed Alek's closest friends knew he'd married a
Shulkin, we'd agreed never to talk about my past. I'd have to step
carefully.

"A brother," I said.

"The funny thing is that my sisters fight with each other constantly,
but they all try to stay on my good side because of Timofei. You must
get badgered by relatives, too? 'Can Alek find a position for my neighbor or an apartment for my cousin?'"

I had the unsettling feeling Tanya had chosen this line of conversation to find out more about me. I didn't want to tell her that most of
my family had either died or left the country. And I certainly didn't
want her to know that my brother was a former Imperial Army officer.

"I wouldn't feel comfortable bothering Alek with that sort of thing,"
I said meekly.

"That must be why he married you—because he knew you'd never
nag!"

Tanya chuckled and patted my arm, to show she was only joking.
Was she, though? Her eyes surveyed my face, as if searching for clues,

and her body practically quivered with curiosity. She had plenty more questions, and the only way to stop them was by shifting her attention elsewhere.

"How long have you known Alek?" I asked brightly.

"Oh, years. He and Timofei were at university together. I was one of the first people to read an early draft of *The Great Flood.*"

The name meant nothing to me, and Tanya looked shocked by my ignorance.

"Alek's book, the one that got him sent to prison. You've never read it?" Tanya shifted to a deeper, dramatic voice. "*The soil of our sacred land will be drenched in the blood of traitors, and the first shoots of freedom will be watered with their tears.* Just thinking about it makes my heart race."

I remembered Alek back in 1914, staring coolly at the antics of Mama's artist friends. Disapproving, detached. Waiting for all that bourgeois foolishness to be destroyed.

"I shouldn't be telling you this," Tanya continued, "but Timofei's always been a little bit in awe of Alek. They all are. For obvious reasons."

Tanya gave me a knowing look that I couldn't reciprocate.

"I'm sorry—I don't understand."

"The promotion. Didn't Alek tell you? He's working directly with Comrade Dzerzhinsky."

That name I knew. He'd been the head of the Cheka, the secret police who'd tortured and killed anyone they deemed an enemy in those first, bloody years after the revolution. Nameless men in black leather coats who'd executed entire families. I'd heard the Cheka was disbanded, its terror tactics unseemly for a government trying to show the world a civilized face. But Dzerzhinsky was still around. Working with Alek. I didn't know much about Alek's job, but he made the Political Directorate sound like a harmless bureaucracy. Was it? Or was it simply the Cheka in a different form?

"Alek doesn't talk about his work," I said, hoping Tanya would tell me more, but she waved her hand in dismissal.

"Forget I said anything."

She stood up abruptly, her fingers fidgety. "It's time we were off, anyway. Timofei will stay all night if I let him, and I know you're too polite to kick him out. Good night, it was very nice to see you."

She practically ran out the door, clearly nervous. When Alek came to bed a half hour later, I gave him an edited version of our talk.

"Tanya was appalled that I'd never read *The Great Flood*. Do you mind that I haven't?"

"No. It's hardly Tolstoy."

For a committed Bolshevik, Alek was surprisingly lenient toward my "decadent" literary tastes.

"I think she's a little scared of you."

"Me?"

It was dark; I couldn't see his face. Only the faintest outline of his profile, the curve of nose and lips.

"She said you'd gotten a new job, then acted all strange when I said I didn't know about it."

It was important to use the right tone: amused rather than aggrieved.

"It's a temporary position—I don't even know how long I'll stay. We're building a whole government from scratch, and things change from day to day."

"Well, I'm sure it will all work out," I said brightly. As if we were making plans for dinner, nothing of importance.

"The work I do . . . it's sensitive. State security. Not a subject for gossip." Alek's voice sharpened. "Tanya shouldn't have said anything."

I felt the chill of his displeasure, radiating outward, and belatedly realized I had no idea what he was capable of. For all Alek's talk of a bright new future, he was working for a man who condoned torture and murder. Would Tanya be punished for one careless remark? I remembered Sergei's warning: *Alek can be so cold.*

"She didn't mean any harm." I spoke breezily, seemingly oblivious to Alek's displeasure. "She idolizes you, she and Timofei both."

In the silence that followed, I could almost hear the gears of Alek's brain twisting. Yes or no, yes or no.

"She's always been a chatterbox," he said at last. "I don't know how Timofei lives with it. I trust you won't go babbling about my job to the next person you meet?"

"Of course not."

"Then let's say no more about it."

I went slack with relief, as if I'd watched Alek drop his pen right before signing a warrant. Whether or not he'd really arrest an old friend's wife for something she said in private, I believed it possible. My own husband might punish me just as harshly, if I said the wrong thing.

When he'd fallen asleep, I crept to the front room and scanned the spines of the books piled on his desk, books I'd never paid attention to before. I found a copy of *The Great Flood* near the bottom, pulled it out, and started reading. It was the story of a wretched peasant family and their sadistic overlords, a cliché-ridden tale of good versus evil. I flipped ahead, dread rising as I read about a peasant's murderous rage as he sought revenge for his suffering. The flood, I realized, was the blood that streamed from necks and stomachs, drenching the soil, cleansing the land. In Alek's telling, murder was a sacrament, achieved by killing the rich. He'd told me he didn't push the Priyalko peasants into violence, but his book made it clear that he saw such uprisings as necessary. Even admirable.

I could almost hear Sergei reassuring me that Alek's book was just a metaphor, that I mustn't mistake art for life. But I couldn't stop my heart from pounding. Couldn't help being afraid. I'd thought marrying Alek would keep me safe, but it had only exposed me to greater dangers. The only solution was to keep myself above suspicion. Avoid any situation that might make me look disloyal.

I began turning down invitations and rebuffing the few neighbors who tried to get to know me. Better to avoid personal connections and the temptation to share confidences. At the few social gatherings I attended, I let Alek's friends believe I was an indulgence of middle age: a pretty little thing he'd chosen for looks rather than brains. I barely spoke, and I professed to have no opinions on anything important. It was safer if they thought I was stupid. It was also crushingly lonely.

Work was my only escape from despair. When Alek told me there was an opening for English speakers in the Commissariat for Foreign Affairs, I jumped at the chance. I met with the man who would be my supervisor, a former professor of British literature, who offered me the job after less than five minutes of English conversation.

"You speak like a native," he said. "Almost no accent. When can you start?"

I'd found the one place in Soviet Russia where my privileged upbringing was an asset, not a weakness. Two days later, I arrived at my new office, a low-ceilinged former private library where a scattering of people sat at wide wooden desks, hunched over their reading. I was directed to my desk, where a stack of newspapers awaited. A pad of paper and a pen sat to the side.

And so, unbeknownst to me, the next stage of my transformation began.

Officially, I wasn't a spy. I was a foreign-media appraiser, compiling reports on what English-language newspapers and politicians were saying about the Soviet Union. Britain and the United States, wary of similar uprisings in their own countries, had been denouncing the Bolsheviks for years. But fears of the so-called Red Tide had eased by the time I started work, near the end of 1922. Diplomatic relations had reopened between Great Britain and Russia; deals were made discreetly with American companies to import machinery. Even in a Communist country, there were profits to be made.

At times, I felt like a fish in an aquarium, gazing through a thick window at a world I couldn't touch. I read about rich girls pulling off their shoes and frolicking in New York fountains. Men who became famous for pratfalls projected on cinema screens. Frivolous antics completely detached from my own sober reality. Gradually, I learned the names of the most important politicians and which writers had the most public impact. I developed a system for taking notes and organizing important themes. I became friendly—to a point—with my coworkers and got a reputation as an efficient, self-contained worker. It was enough. In time, I stopped looking at the advertisements for lingerie and skin creams that had so fascinated me when I first began the job. They weren't important, and they only slowed me down.

And then one day, in the spring of 1924, Alek brought home a dress. I didn't think of myself as vain—in the two years I'd been married, I'd worn the same three outfits, all in shades of brown—but I was immediately entranced. The navy-blue fabric rippled under my fingers like lake water.

"You've been invited to a party," he announced.

"By whom?"

"The politburo." Then, seeing my shock, he smiled and said, "Not exactly, but close enough. A delegation of English and American writers has been touring Moscow and a few of our new industrial plants, with the personal approval of General Secretary Stalin. We're giving them a grand send-off tonight, before they leave for Finland."

"What does that have to do with me?"

"One of them is Alistair Devlin."

Devlin was an influential columnist for a London newspaper, one of a select group whose work I'd been ordered to translate whenever it was published. His self-regard practically wafted off the page, but he was considered a leading voice on political affairs, with an appropriately thick file in my supervisor's office. Paperwork, as Alek frequently complained, was the unwanted stepchild of the revolution.

"I'm surprised he agreed to come," I said. "He's a terrible snob."

"A curious snob. 'The enemy we meet is the enemy we cease to fear.'"

It was a quote from Devlin's column a few weeks ago. Alek must have read the file.

"We arranged for the usual translators and escorts, as we do with any foreign visitors, but Mr. Devlin has been very tight-lipped. There's been some concern about what he's planning to write when he goes home. I suggested he might be more forthcoming with a person who knows his work. Someone who understands the gentle art of flattery."

Alek handed me a small glass bottle and waved toward the bedroom. "Try on the dress."

It felt like money, caressing my body. The neckline skimmed my collarbones, and the hem fell halfway between my knees and ankles, higher than I usually wore. A matching sash wrapped around my hip bones, the ends tumbling theatrically toward the floor. The bottle was cologne, with a label that read *Fleurs du Provence*. I unscrewed the cap and pressed my fingertip against the opening, the way Mama used to do, and spread the scent along my wrists and neck. I checked my reflection in a small hand mirror and saw disjointed images of silk and skin. My eyes, flickering with an unfamiliar glow.

When I came out of the bedroom, Alek looked taken aback by my transformation.

"Very good," he finally said. "I'll call for the car."

Having a driver was one of the privileges I'd already begun taking for granted.

"We're leaving now?" I asked.

"You're leaving. I'm not coming."

The thought of going alone filled me with a sudden panic. How could I be trusted to do the right thing without Alek there to guide me?

"What do you want me to do?"

"Tell Devlin you love his work. Indulge him."

The dress and perfume suddenly felt obscene. "How?"

Alek laughed dismissively. "I don't mean seduce him—as if you could! No, no, you're an admirer, nothing more. But don't introduce yourself as Nadia Semelkova—make up some other name. I don't want it getting around that the wife of a Party official was cozying up to a foreign journalist. I'm sure you can come up with a convincing story. Just find out what he's going to write. That way we'll be prepared."

The car arrived a half hour later, after I'd washed up and neatened my hair. During the drive, I tried to calm my nerves by telling myself it wasn't all that different from our summer theatricals at Priyalko. All I needed to do was create a character that would appeal to Alistair Devlin. So, what type of woman would she be?

The idea came to me fully formed. The daughter of a British mother and Russian father, fluent in both languages. Educated but not worldly, easily impressed by a well-known writer. The kind of shiny, shallow woman who reflects a man's self-admiration back at him.

The driver dropped me off at the Metropol Hotel, the government's approved lodging for foreign visitors. A place for diplomatic meetings and chance encounters, polite smiles and covert scheming. The official face of Communism might be resolutely stark, but the Metropol proved indulgence was still tolerated, for those with the power to claim it. The prewar draperies and carpet had grown shabby, and the kitchen no longer offered the delicacies of years past, but the building maintained its aura of stately beauty. A trio of pretty girls in the café laughed and gestured a touch too showily, and I wondered if they, too, were here on a mission. Or available for the right price.

The writers and their handlers were gathered in a room off the lobby. From a distance, they were shadowy figures engulfed in cigarette smoke, sipping from glasses of vodka. It was only as I got closer that I was able to sort out their different voices and nationalities. It was the first time I'd been around Americans, and I was fascinated by the way they spoke, as if their words were birdseed flung by children in the park, covering as wide an area as possible.

One of the Russian translators caught my eye and walked over. "Comrade Semelkova?"

I quickly shook my head. "Comrade Kishkina. Yulia."

The man understood it was best not to ask questions.

"I'll introduce you to Mr. Devlin. You can talk to the others, if you like, though I don't think they'll provide anything useful. The man with the black hair and loose jacket runs a Socialist press in New York and wants everyone to know he once had dinner with Trotsky. The drunk one in the middle writes novels, or so he says. American, but spends most of his time in France and travels with his own bottles of whiskey. The man next to him writes for the *Saturday Evening Post*. The one with blond hair works for a Socialist paper in London. Loyal to the cause."

Even from a distance, the Englishman he'd pointed out last gave off an impression of boyish, rumpled enthusiasm. Though he looked to be about my age, I felt decades older.

Alistair Devlin, by contrast, was jowly and wrinkled, a face formed by decades of furrowed brows, disapproving frowns, and pursed lips. The buttons of his jacket strained against the outward thrust of his balloonish stomach. It had been a long time since I'd seen an overweight man in Russia.

The translator made a brief introduction, then discreetly drifted away. As I'd suspected, Devlin was more interested in me as an admirer than a person. As soon as I said I'd had the honor of reading his columns, he was off on a monologue about writing, the British press, the idiocy of his literary rivals, and a litany of other complaints I pretended to find fascinating.

"Have you enjoyed your visit to Moscow?" I finally interrupted. If I didn't get some information out of him soon, the whole evening would be a waste, and Alek would be furious.

"It can't compare to London, my dear, but I've been pleasantly surprised. The young folk I've met have a confidence I rather admire."

"We're fortunate to live at the dawn of a new era." I raised my voice, for the benefit of the group's escorts. Just as I'd been told to report back on Devlin, someone else would probably be reporting back on me.

"You lot sound like missionaries, yet you're all atheists. Would you say Communism is your religion?"

"Who needs God when you have Comrade Lenin?"

"Are you trying to shock me? Well done. I like a girl with bite. The Socialists at home are so *drearily* earnest."

I took a step closer, gave him a taunting half smile. "So, what are you going to write about us in your next column?"

"Wouldn't you like to know?"

His singsong tone was intended as flirtatious, as was his puckered mouth. I wondered if his act ever worked on women who didn't want something from him.

"Tell me," I said. "A reward for a devoted reader."

"The headline won't be 'Swooning for the Soviets,' if that's what you're hoping."

I giggled, the response he was obviously hoping for.

"Still, I'll admit your country isn't in such bad straits as I expected. It's quite impressive how much building is going on, all the new factories . . . That will be my theme, I suppose. The Soviet Union as a country to be taken seriously."

I nodded encouragingly, jotting mental notes, as Devlin droned on about his travels. He'd already decided on the opening line of his next column: *The fearsome Communist specter has a youthful, optimistic face.* I recited it mentally as the gathering broke up and I was driven home. As soon as I got back to the apartment, I scribbled down my observations with Alek behind me, peering over my shoulder. I hoped he'd be proud. We now had proof that Alistair Devlin, the voice of London's elite, would be praising the Soviet Union in print.

"What did the other writers say?" Alek asked.

"I didn't talk to them."

Devlin—wanting all my attention to himself—hadn't made introductions, though they were obviously curious about the Russian woman who'd suddenly appeared in their midst. At one point, the young

English reporter circled behind Devlin, discreetly eavesdropping, and I pretended not to notice. When the party was breaking up, and I was saying my goodbyes to Devlin, the reporter was there again, hovering.

"Lovely to meet you," he said, which didn't make sense, because we hadn't spoken. His blond hair and easy smile made him look like the kind of man who'd dance in a nightclub or drive too fast, an apparition from a fantasy world. He was also a distraction. I couldn't risk another conversation, not when my brain was sorting and storing everything Devlin had said.

That brief, wordless encounter didn't make it into my report; I didn't even know the reporter's name. When I'd finished writing, Alek read the pages over, nodding and murmuring an occasional, thoughtful "Hmph."

He laid the notes on the table and straightened the edges. "How's your French?"

"It's my first language. I spoke French before I learned Russian."

"One of the many reasons this country was ripe for revolution." Alek smirked. "There's a delegation coming from France in a few weeks. I could get you attached to the group as a translator."

Was it a serious offer? Or another test of my loyalty? If I showed too much interest, he might snatch the offer away, to teach me a lesson.

I answered hesitantly, acting doubtful. "I'll do it if you want me to."

"You're good at drawing out information. This report proves it."

"It wasn't difficult with a windbag like Devlin."

"You're more devious than I thought. Or maybe it's the dress."

Alek reached around my waist and pulled me up from my chair. His hands ran along my stomach and sides, his rough fingers tempered by the smoothness of the fabric. His lips dug into my neck. I surrendered to his need, as always. Whatever Alek's egalitarian leanings in public, at home he was emphatically in charge.

A half hour later, I lay in the dark, listening to Alek's snores. My skin still held a trace of cologne, faintly detectable beneath the more earthy smells of sex. The exhilaration that had fueled me through the evening refused to ebb, making it impossible to sleep. I remembered what it felt like to walk through the Metropol as Yulia Kishkina. Swaying my hips and flattering Devlin. Catching the attention of a handsome young man with dark blond hair.

For a few hours, I'd become someone else. I'd escaped.

LONDON

1938

To: Director, SIS

Please find enclosed an official statement from Mr. Harold Pinkney, manager of the Hotel Bristol (17 Porchester Terrace, W2). He contacted the authorities on May 18, after seeing a report of Marie Duvall's death in the *Evening Standard*. According to Mr. Pinkney, Miss Duvall checked into his hotel on May 13, four days before the accident. She was accompanied by a Mr. Claude Duvall, whom she referred to as her uncle. Mr. Pinkney did not speak to Mr. Duvall, and therefore cannot confirm he spoke either English or French. We think it most likely he was also an operative, working as a bodyguard or accomplice.

As you will see from the statement, the Duvalls kept to themselves during their stay and did not inter-act with other guests or staff. Police who examined Miss Duvall's room found clothing, a suitcase, and a few books in French. Those are being checked by our cryptography division to see if they contain encoded communications. A complete inventory of the room is attached.

We continue to make inquiries regarding Miss Duvall's travels in London.

—Roger

PARIS

1926

I'd been raised speaking French, reading French, even dreaming in French. When I arrived in Paris for the first time, stepping out from the clamor of Gare de l'Est, it felt surprisingly familiar. As if a land I'd dreamed of turned out to be real.

And as in a dream, I wasn't myself. According to my passport, I was a Frenchwoman named Marie Duvall.

I hailed a taxi and gave the driver an address on Rue de Grenelle. Astoundingly, the city looked as I'd always imagined: grand façades flanking equally grand boulevards; a chaotic ballet of automobiles, buses, and dogged pedestrians; flashes of manicured green gardens amid the gray. Signs over shop windows made me hungry with longing. *Boulangerie. Patisserie.* Even sounding out the names in my head felt indulgent.

But what struck me most were the faces. In Moscow, people looked downward or forward, their expressions determinedly blank. Here, they were laughing and scowling, amused and imperious—expressive in a way that seemed almost indecent. There were glimpses of misery, too, like the legless beggars wearing the tattered remains of uniforms. But compared to Moscow's cool efficiency, Paris felt bracingly alive.

My gawking caught the attention of the driver, who asked if it was my first visit to Paris.

"Yes," I said. Then, daring myself to face the challenge of my false identity head-on, "I'm from the South. A village near Bordeaux."

I'd practiced ways to deflect follow-up questions—"I've got cousins there! Do you know Madame So-and-So?"—but the driver only nodded.

"You picked the right time to come. Rained every day last week. You could almost row a boat down the Champs-Élysées."

It had been the wettest April since before the war, apparently, but I only half listened. I didn't know how long I'd be there, and I wanted to imprint each image on my memory.

When Alek had first mentioned my cousin Mikhail a few weeks ago, I'd been immediately wary. We'd had short visits from Sergei and Vasily in the four years we'd been married, but we never talked about my other relatives. The Shulkins who had escaped.

"I haven't seen Mikhail in years," I said. Twelve years, to be exact. The night of Maria's ball.

"He's living in France," Alek told me. "Styles himself Prince Shulkin, as if the title means anything now."

It means his older brothers are dead, I thought with a pang.

"He's part of something called the Russian Cultural League. An émigré group that puts on Russian plays and concerts. But one of our informers in Paris thinks it might be more. Nikolai Romanov, the tsar's cousin, was spotted at a performance. A few other troublemakers, too. We think the league might be a front for a terrorist organization."

I pictured the talkative boy who'd guided me across the dance floor. "I can't imagine Mikhail mixed up in something like that."

"We can't ignore any possible threat. There are plenty of people who'd happily fund an uprising against the Soviet Union and bring the Romanovs back. We haven't been able to infiltrate the league yet—Mikhail and his friends run a very tight ship—so we need a person who can gain their trust."

Alek gave me a triumphant look, his eyes glittering behind his glasses.

"We're going to Paris?" I asked.

"You're going to Paris. Alone."

I felt breathless. Weightless. Alek was offering me an escape from Moscow, from Russia, from a life that was steadily corroding whatever remained of my true self. But the more he thought I wanted it, the more likely he was to snatch it away. I stared at him blankly, a cowed wife bewildered by her husband's schemes.

"I'm too well known," Alek said. "If word got out that a Political Directorate official was in Paris, everyone would keep their mouths shut and lay low. Do you think Mikhail knows you're married?"

I shrugged. "I don't think so. I lost touch with that side of the family when they left Russia."

"If he does, you can always say you divorced me, because I made you so miserable." Alek let that suggestion hang for a while, to see if I'd squirm. "I'll arrange a temporary job at the Russian embassy, something to do with translations. Then you track down your long-lost cousin and talk about the good old days. All those parties at your mansion."

I no longer wondered why a committed revolutionary like Alek had married a former noblewoman. I'd learned, over time, that Alek had chosen me not in spite of my heritage, but because of it. I was his spoil of the revolution, no different from the clothes and china the peasants had scooped up at Priyalko. He liked to prod at my emotional bruises, and the sooner I showed he'd hurt me, the sooner he'd move on. I allowed myself to remember the front hall of my parents' house, Mama and Papa dressed for a night out, me in my nightdress at the top of the stairs, waving goodbye with Miss Fields by my side. I allowed the grief to run through me and out.

"Mikhail lived in Moscow," I said curtly. "We barely knew each other."

"I trust in your powers of persuasion."

Alek watched me, as he so often did, with an expression that was part amusement, part dare.

"I might have to say things I don't mean, to gain Mikhail's trust. What's to stop one of your informers from reporting me as a traitor?"

"Don't worry about that. If you do find evidence of a conspiracy, the rewards will be considerable. For both of us."

And I'd be betraying my family to the very people who destroyed us. But that was a dilemma for another day.

I made a show of looking reluctant. "If it's what you want."

Even as my false documents were arranged and signed, as Alek plotted out my train route and slid French banknotes into the lining of my suitcase, I didn't quite believe he'd allow me to go. When I boarded the train in Moscow, I expected a last-minute complication, some trumped-up reason to keep me in Russia. At the border crossing with Finland, I began using my false passport, in the name of Marie Duvall, wondering if the forgery was good enough, or if it would get me arrested. All through Finland and Poland and Germany and France, I sat rigid with worry. One suspicious question about my accent, and I'd be unmasked as a fraud. But no one spoke to or more than glanced at me. It was only now, safely in Paris, that my fear started to ease.

"Here we are!" the driver announced.

I stepped out in front of a three-story office building with an understated law-firm nameplate. Only after the driver had driven out of sight did I cross the street to my true destination. Alek had told me to be careful about who saw me going in and out.

The Soviet embassy was an elegant eighteenth-century mansion, the sort of privileged palace revolutionaries like to loot and burn. I passed a guard who sized me up, bored, one hand resting casually on the gun at his waist. The main reception room was forlornly formal, with dusty chandeliers and a tangy odor of mildew. I told the man at the front desk I had an appointment to see Comrade Patlov, and the man himself appeared shortly afterward. He had a round, doughy face, with hair that stood up like scrubbing-brush bristles. I guessed he was in his forties, old enough to have been a Bolshevik well before the revolution. He must have done something noteworthy to be given this plum post.

He looked at me like a cat eager to bat around a new toy. "Miss Duvall! How was your journey?"

"Long."

I smiled to show I was no worse for wear, though exhaustion was belatedly catching up with me. I'd barely slept on the train.

Comrade Patlov escorted me down a hallway, along a carpet stained with muddy footprints.

"The building was empty from 1917 until last year. It took that long for the French to re-establish diplomatic relations. We're still getting things sorted out, as you can see."

He led me into his office, where a few pieces of mismatched furniture looked as if they were under attack by stacks of boxes. He took his place behind the desk, gestured for me to sit opposite him, then pushed a large envelope toward me.

"Everything you need is in there. Money, documents, directions to your apartment. The rent's been paid six months in advance, in the name of Miss Duvall. The landlord isn't the type to ask questions, but we'd prefer he not know you're Russian. He thinks a rich man's rented the place as a love nest for his mistress."

Was there a part of this mission Alek hadn't told me about? "I hope you don't expect me to . . ." I paused, uncomfortable. "Play the role of a mistress."

"Oh no!" Patlov looked reassuringly dismissive. "We tipped the landlord well, to make sure you're left alone. You've also got papers in the name of Nadia Shulkina, in case you need to show them when you're with other Russians. You don't want them knowing who you're married to. No one else at the embassy knows, either."

"I was told I'd have a job, translating."

"Yes, documents related to a new Soviet-French trade agreement. I've gotten you the proper papers, and from time to time, you'll be called in to meetings at the Ministry of Trade. But it shouldn't take up more than a few hours a week. Your real job is with the Russian Cultural League."

"Where should I start?"

"Visit your cousin, Prince Shulkin." Patlov gave the title a sarcastic twist. "Ask what he's been up to, find out how he spends his time. I don't expect him to confess anything at your first meeting, so ingratiate yourself with him and his friends. Go to the shows put on by the league, flirt with the old-timers. When the time is right, confide that you're unhappy in Moscow and wish you could go back to the days before the revolution. See what happens."

Patlov gave me the condescending smile older men use when doling out life lessons. "I don't have to tell you that these are delicate times for the Party and our country. If you help us uncover a plot, it will put you, me, and Comrade Semelkov in a very beneficial position."

In the two years since Lenin's death, the Bolsheviks had split into factions, each battling for what they said was the soul of the Party. For now, Alek was allied with General Secretary Stalin, but who knew how long he'd remain on top? The only way to stay in power—and out of prison—was to prove yourself by rooting out enemies. Suddenly, the true nature of my mission became clear. Alek hadn't sent me here to find out if there was really a conspiracy; he'd already decided there must be one, and he wanted the credit for destroying it.

But what if he was wrong? If there was no plot?

"Now, on to the particulars," Patlov continued. "There are prying eyes and ears all over this place—it's impossible to keep a secret in an embassy. When you have something to report, we'll meet at a café a few blocks away. I've marked it on this map. There's no telephone in your apartment, but I'll send a note in the name of Mr. Pascal if I need to see you. You can send me any messages as Miss Duvall. Understood?"

I nodded, and Patlov stood up, eager to get me out before anyone saw me in his office. I walked two blocks before hailing a taxi and felt my heart sink as we left the grand boulevards behind for narrow streets with soot-blackened walls. The building that would be my new home was four stories of grimy windows and crumbling stone, with a stairwell that smelled of shared toilets and disappointment. What Patlov had referred to as an apartment was in reality a single room, furnished with a squeaky bed, scratched table, and two wooden chairs. A tiny gas stove was crammed in one corner. From the lone window, I saw only the bricks and crumbling mortar of the building next door. So much for Parisian charm.

Settling in took a matter of minutes, given my few possessions. The place needed a thorough scrubbing, yet I was overwhelmed by a wave of unexpected satisfaction. My home might look like a prison cell, but for the moment, at least, I was free.

In my memory, Mikhail was still the gangly fifteen-year-old who pulled me across a dance floor in my first and only party dress. When he opened the door to his apartment, a few blocks from the Tuileries Garden, I saw he'd grown not only taller, but fuller. His dark hair jutted around his forehead in thick chunks, and his black suit was shiny on the shoulders and cuffs from wear. He looked like a tradesman or factory worker. Certainly not a prince.

I was surprised by the warmth of his embrace and the genuine pleasure with which he kissed my cheeks. We took a silent moment to register the changes since we'd seen each other last. I wondered if he was thinking of me in green silk, twirling in a ballroom, surrounded by people who were now dead. He'd seemed so much older than me back then, but now we were twenty-seven and twenty-four, and the age difference didn't seem to matter. I found myself liking him immediately, much more than I'd expected.

Mikhail led me into a spacious sitting room, where the heavy drapes and layered carpets created an atmosphere of lush elegance. China figurines and decorative crystal pieces were scattered across the tables, and I realized it had been a long time since I'd sat in a space so cluttered with useless objects. The family must have some money left, otherwise they would have sold off these possessions.

"I was so pleased to receive your note. Mama and the others have taken the children to the park, but they'll be back soon. They can't wait to see you, too."

He held up a teapot with a questioning look, and I nodded. "Who lives with you here?" I asked.

"Mama, of course. She and Papa bought the apartment years ago, thank goodness. It's impossible to find a place with this much space at an affordable rent these days. Too many Russians swarming in and driving up prices."

Mikhail gave me a wry half smile as he passed me a teacup. A generous portion of pastries was laid out on a platter, but there was no maid to serve us, as I would have expected.

"Two of my sisters are staying here as well—the ones who are widows—and their children. Three other nieces and nephews, the children of my oldest brother."

It would be polite to ask, even if I already knew the answer. "And your brothers?"

"Both dead. The war."

Which one? Before or after the revolution? If Mikhail wasn't going to offer up the story unprompted, I wasn't going to ask.

"So that makes twelve of us in a three-bedroom apartment, which we would have found appalling once. But we manage all right. The boys in one room, the girls in another, and Mama shares with my sisters. I'm lucky enough to have my own room, off the kitchen—it used to be the cook's. Quietest place in the house."

He might look like a workman, but Mikhail still had the manners of a Shulkin. Gracious and well-spoken, trained to be a gentleman, no matter what the circumstances.

"Tell me about your job," he said. "How long will you be in town?"

"I'm not sure. I'm translating for a trade delegation." Five minutes into our meeting, and I'd already told my first lie. "It all depends how long negotiations last. A few weeks, at least."

More if you give me a reason to suspect you. I pushed the thought aside and shifted the conversation to family.

I told Mikhail about Priyalko and Papa and Mama, but there was hopeful news, too. Sergei was still writing, sending cheerful letters from the city that had been renamed—yet again—as Leningrad. Vasily had recently married a woman I'd never met, the sister of a fellow officer, and he'd promised to bring her to Moscow during his next leave. Mikhail, too, had an inventory of losses. During his family's exodus on the overcrowded ships that carried desperate Russians away from Crimea, one of his sisters had died from typhus. He'd seen other Shulkins scatter all over the world, to America, Argentina, Germany, and France. A few had simply disappeared in the chaos of the Civil War.

"We're luckier than most, living here, and we all chip in where we can. It's not easy to get a work permit, but one of my brothers-in-law is a maître d' at a restaurant. The Renault factory hires a lot of Russians—they like former tsarist soldiers, since they're good at following orders. I've been thinking about driving a taxi. The only problem is I've got to learn to drive."

Mikhail laughed, acknowledging the absurdity of Prince Shulkin, who grew up with multiple chauffeurs, shuttling tourists through Paris. True survivors, like Mikhail and me, learned to marvel at such twists of fate, not cry.

"Do you know many other Russians in Paris?" I'd have to come up with something to tell Patlov at our next meeting.

"Oh, of course, they're everywhere. To the Parisians' great dismay."

Mikhail offered me the platter of pastries, but I shook my head, even though I was hungry. They looked store-bought and expensive, an extravagance to impress an honored guest. Better to save them for the children, as a treat.

"We all support each other, as much as we can," Mikhail continued. "Russian doctors can't get a license, but they'll treat us, unofficially. The taxi idea came from a former officer of the Imperial Guard who's started his own fleet and said he'd hire me."

I'd have to nudge harder. "I've heard a lot of artists moved here. That must keep things interesting? I remember you telling me how much you loved the theater."

"Some of it's too avant-garde for my taste—Diaghilev and his crazy ballets. There is a small group I've gotten involved in that puts on concerts and shows that are more traditional. So many wonderful actors and singers came here after the revolution, we've got no short-age of talent. There's a performance next Wednesday, Tchaikovsky and Rachmaninoff. You should come."

Before I had a chance to ask more questions, we heard a clatter in the hallway, and our quiet tête-a-tête was overrun by a flurry of high-pitched children. Soon, I was embracing the rest of Mikhail's family and trying to answer a dozen different questions at once. By the time I finally said goodbye an hour later, I'd barely spoken to Mikhail again, but it didn't matter. I'd done what I needed to do.

The shabby café where I met Patlov the next evening catered to stoop-shouldered, rough-skinned men who drank with grim concen-tration. I told him Mikhail was sentimental about the past and social-ized with lots of other Russians—facts that were suggestive, but not damning.

"He admitted he's part of a group that promotes Russian culture, though he didn't mention the league by name. I'm going to one of their concerts next Wednesday night."

Patlov took a sip of coffee. Ours was the only table without at least one bottle of wine as a centerpiece. "Figure out who the other leaders are. Charm them. Don't ask too many obvious questions, your first time. It's more important to establish trust. I'll meet you here Thursday morning at nine for a report. They serve a good breakfast, believe it or not. The owner's wife bakes the bread herself."

Patlov waved at the waiter leaning against the bar. "Two roast chicken plates!" he called out. Then, with a grin that stretched half-way up his cheeks, "Might as well enjoy a few good meals while we're here, eh?"

Apparently, I wasn't the only one who wanted to stay in Paris as long as possible.

The repertoire of Mikhail's musical evening seemed purposefully selected to provoke wistful tears. The pianist and string quartet mournfully overemoted, and half the audience were wiping their faces by the end. There were a hundred or so of us, perched on tightly packed chairs in the salon of a Russian duchess's palatial apartment a few blocks from the Louvre. The men in white tie and tails were the ones who'd been clever enough to stash their fortunes overseas before the revolution; the others, like Mikhail and myself, wore patched suits and faded dresses. Given such obvious signs of poverty, I found it odd that our hostess for the evening was draped in jewels more suited to a presentation at court. Perhaps, in her mind, it was a gesture of defiance.

After the musicians took their bows, the duchess invited us to an adjoining dining room, where a buffet table was covered with heaping platters of food. I prepared to start mingling, though I could already predict how each conversation would go: we'd exchange names, find out who we knew in common, then tally up our dead. It would be tedious and tiring, and I doubted I'd find out anything useful in such a public setting. I hung back in the salon while the others pushed forward, waiting for everyone to get their food and split into groups. Then I'd decide who to approach first.

From behind me, a voice called out in English, "Hello, there."

I recognized him immediately. Though I'd charmed dozens of foreign visitors in the past few years, using a variety of aliases, I'd never forgotten the young English reporter with dark blond hair and cheerful eyes who'd hovered behind Alistair Devlin at the Metropol Hotel. He held out his hand with almost aggressive friendliness.

"Lee Cooper."

We hadn't been introduced that night, but I'd been posing as Yulia Kishkina. Had he heard someone else call me that? What name should I use?

Thankfully, Lee mistook my hesitation for confusion. "I believe we met in Moscow. A writers' party at the Metropol? I'm sorry, I don't remember your name . . ."

"Nadia Shulkina." I reached out my hand, and Lee gave it a decisive shake. "I'm surprised you remember me."

"Oh, you made an impression. I'd been cooped up with the same men for nearly two weeks. You were the first pretty Russian girl I got to see up close."

I might have been more pleased at being called pretty if I hadn't sensed it was a compliment Lee tossed out often. I also wondered, with my habitual and well-deserved caution, why the same Englishman would just happen to cross my path in both Moscow and Paris.

"What brings you to France?" he asked.

"I'm doing some translation work for the embassy." With the coy flirtatiousness Lee would expect of a pretty girl, I asked, "What brings *you* to Paris?"

"I don't suppose you're familiar with the *Weekly Workers' Bulletin?*"

I shrugged. "I read some of the British papers, for work. But there are so many . . ."

"Not to worry. We take pride in our lack of international renown. I was recently appointed the *Bulletin's* European correspondent."

"And now you're writing concert reviews?"

"I'm not here for work. Purely personal interest. I was quite taken by Russian culture, after my visit. I was quite taken by the country as a whole, to be honest."

Of course he'd been impressed, because foreigners were shepherded to the places most likely to dazzle them. Lee's guides would have shown him spotless workers' barracks, health clinics stocked with supplies, and bustling, modern factories. He wouldn't know those factories were built by forced labor. He hadn't seen horse carcasses with their bones scraped of flesh, or the feral hopelessness of starving children.

"I've tried to learn a bit of the language—the cellist who played tonight has been helping me, though I'm fairly hopeless. My mouth just can't seem to form some of the sounds. Your English, on the other hand, is very good."

"I had a British governess."

I thought fleetingly of Miss Fields. I could never send a letter to England from the Soviet Union, but I could from Paris, if only I knew where she lived. But I had no way of finding out. I didn't know where she'd grown up, where she'd gone to school, or anything about her family. I didn't even know her first name.

"Shall we get something to eat?" I asked, tilting my head toward the dining room.

"With pleasure. I'm glad you're not one of those women who pretends she's never hungry."

I could hardly tell him that after the winter of 1919, I never turned down a chance at food. Or that, in private, I wasn't above licking my plate clean. "Do you like Russian food?"

"I do, most of it. Can't say I'm mad for caviar, but most everything else is all right. I like trying new things. It's one of the advantages of travel."

Lee handed me a plate and followed behind as I served myself dumplings and stuffed cabbage. When I was done, I hovered by the edge of the table, unsure of where to go next. The other concert-goers had broken into groups of three and four, each producing a torrent of animated Russian. I couldn't muster up the will to interrupt any one of those conversations and go through rounds of introductions and questions. Talking to Lee was so much easier.

"Nadia!"

Mikhail, across the room, raised his hand to get my attention. I turned to see if Lee was still behind me, but he'd already been claimed by a tall man in a tuxedo.

"My cousin," I tried to explain, but Lee only nodded distractedly. I wasn't sure if he'd heard.

"Making friends?" Mikhail asked when I reached him.

"Practicing my English," I said. "He works for a British newspaper."

"What's he doing here?"

I shrugged. "He likes Russian music."

"And Russian girls."

"Stop."

I popped a dumpling in my mouth and looked away, so Mikhail wouldn't see me flush. Alek would have kept prodding me, prolonging my discomfort, but Mikhail swiftly changed the subject.

"Let me introduce you around," he offered.

The men and women I met were former nobles and businessmen who spoke of their new circumstances in terms ranging from grief to amusement. To the Bolsheviks, they were all interchangeable class enemies. Each of them, however, had their own story of upheaval and death, their own burdens of memory. Though I didn't recall meeting any of them before, many names were familiar from Saint Petersburg and Moscow social circles; some of the older military types had met my father, and my mother's name drew knowing nods. In this room, with the duchess's jewels twinkling in the lamplight, I even had the jarring sense that nothing had changed, that I might turn and see Papa in his uniform, one hand clasped possessively on the hilt of his ceremonial sword.

Then I noticed the scuffed shoes and ragged hemlines. The undertone of sorrow that permeated the room. No—nothing was the same.

A trio of men formed a focal point in the center of the room, attracting a stream of guests in and out of their orbit. I glanced their way a few times, wondering who they were. Mikhail, noticing my interest, took my arm and walked me toward them.

"The one on the left will try to flirt with you," he murmured. "Go along, and you'll make an old man very happy."

Mikhail presented me with a flourish, his honored guest. The men's names were familiar—all aristocratic families—but Mikhail made the introductions so quickly that I forgot who was who and mentally labeled them the General, the Count, and the Duke. All were in their sixties or seventies, though the General's impressively waxed moustache and hair were dyed black. They fawned over me like beaus at a ball, and when they heard I'd come from Moscow, they all talked over each other, fighting to get their questions in first.

"Does Stalin know what he's doing? I hear he's losing followers."

"Have you met him? He's supposed to be a brute."

"Can't be worse than that madman Lenin, can he?"

"His body should be rotting in the ground, not laid out for worship in the middle of Red Square. Tell me, what does it look like?"

I did my best to answer: I hadn't met Stalin, the political situation changed from day to day, and yes, I'd seen Lenin's embalmed body in its glass case. Once had been enough.

"Only a matter of time before it all falls apart," the Count said, a phrase he'd probably been repeating since 1917. "The peasants were never behind the Bolsheviks—they got duped by Lenin's lies."

"I've said all along, it's the politicians' fault," added the Duke. "After the tsar abdicated, they all fought each other, and Lenin walked off with our country."

This was followed by debate about what they'd have done if they'd been in charge, and Mikhail gave me a quick, apologetic grimace. The conversation had the rote rhythm of a long-running play, with the same lines repeated ad nauseum.

"Gentlemen," Mikhail eventually interrupted, "may we leave the politics aside? I promised my cousin a musical evening, not a recounting of old battles."

"The music was wonderful," I said. "I'm so glad I came."

The Count stepped closer, claiming my attention for himself. "Russia's cultural heritage is the one treasure the Bolsheviks can never take from us. So many of our country's finest musicians and theater artists live here on practically nothing, and it breaks my heart to see their talents go to waste. It is our patriotic duty to support them."

"You can thank these gentlemen for tonight's performance," Mikhail explained. "They're the founders of the Russian Cultural League, the group that arranges these evenings."

It was the name I'd been waiting to hear, proof I was on the right track.

"We're financing a production of *The Seagull* in May," the General said. "You must come."

"With Daria Andreyevna Orlova as Arkadina," the Duke gushed. "I remember seeing her at the Moscow Art Theatre, years ago. She had the whole audience in tears."

"I'd love to see it," I said.

"How refreshing, to meet a young person who appreciates the classics," said the General, who'd shifted so close that his onion-scented breath wafted across my face. "You strike me as a woman of impeccable taste."

I pretended to be embarrassed and glanced away. The dining room was half-empty, and servants had begun clearing the table. I couldn't see Lee. Had he left without saying goodbye? The thought of it stung, and the evening soured. I'd confirmed the existence of the Russian Cultural League, but the people behind it were still trapped in the past, content with dim replicas of their former glory. They certainly didn't seem like a threat to the Soviet Union.

"I should get home," I told Mikhail. "I have work in the morning."

"Should I come with you? It's late . . ."

I waved him off and nodded to a group of men nearby who were waiting to speak with him. "I shouldn't keep you from your admirers."

"Promise you'll come for tea soon. Let's say Friday."

"Friday," I agreed, giving him a quick kiss goodbye.

I retrieved my hat from a maid hovering by the door, then stepped out onto the landing. The tight-fitting cloche dipped across the right side of my face, and I was adjusting the brim when I heard footsteps clattering up the stairs.

It was Lee, and he looked delighted to see me.

"I nearly missed you!" he said. "So glad I didn't."

The torpor that had engulfed me only seconds before instantly dissolved.

"I was helping a princess down the stairs," Lee said. "Only this one was considerably older than the ones in the storybooks, with an arthritic hip. It took ages. Were you leaving?"

I wasn't sure what to say. I wanted to do whatever Lee was doing; if he was staying, so would I.

I heard voices approaching from inside, a group of friends joking in raucous Russian as they said their goodbyes. Lee, making the decision for both of us, leaned back against the handrail, making space for me to walk down.

"Shall we?"

I went first, down two flights of stairs, and we emerged onto the busy Rue Saint-Honoré. Lee paused on the pavement, and a chilly breeze triggered goose bumps on my bare arms. It had been warm when I left my apartment, and I hadn't thought to bring a coat. We were silent for a moment, reluctant to part.

Lee's voice, when he spoke, was tentative. "There's something I wanted to ask you."

Anticipation made me even shakier than the cold. The way he was looking at me, his nervousness—it could only mean one thing. How in the world would I respond?

"I'm writing a book about my travels in Russia," Lee explained. "I've already got a publisher—everyone's interested in the Bolsheviks these days—and I collected all sorts of papers and pamphlets when I was there that I'd like to consult, but I can't read Russian. I was wondering, might you be available for some translation work?"

I managed to keep my expression cool as my skin prickled with shame. How could I have deluded myself that Lee was interested in me romantically? I was a married woman, working for the Soviet government. I couldn't make stupid mistakes.

"That is, if you're not too busy?"

I could see how much he wanted me to say yes. I'd misinterpreted the nature of his interest, but it was still gratifying to be looked at so eagerly. To feel wanted.

Perhaps Lee offered another kind of opportunity.

"I'd like to. I'll have to check my work schedule."

That is, check with Patlov. I'd need his approval before doing this, and I'd have to come up with a very good reason for spending time with a handsome Englishman. Despite the kindly uncle manner, Patlov was no fool.

Lee reached into his jacket pocket and handed me a card. "Give me a ring when you have it sorted out."

My mind was already spinning with ways to make Patlov say yes.

"Which way are you walking?" Lee asked.

I nodded to the left.

"You live nearby?"

"Oh no, I can't afford this neighborhood. I'm taking the bus, to the Marais."

"I've got a flat in Montparnasse." The other side of the river, the opposite direction from where I lived. "But I could walk you to your stop?"

I nodded and we started off, our steps leisurely, a mutual understanding that neither of us was in a hurry to leave.

"How long have you been in Paris?" I asked.

"Two months."

"What do you think of it?"

"Paris is Paris, wouldn't you say? The things I love about it are also the things that drive me mad."

I asked him what he meant and laughed as he described the quirks of his building's plumbing and the irritable old neighbor who scowled at everyone yet fed an army of stray cats. Lee was clever and funny, describing even the things he disliked with good-natured humor, as if he saw the world bathed in the same sunniness he projected. That night, I would have given anything for a transit strike or traffic jam, some obstacle that would have given us more time together. But the bus screeched toward the stop almost as soon as we arrived. I fumbled in my bag for the fare, and Lee stepped back. The last I saw of him, through a moving window, was the blur of his waving hand, obscuring his face.

Patlov was right: the grimy café where we met served a surprisingly delicious breakfast. And it was unexpectedly easy to convince him that Lee Cooper, an unknown writer for a little-read newspaper, was a potential spy.

"As far as I could tell, he was the only non-Russian at the concert," I told Patlov. "Why was he there? He told me he's interested in Russian culture, and he's friends with one of the musicians. But he didn't seem particularly interested in talking about the music. When he made his offer, I thought it might be a good way to find out more about him."

"I agree that his presence at the concert was odd," Patlov said. "There are a few possibilities. He could be writing something for his paper that he doesn't want anyone knowing about—perhaps an exposé on Russian émigrés. He could be a British government informer. Or he may be exactly what he says, a loyal Socialist and potentially useful ally."

Patlov held up his cup and signaled for more coffee.

"It wouldn't hurt to meet with him. Look through his papers and get a better idea of what he's up to." He pointed to a telephone on the far end of the bar. "Call him. Set up a time."

Lee's telephone rang at least ten times before he answered, and his *"Allo?"* was husky and brusque. I'd clearly woken him up.

"Mr. Cooper? It's Nadia Shulkina. From the concert."

"Miss Shulkina, of course." His voice brightened, and I could imagine him straightening up, smoothing his hair. "Lovely to hear from you."

"I'd be happy to help with your translation. I have time in the next few days, if you'd like me to get started."

"Don't suppose you'd be free tomorrow afternoon?"

"Yes, that would be fine."

"Smashing. The *Workers' Bulletin* can't afford an office, so I work out of my apartment, if that's all right with you. Say, two o'clock?"

I agreed, and he gave me the address as I looked pointedly at Patlov and nodded. He looked pleased, but the blissful surge that carried me back to the table had little to do with my handler's approval. I had no intention, then, of befriending Lee—let alone seducing him. I was content just knowing I'd be seeing him again. That I'd get to hear him

laugh. Years of deprivation had taught me that you can still take pleasure in something you'll never possess.

That didn't stop me from making an effort before our next meeting.
That morning, I washed my hair and coaxed it into waves. I polished my
shoes and fingernails. I couldn't compete with Parisian women when it
came to fashion—my three dresses were all interchangeably plain—but
if Lee moved in Socialist circles, he'd be used to seeing women in drab
browns and grays. All that mattered was that I make a good impression,
so he'd hire me for as long as possible.

I arrived at the address Lee had given me five minutes early, but he
was already waiting outside. The apartment building was grander than
I'd expected, with an ornate stone façade. A set of oversized wooden
doors at the center opened into a central courtyard. The concierge,
Madame Gournier, sat a few feet inside, surveying her domain. Dressed
in head-to-toe widow's black, she gave me the hardened stare of a judge
who hands down harsh sentences.

Lee introduced me, his French impressively fluent. "I've hired
Mademoiselle Shulkina to assist me with the book I'm writing. She's a
very talented translator."

"Mr. Cooper flatters me," I said, equally flowery. "It's an honor to
be part of such important work."

Our display of mutual admiration softened Madame Gournier's
scowl.

"A pleasure to meet you," she said, tipping her head to me. Then,
to Lee, "The plumber is coming tomorrow, if you're still having trouble
with the sink."

"Marvelous." He pressed one hand against his chest and gave her a
look of misty-eyed devotion. "I am so grateful."

Madame Gournier's sudden smile transformed her from a gruff
watchdog to a sentimental grandmother. Apparently, I wasn't the only
one susceptible to Lee's charm.

I followed Lee to the top floor, assuming a dimly lit attic was all he could afford on a Socialist writer's salary. I was surprised when he led me into an expansive sitting room, with a Victorian claw-legged sofa and upholstered armchair to the right and a large, cluttered dining table in the center. Unlike my dismal lodgings, it had high ceilings and large windows, which gave the space a brightness that more than compensated for the shabbiness of the furniture. Through an arched doorway, I glimpsed a stove, and there were two closed doors on the opposite side of the room. Bedrooms? Was it possible he had the luxury of a private bathroom?

"Sorry for the mess," Lee apologized, pushing books and papers aside to clear one end of the table. "I tried to sort everything I collected in Russia, but since I can't read any of it . . ."

He gave up on his attempt to create order from the chaos and let out an exaggerated sigh.

I walked around the table, mentally cataloging what I saw. There were stacks of books in English and French. Mostly history and economics, but a few novels, too. Piles of newspapers, from Paris and London, as well as past issues of the *Workers' Bulletin*.

Lee pulled out two chairs and set them side by side. "Shall we get started?"

He pushed forward a tottering pile of pamphlets, brochures, and other miscellaneous papers. All seemed to be in Russian, aside from a few handwritten notes. It was a daunting mess that would take multiple visits to sort out. Exactly as I'd hoped.

"How do you keep track of what you have?" I asked hesitantly. "Is there a system?"

Lee's laugh was the burble of a mischievous child. "God, I wish there was. You'll have to help me with that, too."

I was struck by how effortlessly Lee spoke and moved. There was no self-consciousness, no pause between what he thought and what he said.

"I picked up things here and there and tossed it all in my case. I didn't know what might prove useful later on. If you could put this in some kind of order, that would be a good start."

Lee passed me a pencil and a new, blank notebook. As I began skimming through the documents, sorting them into piles, Lee picked up a book and went to read on the sofa. I glanced at him from time to time, furtively, looking back over my shoulder. He sat with his legs outstretched, crossed at the ankles, the book resting on his stomach—as if I wasn't there. After about an hour, he offered me tea, and as we waited for our cups to cool, I showed him the tentative categories I'd written down. We sipped and talked, as I explained what certain pamphlets said and why they might or might not be helpful. Lee took anything I judged unimportant and tossed it off the table. Discarded papers carpeted the floor by the time I realized the light had darkened to the amber glow of late afternoon.

"I didn't realize it was so late," I said. "I'm sorry—I didn't do much translating."

"You've been awfully helpful," Lee said. "At least now I know what I've got. Would you like to take the newspaper articles to start?"

It took me a moment to understand: he wanted me to take the papers home and bring them back when they were translated. No matter how much work I did, my time with Lee would be limited to brief conversations and exchanges of files.

No. It wasn't enough. For the past few hours, I'd felt surprisingly at home. Lee's worn-in furniture reminded me of Priyalko, where comfort mattered more than style, and the sunlight streaming through the windows had restored me. I wanted to come back. Not for any mission—for myself.

"Would it be a bother if I worked here?" I tried to sound nonchalant, as if the thought had just occurred to me. "It would be easier if I had access to all the material at once."

I was becoming a connoisseur of Lee's smiles. The one he gave me now was tentative but warm.

"I might have questions," I began, right as Lee said, "That makes sense," and our laughter intertwined. Perhaps he was lonely and welcomed the company, though I couldn't imagine Lee lacked for friends. He seemed like the kind of person who drew people toward him. Women, especially.

We agreed I'd return in two days. When he asked for the best way to reach me, I told him I didn't have a telephone, but he could send a message to my apartment. I scribbled the address at the top of my notes, only belatedly realizing he'd be writing to Nadia—a woman who didn't officially live there. Frantically, I tried to work out a solution, hoping Lee didn't find my sudden hesitation strange. Finally, I wrote, *Marie Duvall.*

"I'm staying in her apartment while she's out of town. You'd better put her name on the envelope, to make sure I get it."

"Will do," he said, handing me my first payment of ten francs. Tangible proof—in case I was tempted to forget—that his interest in me was purely professional.

I spent half the money at a bakery, giddy at my extravagance. It was only once I'd arrived home and taken my first bite of *pain au chocolat* that the doubts began to seep in. Lee was charming and confident, a man with seemingly nothing to hide. But how could a reporter for a Socialist newspaper afford such a big apartment? Why did he have nothing better to do this afternoon than lounge on the sofa and read?

Something wasn't right. Which meant the suspicions I'd invented for Patlov might have some truth to them, after all.

LONDON

1938

To: Director, SIS

I regret to inform you that despite two weeks of dogged investigation, our team has made little progress in the matter of "Marie Duvall," aka Red Mistress. Our most promising discovery was a ticket receipt found in her hotel room, for the British Museum, dated May 14 (three days before her death). After showing her picture to museum staff, we found a guard who confirmed seeing her on the date in question. He told us she was accompanied by a gentleman whose description matched the accomplice who checked in alongside her at the Hotel Bristol. The guard was unable to say if either the woman or the gentleman spoke to anyone else and noted the museum was quite crowded that day.

While it is possible Red Mistress went to the museum for her own recreational interest, we think it highly unlikely that an agent of her standing would choose to spend her time in this manner. As you and I well know, busy public spaces are often chosen as locations for secret meetings, document exchanges, etc. Therefore, we will be interviewing all museum staff at length to discover if anyone saw Red Mistress make contact with another visitor that day.

I hope to have news of further developments soon.

—Roger

PARIS

May 1926

I'd been in Paris a month before I first heard of the Patriot.

Day by day, I'd laid the foundations of a new life. I became a regular customer at the local bakery and exchanged morning greetings with the Blanchards, a pair of elderly, unmarried sisters who lived on the ground floor of my building. Sometimes I gave a coin or two to the soldier who begged at the corner, his face sunken into a military jacket with one empty sleeve. I brightened the walls of my apartment with colored postcards of seaside villages and fields of flowers, places I'd probably never visit but liked to imagine I could. Gradually, the dingy space began to feel almost welcoming.

I made dutiful appearances at the French Ministry of Trade, where I sat at a tiny desk in a tiny room and translated contracts from bureaucratic French into bureaucratic Russian. But most of my time was spent with Russians émigrés, gradually constructing my newest persona: a young woman who worked for the Communists, but no longer believed their promises. It was a delicate process, one that made me think of Elena making bread dough in the kitchen at Priyalko. I'd watch as she sprinkled water into the flour, gently pushing and prodding, telling me to be patient. Move too fast, she'd tell me, and you risk ruining the whole thing. I'd drop hints of my disloyalty into every conversation, hoping word would build and spread. I couldn't imagine Mikhail involved in a conspiracy—he'd never put all the relatives who depended on him in danger—and the leaders of the Russian Cultural League were too old and stuffy to be serious threats. But I believed there really were people working against the Soviet Union, and if I got a reputation as a would-be Soviet turncoat, it was only a matter of time until they approached me. Patlov would get his proof of a plot, I'd achieve my mission, and the Shulkins would no longer be under suspicion.

And then I'd be called back to Moscow. But I tried not to think about that. At a dinner with the Russian Cultural League leaders and their wives, I talked about my love of art and lamented that the Soviet system was crushing creativity along with everything else.

"All I'm allowed to draw are muscled factory men and happy farmers." I spoke slowly and emphatically, as if I'd had too much to drink. "Soviet art has no soul."

The General reached for my hand—he always found some excuse to touch me—and nodded. "It does my heart good to know that not all young people have been brainwashed by the Communists."

"I'm not saying they're all bad. But there are times . . ."

I glanced around the table, dramatizing my hesitation. My voice dropped to a whisper.

"There are times I'd do anything to go back to the way it was."

"Wouldn't we all," murmured the Duke's wife. I caught a glance between her husband and the General. Another drop had been added to the mix.

I'd hoped to make similar progress with Lee, but he remained maddeningly inscrutable. My visits had developed a routine: two or three afternoons a week, I'd knock on his door, heart thudding, and be greeted with an encouraging smile. I'd take my seat at the dining table, where he'd either work alongside me or move to the sofa to read. After an hour or so, we'd take a break for tea and conversation, covering the same limited topics: my latest translation, the weather, or the book he was reading. Lee's pleasantness was an impenetrable shield, deflecting any question that was remotely personal, and after a few weeks, Patlov began asking whether he was worth my time. I'd come up against an impossible choice: tell Patlov that Lee was harmless—which would mean the end of my visits—or lie about him so I could keep visiting.

I hadn't yet decided what to do when Lee answered the door one day looking bleary-eyed and pale. His hair stuck out at odd angles, and a sprinkling of stubble darkened his cheeks.

"Late night," he mumbled.

I followed him inside. With a vague wave toward the table, he said, "I'll leave you to it," then shuffled off to his bedroom, closing the door behind him.

I began writing out the English translation of a pamphlet that announced the opening of a new factory: *A new day dawns for the People . . . No longer will they be denied the fruits of their labor.* When I heard the gentle rumble of snores from behind the bedroom door, I put down my pencil. At last, I'd have a chance to look around without Lee watching. I carefully flipped through the stacks of books on the table and shook each one to see if anything had been slipped inside. Nothing fell out.

I moved through the room, searching for likely hiding spots. I slid my hands under chair cushions and lifted up lamps. All I found were cigarette butts and wads of lint. In the small but well-stocked kitchen, I inspected the coffee and tea canisters (nearly empty), the breadbox (completely empty), and the cabinets, which held only dishes and cutlery. I was about to open the icebox when I heard the distinctive creak of bedsprings and hurried back to the table. By the time Lee emerged from the bedroom, I was back where he'd left me. His clothes were still rumpled, but his face looked less haggard.

"Sorry about before. I should have said no to the final round of whiskey last night."

I'd never tried whiskey, and judging from its effects on Lee, I wasn't interested. "I'm glad you're feeling better."

"I'm going out for some food. Do you need anything?"

"No, thank you."

Lee picked up a jacket he'd left hanging on the back of a chair and put on his hat. Then he was gone, leaving me alone in his apartment for the first time. Had he gone to a restaurant for a leisurely meal? Or was he buying a few things at a shop and bringing them home? There was no way of knowing how much time I had, so I'd have to move fast.

The bathroom had no obvious hiding places; there was barely space for the toilet, sink, and rust-stained tub. I quickly moved on to the bedroom. It was darker and more austere than the front room, with a distinctly masculine smell. There was one small window, which opened onto the courtyard, and an iron-framed bed sat flush against the adjacent wall. A thin blanket had been thrown across a wad of sheets, and the pillow was flattened on one side. For a brief, vivid moment, I pictured Lee's head on that pillow, his legs tangled in those sheets.

Then I wrenched my thoughts away from such foolishness.

I searched everywhere I could think of. Under the mattress; inside the suitcase stashed under the bed; inside the pockets of the jacket and robe hanging on the back of the door. I methodically unfolded and refolded every piece of clothing stored in the squat bureau—mostly underwear I felt awkward touching. A stack of handkerchiefs embroidered with Lee's initials held a lingering aroma of perfume, though I didn't find any other trace of a woman's presence. Still, I told myself, I mustn't act disappointed if he introduced me to a special female "friend" one day.

The bottom drawer was a mishmash of household items: shoe polish, pens, nail scissors, and bandages. It was only once I'd cleared most of it out that I saw a small diary wedged in a corner at the very bottom. It was for the current year, with two pages allotted for each week, three lines per day. The only things written inside were names, jotted in Lee's spiky handwriting. Some days were blank, others had only one or two notations, but on certain pages, a dozen or more names were crammed in, the letters so shrunken that they were almost unreadable. I flipped back and forth, trying to find a pattern. There seemed to be a mix of nationalities—French, Russian, English, German—but I couldn't find any apparent link between them. Then I saw it.

Mikhail Shulkin
Nadia Shulkina

Lee had written down our names on the date of the musical salon. Why?

I heard a key rattle at the front door. I slammed the diary shut, dropped it back into place, and called out, "Mr. Cooper?"

When Lee appeared in the doorway of the bedroom, I was leaning toward the half-open window. "Sorry—I heard a strange noise and wanted to see what was going on."

As Lee walked past me, I glanced around the bedroom to make sure I'd left nothing out of place. The pillow and blanket had shifted when I rummaged under the mattress, but I was fairly certain Lee wouldn't notice. The bed had been just as messy when he left.

"A pigeon?" Lee suggested. "Or it could have been children. They play in the courtyard sometimes."

"That must be it." Distraction was one of the many tricks I'd learned from Alek: keep talking, keep moving. "Do you have a moment? I have a question."

Lee followed me back to the front room, and I showed him a passage I'd been struggling with, which could be translated two different ways. If my attraction for Lee had begun as a girlish appreciation of his good looks, I'd come to like him best at times like this, when we worked together as colleagues. Each conversation was like a dance, and we matched each other step by step, speaking the same rhythm. He didn't seem bothered that I'd been in his bedroom, which meant the diary wasn't necessarily suspicious. Lee was a journalist, after all. It was natural that he'd keep a list of the people he'd met, for use in future stories.

So why had he hidden the diary away from his other work papers?

I knew I should tell Patlov. I almost did, countless times during our next meeting. Instead, I shared the latest gossip from the league—there were always petty feuds over who got credit for what—and assured him Mikhail still hadn't said anything suspicious, despite my frequent prodding. By the time Patlov was finishing his second cup of coffee, I'd convinced myself I needed more information before telling him about Lee's diary. If I could sneak another look at it, I'd copy down the names and bring the list to Patlov. Come to him with evidence, rather than suspicions.

"Have any of them mentioned the Patriot?" Patlov asked.

I'd let my mind wander and lost track of the conversation. Using another method I'd perfected during my marriage, I pretended to give the question careful thought. Eventually, as I'd hoped, Patlov was the first to break the silence.

"It's a name we've heard, from a few sources."

"I don't think so. Who is he?"

"We don't know. Someone within the Soviet leadership who's made contact with émigrés in France." The normally imperturbable Patlov looked flustered. "It may be nothing. A rumor. But keep your ears open, will you?"

"Of course."

Was this a test? If so, I'd failed. There were webs of secret alliances all over Paris, and I had yet to find my way into any of them. Alek wouldn't let me keep searching forever.

The Patriot was still on my mind the following day, when a blustery wind seemed determined to sweep the streets clean. The Blanchard sisters had their front door closed when I left my building—no chitchat today—and the begging soldier looked more wretched than usual, his chest curled over his bent-in knees. I looked away as I walked past, telling myself I shouldn't feel guilty that I had no coins for him today. I did, anyway.

By the time I reached Lee's apartment, it had begun to rain. I made it inside without getting wet, but the staccato splatter of water against the windows made it impossible for me to concentrate on work. Lee was similarly restless, flipping impatiently through a newspaper, shuffling folders at the table, then settling down at his typewriter. He rolled in a blank piece of paper and stared at it, while I waited for him to either start typing or start talking. I'd been rereading the same paragraph over and over, remembering nothing. The rain died down to a trickle, then stopped, yet neither of us seemed able to capture our usual rhythm.

Lee pushed back his chair and exhaled dramatically.

"Does it feel hot in here?"

I shrugged, but he'd already strode off to the window. He pushed up the sash with a grunt, and a rush of wind swept in and around him, scattering papers to the floor. I jumped up to grab them, and Lee waved his arms to catch one drifting past. I had a sudden image of farmers chasing chickens, which made me laugh. Lee joined in, and soon we were breathless with giggles, brandishing each page we caught with exaggerated triumph. When Lee gathered them all together and imprisoned them with a paperweight, I felt light-headed with glee. For one wild moment, I wanted to rush forward and kiss him.

Lee put his hands on his hips and grinned. "I'm starving. Would you like to get something to eat?"

It was three o'clock in the afternoon, and I wasn't particularly hungry. I could decline Lee's offer and use this opportunity to take another look at his diary.

"I'd love to," I said instead.

The Paris of those years has been distorted by the gauzy lens of nostalgia. Not every shop was quaint, not every corner picturesque. Cars screeched and honked, and warm days brought an overripe stink from the Seine. But anyone who walked through Montparnasse that spring could sense the city's vitality. Lee and I navigated sidewalks filled with people, drawn outside by the respite from the rain. Two women draped in silk strolled past us, arm in arm, their hat brims touching as they exchanged hushed confessions. A huddle of young men argued outside a tobacconist's, talking over each other, using hands and elbows and shoulders to punctuate each phrase. The air hummed with expectancy, the feeling that anything could happen.

Lee asked if I'd been to Le Dôme, and I shook my head.

"Then that's where we'll go. It's one of my favorite spots in Paris."

The restaurant's broad awning stood sentinel over a densely packed seating area, crammed with customers who seemed to have no other responsibilities on a weekday afternoon. Coffee cups and ashtrays fought for position on the tiny, circular tables, with chairs positioned at odd angles to fit the spaces in between.

"It'll be quieter inside," Lee said. "Bonjour, Henri!"

A maître d' with an impressively bristly moustache and cheerful eyes opened the front door for us. I stepped into a hushed atmosphere of dark wood and red velvet. Though the interior seating was as cramped as outside, only a few of the tables were occupied. Henri led us toward a booth in the back. We passed a group of men whose overflowing ashtrays indicated they'd been there for some time, and one of them looked at me with what seemed like more than casual interest. Before taking my seat opposite Lee, I pretended to adjust my dress, so I'd have an excuse to look at him again. The man had turned back to his companions, and though I couldn't hear what they were saying, it sounded like they were speaking Russian. Had Patlov sent him to follow me? It didn't make sense; he'd already been here when I arrived.

Lee handed over a menu. "Have a look. I always get the duck."

When was the last time I'd eaten duck? It must have been at Priyalko. Yuri would bring them, freshly shot and plucked, to Elena in the kitchen. Papa would beam in delight and invariably declare, "Perfection!" after taking his first bite. Vasily would slide half the meat off the platter as Mama protested, "You can't possibly eat all that," even though he always did. I remembered the grease that coated my lips, the napkin I kept in one hand to wipe it away.

"I'll have duck, too," I said.

Henri seemed to appear out of nowhere, and Lee placed our orders, including a bottle of wine. When it arrived—swiftly enough to confirm Lee was a favored customer—Henri poured me a generous serving. What I'd intended to be a small sip turned into a nervous gulp, and the sudden bitterness in my throat made me cough.

"Are you all right?" Lee asked.

I wasn't, of course. I was dining out with a man who wasn't my husband, being stared at by a mysterious stranger, drinking wine that could tempt me into saying things I shouldn't. Being the center of Lee's attention felt like squinting into the sun.

"I'm not used to eating in restaurants," I said.

"It suits you, though. May I ask you something, of a personal nature?"

I gave him a cautious nod.

"You told me you had an English governess. I've wondered—well, there's no delicate way to say this, but it made me assume your family was well-off, before the revolution."

I nodded again.

"I'm only asking because you're so different from the other women I met in Russia. You must have some standing in the Party, to be an official translator, but you seem to have no interest in politics. You never denounce my decadent capitalist ways."

"I thought you were a Socialist."

"I am, in the most general sense. I believe in fair pay and workers' rights and taxing the rich to lift up the poor. But I don't like being told what to believe. I prefer to work things out for myself."

How lucky he'd been, to have that freedom. "I was not brought up as a Socialist. Much less a Communist."

"So, you joined the Bolsheviks to rebel against your parents."

I could feel the confession taking shape, words forming themselves into sentences. A torrent of emotion urging release.

Lee watched me intently, his blue eyes crinkling with compassion. "Tell me."

I'd spent so many years hiding my true self. Trying to be less visible. Now, I was sitting across from someone who wanted to see beyond my aloof outer self. Is there anything more flattering?

"My father was the one who hired Miss Fields—he loved England. He'd visited once, for a military conference, and he promised to take me, when I was older. He was an officer, in the army . . ."

I'd meant to tell Lee only the basic facts, but once I started, I couldn't stop. In Russia, talking about Papa was tantamount to treason, but here, with Lee, it was safe to remember. To mourn the man I'd loved most in the world. By the time the duck arrived, I'd moved on to Mama, which, in turn, led to Vasily and Priyalko. I described the rye fields on a summer evening. Mama's camera and our theatrical performances and Miss Fields reading excerpts of Jane Austen. The drawings I'd made that Elena pinned along the upstairs hall. I led Lee through the house and the grounds, showing him the places that lived on in my mind, sheltered in the alcoves of memory.

Lee followed alongside me, nodding and smiling. He tipped the last of the wine into my glass, and I wondered how much I'd drunk. Lee had finished eating, but I'd made it only halfway through my meal.

Henri appeared and frowned at my plate, as if the unfinished food was a personal affront.

"Another bottle?" he asked.

"Non, non," Lee said. "Coffee."

As Henri walked off, I gave Lee a mock-serious grimace. "I'd better finish. I don't want to hurt his feelings."

"Take your time." Lee finished his wine in one long, smooth swallow. "I'm in no hurry."

My body felt wispy and loose, the wine softening the barrier between what I thought and what I said. "I hope I'm not boring you."

"Quite the opposite. I find other people's lives fascinating."

"Is that why you became a reporter?"

Lee tilted his fork between his fingers, taking his time in answering. I hadn't thought it was a difficult question.

Finally, he said, "I fell into writing, really."

I sliced the remains of my duck and waited. Henri brought the coffee, and Lee added cream and sugar, stirring them in slowly.

"Go on," I urged, midchew. "Your turn to talk."

"My father's a military man, like yours. Very keen on discipline and running a tight ship. My mother died when I was ten. She was lovely—one of those people everyone adored. I did, certainly. After she was gone, Father couldn't pack me off to boarding school soon enough. One of those miserable places run like an army camp. I hated it, but Father wouldn't hear of me leaving. 'Suffering builds character,' he'd tell me."

Lee's voice was quicksilver smooth, but I could hear the hurt lurking underneath. I knew, all too well, the façades we erect to seal away grief.

"When you were talking about your papa encouraging your art and applauding your shows—well, I couldn't imagine my father doing that. He never showed much interest in anything I did. I don't think we've ever had an honest conversation."

"That can't be true."

"Oh, we speak. But never about ourselves. Not like you and I are doing right now. The only thing that matters is that his children don't embarrass him. Do well in school, but not too well. Avoid drawing attention. My two older sisters did exactly as they were supposed to. Sally lives in Liverpool with her husband and two children, and

Harriet's marrying a banker in a few months. Thank God, because it's given Father something other than me to focus on."

"Where did you grow up?"

Again, Lee seemed oddly hesitant.

"London, for the most part." Then, with a shamefaced smirk, "And a country house, in Wiltshire. Passed down from my mother's family."

Now I understood his reluctance to tell me. "An unusual upbringing for a Socialist."

"Which is why you must cross your heart and promise not to tell."

"You're the one who rebelled, not me."

"My father loathes Reds more than anything, even the French. There'd never been any question of me following Father into the service, and there I was, fresh out of military school, a commissioned officer at nineteen years old. Not because I'd done anything to deserve it, but because I came from the right family and the officer corps had been wiped out during the war. There was something so ludicrous about me being in charge of men who were older than me—and certainly braver. I started going to Socialist meetings only to stir Father up, but once I was there, what I heard made sense. What's so wrong about agitating for an equal share? I went to parts of London that were utterly appalling, straight from a Dickens novel. I couldn't see that suffering and ignore it."

He sounded just like Alek.

"I've made you smile," Lee said. "What is it?"

"You remind me of someone I know, back in Russia."

"Who?"

The wine urged me on, whispering that it would be fun to flirt with the truth. "A man who wants to change the world."

Lee leaned forward, intrigued. I looked away, immediately regretting my flippant tone. I didn't want to think of Alek. Not here.

"You still haven't told me how you became a reporter," I said.

"I wanted to travel, and meet new people, and possibly do some good along the way. I wrote letters to a few old friends, disaffected former soldiers like me, and one of them had an aunt who was funding a new Socialist paper—a suffragette who'd inherited a fortune from her husband and was looking for a cause to spend it on. The *Workers' Bulletin* is, in effect, a rich widow's vanity project that allows me to live the life I've always wanted. But that must remain our secret."

"I won't tell a soul."

Henri strutted past our table, leading a group of men and women to the table opposite us. The café was filling up, surrounding voices growing louder. Lee caught Henri's attention and pulled out a money clip. I wanted to stop him—to ask for more wine, more time. Instead, I watched Lee settle the bill.

When he was finished, he told me, "I'm off to Marseilles tomorrow. The dockworkers are going on strike."

Another pang of disappointment. "How long will you be gone?"

"Can't say. I won't need you the rest of this week, in any case."

It was only Tuesday. The thought of all those days without him hurt more than it should.

"There's not much more to go, in any case, is there?" he asked.

"I don't think so."

I'd been translating Lee's papers as slowly as I could without looking incompetent. If I'd been working at my true capacity, I'd have long since finished.

"When will you be going back to Moscow?" he asked.

I shrugged. "I'm not sure."

"There must be people you miss. That man you mentioned earlier, perhaps?"

He was teasing, but my pulse began to thud. I shook my head— embarrassed? dismissive?—and Lee, ever the gentleman, stood and adjusted his jacket. "Shall we go?"

My heart sank at how quickly he shifted back to formality. It had felt, for a time, that we were friends. As I straightened my skirt and placed my bunched-up napkin on the table, I reminded myself that this had been only a temporary escape from the constraints of our very different lives.

As Lee and I squeezed through the narrow opening between tables, I saw that the man who'd looked at me earlier was still there, with the same friends. He stared at me again, and this time, I stared back. He had thick, reddish hair and an unkempt beard, and judging by the height of his shoulders, he was taller than average. Middle-aged, most likely somewhere in his forties. I still couldn't place him.

I hesitated as I passed, and my obvious curiosity prompted him to speak. "Madame Semelkova?" he asked.

I stopped, stunned at the sound of my married name, and Lee bumped against my back. Had he heard?

In Russian, the man continued. "I'm sorry if I startled you. I'm an old friend of your uncle Sergei—I stayed at your summer house once . . ."

And then I remembered: Boris the poet. He and Alek had been part of Sergei's bohemian circle. I could picture Boris in Mama's favorite clearing, scribbling in his notebook, clasping it protectively against his chest when Sergei threatened to read his latest verse aloud. I saw all of them: the Volodnovs, with their paint-stained fingers and flamboyant flirtations; Princess Nemerova and her haughtily handsome dancer-companions; Mama with her camera, tugging at arms and nudging people into the perfect pose.

The memories flashed in bursts, disorienting amid the clashing conversations and clatter of dishes. "Could we speak outside?" I finally managed.

Boris, Lee, and I pushed our way through the crowd packed into the café's entryway, most of them gesturing in vain toward Henri. Every chair outside had been claimed, the occupants sitting leg to leg as dozens of voices blended into a single hum. As Boris led us away from the crush, Lee leaned in toward my shoulder and asked, "Shall I go?"

"No, please stay. I knew him, back in Russia, but not well. We won't be long."

Boris leaned into the recessed doorway of a shoe-repair shop that had closed for the day. I stood opposite him, Lee by my side. I introduced the two men in French and explained that Lee worked for an English newspaper. If Boris was curious why a married Russian woman was dining out with a British reporter, he didn't show it. He pulled a package of cigarettes from his trouser pocket and offered it to me. I shook my head, but Lee took one, nodding his thanks. Lee provided the matches, and I waited as each man inhaled his first mouthful. Boris sucked at his cigarette in quick bursts, while Lee was more deliberate. I felt jittery with dread.

"Do you live in Paris?" I asked Boris.

He nodded. "You?"

"Visiting."

"Alek, too?"

"He's in Moscow."

I glanced at Lee, who'd stepped away and was leaning against the wall. Silently, I acknowledged the question Boris hadn't asked aloud: *Lee doesn't know I'm married.* Boris gave an indifferent shrug.

"It's not easy to get travel papers these days," Boris said. "You must have connections."

"Alek does."

"I heard he's risen in the Party." Boris's tone implied that he wasn't impressed. "How is your uncle?"

"Still in Leningrad. The magazine isn't what it once was, of course, but they keep him on as a writer. He's grateful for that."

"He was the first person to publish me. I wrote a poem about a bird as an allegory of freedom. Sentimental garbage, but Sergei saw promise in it."

"He always liked discovering new talent."

"I was surprised when I heard Alek had married Sergei's niece. I assumed all the Shulkins had left Russia."

"The others did."

Lee tossed the stub of his cigarette to the ground and crushed it under his shoe, his face dim in the shadows.

Boris, sensing my restlessness, spoke quickly. "Be careful."

An icy chill spread down my back, my arms, my stomach.

"I've known Alek a long time. I thought we wanted the same thing—the freedom to live and speak as we wished. That was the goal of Sergei's magazine and everyone who worked on it. After the revolution, everything changed. I didn't want to write hackneyed celebrations of factory workers who'd never read a verse of poetry in their lives! I wanted to write the truth about what I saw. When did that become a treasonable offense? Sergei was the one who warned me I was about to be arrested, so I left, with nothing."

"I'm sorry."

"Alek was always self-righteous, but it didn't matter when we were both poor and fighting for the same cause. I didn't understand how quickly he'd turn on friends who questioned his version of the truth. It's none of my business why you married him, and I hope he's a good husband. But you should know, he's ruthless with anyone who crosses him."

Boris looked pointedly at Lee. I started to protest that I'd done nothing wrong, but did it really matter? If Alek had seen me in that café with Lee, he would have assumed what Boris assumed. And he would punish me accordingly.

Boris turned to Lee and spoke in heavily accented French. "A pleasure to meet you, Mr. Cooper." Then, to me, "Good luck."

As soon as Boris turned back to the café, I began walking hurriedly down Boulevard Montparnasse, nudging my way blindly through the crowds. Lee's footsteps thudded along the sidewalk just behind.

"Are you all right?"

I wasn't, but I didn't want him to see me upset, and I couldn't come up with a convincing lie. Lee moved up next to me, his left arm hovering by my right shoulder. I sensed him looking at me, but I stared resolutely ahead. When we came to a cross street, I barely paused before stepping off the curb. A bicycle whipped past, and Lee grabbed my elbow, pulling me back. I staggered and sagged against Lee's chest, his body steadying mine. Then I pulled away.

"Thank you," I said, shaken.

"That man, at the café. Did he threaten you?"

"No."

The strain on Lee's face eased.

"I wanted to make sure. You looked upset."

"We talked about old times. It's not always easy to remember."

We continued in silence, as close as we could be without actually touching, following the route to Lee's apartment. The streetlights had come on, signaling the imminent arrival of another sparkling Parisian evening. But I remained alert with nervous energy. It felt like people were staring at me, hovering uncomfortably close. Was I being followed? I risked a glimpse backward, over my shoulder. Directly behind me was a woman whose eyes bulged beneath dramatic false eyelashes. To her right I saw a red-faced man lustily sucking on a cigar. A few feet back, a man in a dark hat and suit strolled at a leisurely pace. Had he turned his face when I looked back? Or had Boris's warning made me overly suspicious?

I turned my ankle and pretended my heel had slipped. Lee paused alongside me as I adjusted my shoe, my head facing down while my eyes peered back. The man in the suit had stopped half a block behind us. Coincidence? He was holding a cigarette, focused on lighting a match.

I stood up and kept walking, waiting another block before checking the reflection in a shop window. The man was still behind us, far back enough that I couldn't see his face. The upcoming corner was filled with a gaggle of middle-aged women. Americans, arguing over the way back to their hotel. There were people coming and going in all directions, fish swimming in conflicting streams. An opportunity, if I moved fast enough.

I tugged at Lee's sleeve and picked up my pace. He looked at me quizzically but followed as I slipped around the women and abruptly turned onto a narrow side street. I stepped gingerly along the cobblestones, landing on the balls of my feet to avoid making a sound. Huddled against a building, outside the streetlights' range, I saw the mysterious man elbow his way through the tourists and continue along Boulevard Montparnasse. By the time he realized he'd lost me, he'd have a half a dozen options of where to retrace his steps. I could only hope he didn't choose this one.

"Follow me," I urged Lee.

We continued along the street as it narrowed into a twisted lane, a remnant of Paris's medieval past. When we'd gone what I considered a safe distance, I stopped to catch my breath. Lee's cheeks were flushed, his voice sharp.

"What's going on?"

I couldn't tell him we were being followed, because he'd ask why. Was it even true? In the café, Lee's gentle curiosity had put me at ease. The mood between us was different now, as my pent-up impulses sparked against his. Shadows masked everything but Lee's eyes, and they locked on me as he pulled off his hat. He stepped forward, and I leaned in, my hands fluttering up against his chest.

He kissed me slowly, carefully, and his arms reached around my shoulders, welcoming me in. I loosened into the sensation flooding through me, a woozy sense of relief. Paris disappeared. All that existed was the kiss and Lee.

Until my heel slid into a gap between cobblestones, jolting me back to reality. I twisted my head away, and Lee ran his lips along my cheek.

"You're full of surprises," he murmured.

I felt flustered and confused, almost dizzy. Perhaps, for Lee, this was nothing out of the ordinary. Women probably threw themselves at him all the time.

I wrenched myself from his embrace. "I'm sorry," I muttered, looking down. I couldn't risk looking at him, not yet. I didn't trust myself not to kiss him again.

"Don't be. I quite like kissing you."

"I should go."

"Must you?"

For him, it was a game: the delicate tussle of will-she-or-won't-she. He had no idea of the risk I'd taken, or the danger I'd put us both in.

"I have to go home."

The firmness in my voice had the desired effect. Lee pulled back and put on his hat, his expression nonchalant. I wanted him to protest. Shatter my self-possession with more kisses.

"All right. Shall I walk you to the bus?"

"You don't have to. I can find my way from here."

"Well, as I said, I'm leaving tomorrow. I'll send a note when I'm back in town. Have a good evening."

He turned and left, his footsteps echoing off the stones. Calm and deliberate, as if nothing had happened. As if my entire world hadn't teetered on the edge of collapse.

I blinked away tears the entire bus ride home. If someone was following me, I couldn't let them see me upset. I walked briskly from the bus stop to my building, my steps heavy to scare off the rats that would be emerging with the dark. When I saw a man pacing by the entrance, I pulled out my key, ready to make a quick entry.

It was only as I got closer that I realized it was Alek.

"Hello, darling."

Paralyzed by shock, I could only stare. He kissed me on both cheeks, his lips stinging my skin.

"What are you doing here?" I hissed, before realizing that was hardly an appropriate response from a supposedly devoted wife. I mustered an apologetic smile. "You startled me."

"Comrade Stalin needed some documents hand-delivered to the ambassador. I volunteered. It was very last-minute—I didn't have time to write."

But he would have had time to cable the embassy, and Patlov would have been informed. They'd chosen not to tell me. I worried my face was blotchy from crying, my lipstick smudged. Hopefully it was dark enough that Alek wouldn't notice.

"It's good to see you," I said. "Come in."

I heard a baby shrieking as we climbed the first flight of steps; on the next floor, a couple's vicious argument raged behind their front door. Through Alek's eyes, I saw the peeling, mildewed wallpaper, the scratched wood floor. The decay that leached through every surface.

I opened the door to my apartment and turned on the lamp. The dim light did little to alleviate the gloom.

"As you can see, I live very simply."

Alek wasn't one for luxuries, but he looked surprised. "They've given me a room at the embassy," he said. "We can stay there, if you like."

"I was told to avoid the embassy."

Alek sat down on the bed. "I suppose that's for the best."

I went to fill the electric kettle. While my back was turned, I wiped my lips with a kitchen towel, just in case.

"What's this?"

Alek was holding up a folder Lee had given me a few days before.

"It's the first chapter of a book, by a British reporter, Mr. Cooper." It took all my strength to keep my voice level. "It's about his travels in Russia. He asked me to read it and tell him what I thought."

Alek made a show of looking through the pages, though I knew his English wasn't very good.

"I heard you've been working for him."

"Comrade Patlov encouraged me to. It's only a few hours a week. I still have time for my other duties."

"Some duties are more enjoyable than others. Have you learned anything useful from Mr. Cooper?"

My time in Paris had weakened my defenses against Alek. I could tell he was trying to provoke a reaction, so I responded with a half-hearted shrug. Though the water hadn't yet boiled, I poured it into the teapot so I'd have an excuse to look away.

"This must be the day for unexpected reunions," I said, eager to change the subject. "You'll never guess who I ran into this afternoon. Your old friend Boris, the poet."

"He lives in Paris?"

"I think so," I said. "He was with friends—we barely talked."

"Boris was always good at making friends. The kind who pay for his drinks." Alek's tone was dismissive. "I used to think he had talent, but he proved me wrong."

I brought our cups to the table, where Alek joined me. I'd gotten used to sugar and cream, but Alek declined both with a swift shake of his head, as if he refused to be tempted into Western luxuries.

"Comrade Patlov speaks well of you," Alek said.

"You've seen him?"

"Only for a few minutes. He says you're very diligent, but you haven't made much progress with your cousin."

"It's taken time, to establish trust."

I thought of Mikhail, learning to drive. Of his mother, the former princess, who dressed so simply she could pass for her grandchildren's nanny. Both of them accepted where life had led them. They were adapting to their new circumstances, not plotting revenge.

"Mikhail hasn't said anything suspicious, so I'm making friends with other members of the Russian Cultural League. Dropping hints that I'm unhappy in the Soviet Union, as you suggested."

"And what have you found out?"

I had to tell Alek something, to prove my worth. "There's been talk about someone called the Patriot." He didn't need to know I'd gotten that information from Patlov, not the league.

Alek looked surprised. "What did you hear?"

"Not much—only that there might be a spy of some sort inside the Soviet government. Do you think it's true?"

"Nothing's that simple inside the Kremlin. There are rumors, and rumors about those rumors. That's why we need people like you, on the outside. Is Mr. Cooper part of the league?"

Wondering at the sudden shift back to Lee, I said, "No."

"Then why spend so much time with him?"

"Patlov said—"

"Patlov told me you suggested keeping an eye on Mr. Cooper. Or perhaps more than an eye?"

He was baiting me. Trying to stir up a flicker of feeling so he'd know if Lee was another potential way to hurt me.

"You told me once I have no talent for seduction." I kept my eyes downcast, lips prim. A woman too self-effacing and modest to ever betray her husband.

Alek stood abruptly, the chair rattling beneath him, and grabbed my upper arm. "Tell me. Why are you so interested in Mr. Cooper?"

Alek wanted me frightened, so I complied. I wilted against his grip and spoke in a whisper. "He could be a useful ally. His book will bolster the Socialist cause in England."

"You like him."

It hadn't been Alek, following me from the café. But it could have been someone who worked for him.

"He's a womanizer," I said. "He thinks he's charming, but I see through it."

Alek smirked, and I knew I'd found the right lie. I had to make Alek believe I disapproved of Lee's flirtatiousness.

"It's good to see Paris hasn't changed you. Still tough as nails."

His lips attacked first, sucking mine insistently. Then his arms were around me, pulling me to the bed, and I went limp as he collapsed on top of me. I thought, fleetingly, of the way Lee had kissed me, each touch rousing a surge of delight. Alek's kisses were an assault, forcing a retreat. As his hands tugged at my clothes and kneaded my skin, I lay still, a blank vessel for his pleasure. When he climbed on top of me, his weight pressing my back into the iron bedsprings, I closed my eyes and imagined what it would be like if I was with Lee instead.

Grunting and thrusting, Alek pushed harder, as if he sensed the presence of someone else between us. Claiming and punishing me, at the same time.

LONDON

1938

I've only got time for a quick note, old chap—meeting with the director in a half hour and bracing myself for a thorough thrashing. Things aren't going well with the "Red Mistress Disaster," as I've come to think of it, and my head will be the first to roll if it all goes to hell. You've done this job long enough to know what I'm up against. The woman was known to be an expert with disguises, as well as utterly ruthless. (You saw the photos of that murder scene in Paris—I wouldn't have wanted to cross her.) She left no compromising evidence in her hotel room and no clues as to why she was here. I've questioned hundreds of café owners, hotel guests, and taxi drivers, without finding a single person who saw her.

The director's got the Home Office and the Foreign Office on him about the "Soviet menace" and spies invading our shores, and I can't blame him getting snippy, but there's only so much we can do. We all suspect, with good reason, that she was run down by her own side, but proving it is another matter.

Privately, I say good riddance. One less Bolshie in the world.

Hope to see you at the club soon—I've been so busy, I haven't been there in weeks.

Best,

Roger

PARIS

June 1926

Alek stayed in Paris three days. More than once, I gave thanks for the Marseilles sailors' strike, which kept Lee safely out of town. Alek spent most of his time at the Soviet embassy, and other than one lunch with Patlov at his favorite café, we avoided being seen in public together. It felt as if I was holding my breath from hour to hour, unable to exhale until Alek finally told me he was going back to Moscow alone.

"Patlov believes you're close to a breakthrough," Alek said. "He's convinced me to give you more time."

No doubt Patlov was looking out for himself, as well. The longer I stayed in Paris, the longer he could justify his own position as my supervisor.

"This extension has its limits," he continued. "If you don't find convincing proof of a conspiracy soon, you're coming home."

I could hardly tell Alek that I felt more at home in my modest Paris apartment than I ever had with him.

Even after Alek was gone, his influence lingered, like a perpetual shadow. It had been easy, before, to gloss over the repercussions of this mission. I'd been flirting and making small talk, waiting for someone to approach me, playing only a small part in a much larger game. Now,

I understood the true stakes; whoever I reported to Alek would probably be killed. But I had no choice. Alek was already impatient, and he hadn't looked convinced when I assured him Mikhail was innocent. If I didn't give Alek another name soon, he might have my cousin killed, no matter what I said. It was time to stop waiting and start acting, and the mysterious Patriot provided the perfect opportunity.

I'd never seen *The Seagull*, and I found the league's production unexpectedly poignant. Starring Russian stage veterans who were applauded as if they were royalty, the play summoned a world that felt achingly familiar, with artistic-minded characters who reminded me of Mama and Sergei. The cheers at the end were heartfelt and sustained, the actors taking bow after bow, all of us reluctant to leave.

I'd been invited to the backstage celebration afterward, and I greeted the league's founders with lavish affection, giving the General special attention. I leaned in to ask breathy questions, my hand lingering on his arm, and pretended to be scandalized by his off-color jokes. Eventually, I maneuvered him into the wings as he leered at me, intrigued.

"I need your help," I said.

Realizing I hadn't pulled him aside for a tryst, he shifted his expression to concern. "What's wrong?"

"You know I'm a translator, for a Soviet trade delegation."

The General nodded.

"I work mostly at the French Ministry of Trade, but I was told to fetch some documents from the Soviet embassy a few days ago. I was in the file room when I heard two men talking outside. I don't think they knew I was there."

I paused, to ensure I had the General's full attention. "Have you ever heard of the Patriot?"

His moustache twitched, but he didn't answer.

"The men said the Patriot had friends in Paris, and it was time to hunt them down. Do you know what that means? I'm afraid I'll be in trouble if they find out I was listening."

"It's nothing you should concern yourself with."

He was putting me off, glancing back at the party. It was clear he'd heard of the Patriot, but how much did he know? Time to drop more breadcrumbs.

"I hate them," I whispered. "Those men at the embassy, the Bolsheviks—they're all murderers. They've destroyed everything."

It wasn't hard to summon tears, not when I had so much to mourn.

The General's hand brushed my breast on its way to my shoulder. "Don't lose hope," he whispered, his liquor-drenched breath ruffling my hair. "The Russia you love will rise once again."

He was so close to a confession; I could sense the temptation nudging him forward.

I clutched his fingers. "What do you mean?"

"You're better off the less you know."

"I'm willing to help. Go back to the embassy, look through files . . ."

The General tut-tutted and dropped his arm to pat my backside. "No, no, you mustn't. Better to forget you heard anything at all."

If I kept pushing, he could get suspicious. But at least I'd found out one thing: the Patriot existed. "You're right. I'm sorry for bothering you."

"As if a pretty thing like you could ever be a bother! Now, if you hear anything else about this matter, you come to me first. Agreed?"

I gave him a worshipful smile, and we rejoined the party. I made a half-hearted circuit of the room, but I didn't have the energy for any further intrigue. My mind was too caught up in what to do next. If I told Patlov I'd found a possible connection between the league and the Patriot, what would that mean for Mikhail? As I was extracting my hat from a teetering pile, the very person I'd been fretting about sidled up and thrust his arm through the crook of my elbow.

"Come with me," Mikhail ordered.

His curtness caught me off guard, and I followed, bewildered, as he led me through a narrow backstage hallway. We walked down stairs

that led past the orchestra pit and then farther underground, to the theater's hidden mechanics. Storage rooms extended across one wall, and
Mikhail pointed me toward a sign marked "Costumes." He followed me
in, turned on the lights, and shut the door behind him.

There was barely space to move among the racks of clothing. I
smelled damp wool and sweat stains, the sharp stink of shoes that
needed a good airing. Mikhail glared at me, and the confused look I
gave him was genuine, because I had no idea what I'd done to make
him so angry.

"The General told me you were talking about the Patriot." Mikhail's
voice was clipped, the same tone Papa used to chide disobedient servants. "How could you be so stupid?"

I didn't have to fake my indignation. "I don't know who or what
the Patriot is!"

Mikhail sighed, his head dropping in a silent apology. "Why did
you ask the General instead of me?"

"You know what a busybody he is. If there really is some kind
of plot against the Bolsheviks, I assumed the General would know
about it."

"You have to be more careful."

Only belatedly did I realize what I should have known from the
minute Mikhail pulled me aside. He knew all about the Patriot, maybe
even more than the General. Before that moment, I'd truly believed
Mikhail was innocent. That he and the rest of the league had accepted
their lackluster fates. I didn't want to ask. Didn't want to hear that Alek
had been right. But I had to know the truth.

Gently, I asked, "Who is the Patriot?"

Mikhail's voice was feather-soft. "A shadow."

I allowed the silence to expand between us, soothing his concern.

"I've heard different rumors," he finally said. "The latest story is that
he's an officer in the Red Army."

"Do you think it's true?"

Mikhail threw up his hands. "Who knows? It makes a certain sense. The Bolsheviks are tearing themselves apart, breaking into factions and accusing each other of treason. They're vulnerable, and they know it. What's the only institution powerful enough to defeat them? The army. Soldiers are loyal to each other, not Stalin. A strong Red Army leader would have the support of the troops and the people."

"How would that be any better? The Red Army is Communist—you'd have all the same problems."

"The Patriot—if he even exists—claims to have no interest in power for himself. Once the Bolsheviks have been defeated, he will clear the way for a new government."

"Led by Grand Duke Romanov. The tsar's cousin."

"Grand Duke Romanov would like to think so. Personally, I don't think we can ever go back to autocracy. The world's changed too much for that. Russia deserves a modern, democratic government. One where families who've been in public service for generations can do some good."

"Families like the Shulkins."

"Why not?" Mikhail managed a faint smile. "It's all talk for now. Most likely nothing will come of it."

"But if it did . . ."

"We'd get our country back."

I felt a pang of longing. Was the future Mikhail described really possible? Could the Soviet government be overthrown? If it was, Alek would have no more power over me. I could divorce him. Be free.

Such thoughts could also get me killed.

I declined Mikhail's offer to take me home; the nearest Metro stop was only two blocks away. I surveyed the platform in the way all women do when they're traveling alone at night and was reassured to see at least a dozen people waiting alongside me. There was no reason to be nervous, yet I was. My feet shifted from side to side; my fingertips drummed against the side of my handbag. When the train pulled in, I hung back and allowed the people around me to board first. A man stood at the other end of the platform, a few steps back from the train. As the doors in front of me began to close, I slipped inside, glancing back to see a parallel flash of movement a few carriages down.

Unease thickened into fear. This time, I was certain I was being followed. When the train arrived at my station, I stepped out and paused near the wall, pretending to search my bag. Three men and one woman walked past me; none of them paid me any attention. I heard their footsteps clatter up the stairs and waited, alone, in the empty station.

Was that the plan all along, to corner me here? Feeling suddenly exposed, I ran upstairs and onto the street. A lone taxi drove by, and I heard faint laughter in the distance. Otherwise, it was quiet. I looked around the intersection I'd have to cross to get to my apartment. A man in a dark hat and suit was leaning against the side of the building to my right, lighting a cigarette. His hat was tilted low, hiding his face, but I'd seen him get off the train. I'd also seen a man fiddle with a cigarette in exactly the same way on Boulevard Montparnasse, when I was with Lee.

If I went back to my apartment, he'd find out where I lived. Then again, he might already know, if he'd been hired by Alek or Patlov. Before I could decide what to do, the man tossed his match and turned away, strolling in the opposite direction. I watched him go, never looking back, and when I took a roundabout route to my apartment, I didn't see or hear anyone behind me. If the man had been following me, he'd already found out what he wanted to know.

I spent the next day at the Ministry of Trade, alert to every face I passed on the way there and back. Trudging home in the late afternoon, I saw the one-armed veteran had returned to his corner, and I dropped a few sous in the cup at his side. He grunted his thanks—he never spoke—and I wondered if his throat had been injured, too. I'd heard terrible stories about poison gas. The Blanchard sisters had brought chairs outside to enjoy the sun, and I gave them a quick wave, avoiding their attempts at conversation.

When I stepped inside, I found a short note from Lee in my mailbox: *I'm back in Paris. Please let me know if you're available this week.*

The news made me flush with a mix of joy and apprehension. I hadn't seen him since our kiss on that cobblestoned backstreet. I thought of the sunlight in Lee's apartment, the click of his typewriter. The look in his eyes as he pulled off his hat and leaned down toward me.

I was too impatient for the back-and-forth of letters and messengers. I'd memorized Lee's telephone number—I called him occasionally from the Board of Trade—and the Blanchard sisters were more than happy to let me use their phone in exchange for a small payment.

"Miss Shulkina!" Lee greeted me, seemingly unbothered by the awkwardness of our last encounter. "I was hoping you might be free tomorrow."

I knew I should end it. Make a quick, clean break and protect Lee from Alek's suspicions. But it didn't seem right to tell him over the phone.

"Two o'clock?" I suggested.

"Very good, I'll see you then."

The line disconnected with a click. I'd spoken only a few words, but my insides were quivering.

I came outside to tell the sisters I'd finished, and the smaller one, Céline, asked, "Are you all right?"

The other one, Céleste, gave me a sympathetic look. "Trouble with your man?"

I stared at her, bewildered. How did she know about Lee?

"Don't worry," Céline said. "Whoever pays your rent is your business. But if he leads you on by saying he'll leave his wife, don't believe him. They never do."

Belatedly, I remembered the story Patlov had told the landlord about a rich benefactor. The chatty Blanchards must have told half the building that I was a well-off man's mistress. As the sisters nudged me for information about my "friend," I watched the soldier at the corner. With jerky, stiff movements, he stood and straightened his jacket, tipping the contents of his cup into a front pocket. He shuffled away, his feet barely leaving the pavement, and it suddenly hit me: *the boots*. The man who'd followed me off the Metro—and before that, in Montparnasse—had been wearing a plain, dark suit, the same kind worn by hundreds of other Parisian men. I'd realized, subconsciously, that something was off, but couldn't figure out what it was. Now I knew: He'd been wearing scuffed military boots. The same kind as the man who'd been sitting for weeks within viewing distance of my apartment.

My first impulse was to run. Most likely he was headed for the Metro, and if I hurried, I could probably catch up. Then what? He could lead me anywhere in Paris, for who knew how long. I was already tired, and if he caught a glimpse of me, any advantage I had would be gone.

The begging-soldier disguise implied this man was a professional. I couldn't just follow him blindly and risk being spotted. There was only one way I could find out who he was and who he worked for.

I'd have to become someone else.

Madame Gournier walked over to greet me when I arrived at Lee's building the following afternoon.

"He came back from Marseilles completely exhausted. Make sure he doesn't work too hard."

"I don't think I'll be staying long."

I trudged up the stairs, hardening myself with each step forward. The kiss had been an impulsive mistake. Even if Lee and I agreed to put it behind us, we could never go back to the way things were. I'd always be worried about Alek making another surprise visit. Cutting off all contact with Lee was the only way to keep him safe.

When Lee opened the door, he looked like he hadn't slept in days. "Hello, there."

His dutiful smile looked forced, a paper-thin layer of politeness.

I stepped inside and saw that the dining table was more cluttered than usual. A wrinkled jacket lay across the back of the sofa, and the room smelled of stale coffee and damp clothes.

"Tea?" Lee asked.

It would be easy to say yes. To take my usual seat and stir in cream and sugar. But if I fell into the usual routine, it would be that much harder to pull myself out.

"No, thank you. I can't stay."

Lee leaned back against the table, his hands grabbing the edge for support, as if even this brief conversation had worn him out. I'd brought the book chapter he'd asked me to read, and as I set the folder down, I could feel the apprehension simmering behind his nonchalant façade.

"It's very good," I said.

"You think so?"

I watched Lee's eyes come alive, his good humor restored. *Remember this,* I told myself. *Remember him like this.*

"You have a good eye for descriptions. I look forward to reading the whole book one day."

"You can start with the next chapter, if you like. I finished it on the train ride home."

It was important to speak without emotion. Make a clean break. "I can't work for you anymore."

Lee looked more confused than surprised. "Because of what happened, after Le Dôme? Consider it forgotten."

"I'm married."

The truth cut like a knife, slashing us apart. Lee stiffened, and I looked away. I couldn't bear his hurt, knowing I'd caused it. I could hardly bear my own.

"Your husband," Lee said softly. "Is he in Paris?"

I shook my head. How could I explain that Alek *was* here, in spirit, infecting these final moments? Lee's apartment had been my refuge, a place where sunlight dispelled my inner shadows. With Lee, I'd been my truest self, free of doubt and worry. It had been an illusion. I'd never been free, even here.

Tears welled up like a sudden storm. I could have stopped them; God knows I'd stayed strong in the face of worse horrors. I chose to let them flow, to show Lee the depth of my regret.

"I'll be going back to Moscow soon," I sniffed, the wetness on my cheeks strangely exhilarating. "It's best we don't see each other again."

Neither of us had moved, but it sounded as if Lee were speaking from miles away. "If that's what you want."

"I'm sorry."

If I didn't leave soon, I'd weaken. Already, my chest was tightening from the pressure of unreleased sobs. I turned away, toward the door. Lee said nothing. I had no idea if he was sorry or relieved to see me go.

It was important to keep moving, to remember the reason for my sacrifice. Ten minutes and one bus ride later, I was at the theater where the league had put on *The Seagull*. A bored porter half-heartedly guarding the back entrance easily accepted my story about a lost earring, especially when I finished it off by handing him a few francs. I didn't see anyone else as I crossed backstage, or when I went downstairs to the costume room. I picked out the gaudiest items I could find: a low-cut purple dress speckled with sequins; faux-alligator shoes; a green velvet coat with a fur collar; and a wig of wavy auburn curls. I wrapped everything inside the coat, wrapped the bundle with a scarf, and kept it hidden behind my back when I slid back out past the porter.

The begging soldier was in his usual position when I arrived home, close to five o'clock. I kept to the opposite side of the street, purposely avoiding him. Once upstairs, I began my transformation. The dress's fabric looked even cheaper in the daylight, and the shoes—higher than I usually wore—pinched at my toes. I lined my eyes with thick streaks of kohl and swiped on red lipstick. The woman I saw reflected in my small hand mirror was the polar opposite of a sober Communist wife. She was brash and a little bit dangerous, the kind of loose modern woman that makes old-timers scowl in disapproval.

I was finally face-to-face with Marie Duvall.

I'd never seen the begging soldier out past sunset, so I decided to start tracking him at six o'clock. I listened to make sure the stairway was empty before leaving my apartment. I tiptoed down the stairs and past the Blanchards' open door, keeping my face turned away. Outside the building, I took a quick glance at the corner to confirm the soldier was still there, then walked in the opposite direction. I made a careful, slow rotation of the surrounding blocks, keeping an eye on my prey, thoroughly regretting my choice of shoes. Finally, I took a seat at a small café on the main shopping boulevard, where I could see the soldier if I craned my neck at a particular angle. Over two cups of coffee, growing increasingly bored, I waited. Close to eight o'clock, with darkness descending, he rolled up his blanket, his empty right sleeve flapping at his side.

He shuffled up to the boulevard and raised his hand to hail a taxi. I leaped up to follow, my previous lethargy gone. My entire body pulsed with an unfamiliar energy: that of the pursuer, rather than the prey. A taxi stopped for me only a few seconds after the soldier had stepped into his, and I told the driver to follow it. I didn't know how far we'd be going, or if the handful of francs I'd stuffed in my coat pocket would be enough to cover the fare. Flush with the thrill of the chase, I didn't care.

As we moved in jerky stops and starts through the crowded streets, I thought through possibilities. I'd never gotten a close look at the man's face, but I was certain I'd never seen him at the Ministry of Trade or any league events. Who had hired him to follow me? Patlov was the most likely culprit, one spy keeping an eye on another, though I'd thought he would trust me by now. During the six weeks I'd been in Paris, I'd never gone anywhere or met anyone without telling him. Could the soldier have some connection to Lee? I couldn't think of a good reason Lee would want to keep track of my whereabouts, but he had secrets, too. The hidden diary, for example. I'd never gotten another look at it or found out why my name was listed inside.

The taxi we were following stopped, and my taxi did the same, a half block behind.

"Where are we?" I asked the driver.

"Montmartre."

I'd heard of the neighborhood, but never seen it for myself. When I stepped outside, after using almost all my money to pay the fare, I felt assaulted by the noise and lights of pleasures offered up for profit. A clump of young men heckled each other outside a doorway lit by pink lamps, the sure sign of a brothel. Nearby, a woman in a transparent blouse was offering her services more directly, by calling out to potential patrons. Accordions wheezed from a nightclub, where I could hear the thuds of dancing feet. All around me, Montmartre promised release. A bus passed, with blurry, pursed-lipped faces framed in its windows. Tourists, come to gawk at the depravity.

I would have been gawking myself, if I weren't so fixed on my target. He was walking briskly ahead of me, a man with a specific destination. His right sleeve was no longer hanging loose; the supposed injury had been part of his disguise. When he turned off the main road, I hung back, wary of following too closely. Eventually, I leaned my head around the corner. The side street he'd chosen was quiet but not deserted; a few lit windows indicated that here, too, entertainment was on offer, albeit more discreetly. The man entered a building about halfway down, where lamplight glimmered through the gaps in the curtains. I waited a few breaths, then walked closer. I heard voices, music. There was no sign out front, and I hesitated to enter a place I knew nothing about. On the other hand, this might be my only chance to find out who this man was.

Curiosity won out over fear.

I opened the door and entered a small foyer, with a staircase directly to my right. At one time, it must have been a private home. To my left, what had once been the front room had been transformed into a makeshift café, with mismatched chairs and a scattering of tables. Shadowy figures sat against the walls and mingled in the center, but I couldn't see them well enough to know if the man was among them. As I was gathering up my nerve to continue inside, a woman stepped briskly forward.

"Good evening, *chérie*." Her voice was crisply confident, and her face, though wrinkled, was animated and warm. Her hair was wrapped in a turban, and bracelets jangled against her wrists. "Are you meeting someone?"

I was aware of conversations behind us slowing down, of heads turning to look. It was clearly a private club of some kind, and the last thing I wanted to do was draw attention to myself.

"I'm sorry," I mumbled. How could I come up with a convincing lie when I didn't even know where I was?

"There must be a reason you're here?" The woman smiled, willing to be convinced.

The wig's curls tickled my cheeks, reminding me that I was here as Marie, not Nadia. Shrugging nonchalantly, I said, "A friend told me she'd been here. I was curious to see it for myself."

"What's your friend's name? Perhaps I know her."

"I'd rather not say."

My coyness amused her. "You're welcome to make new friends, if you like. Starting with me. Madame Girard."

The owner, I assumed. With the easy grace of an experienced hostess, she led me past the tables to an adjoining room, where a bar sat opposite a dance floor. Brassy music rang out from a gramophone, and a few couples were doing an approximation of dancing—holding on to each other and moving roughly in time to the rhythm.

"A drink?" Madame Girard asked. Then, before I could answer, she declared, "Pernod."

The sunken-cheeked young bartender was too thin for his tuxedo, which was either borrowed or bought secondhand. He poured two glasses and pushed them forward.

"Your first is on the house," said Madame Girard. "To your health!"

We clinked glasses, and I took a careful sip. The drink was bitter, but cool enough to taste refreshing.

"Time to get acquainted," said Madame Girard. "You know my name, but I don't know yours."

"Marie."

"Just Marie, eh?" Her eyes twinkled. "Well, that's good enough for me. You're not from Paris, are you?"

"No, I'm from the South. A small town no one's ever heard of."

"And you left as soon as you could. Smart girl. A pretty thing like you would be wasted in the country. Tell me. What are you here to *do*? What is your *passion*?"

"I'm an artist." Why not? I was certainly dressed the part.

"How wonderful!" She looked me up and down as if reassessing my worth. "Are you here because of Maya?"

I stared back at her, confused.

"Maya de Severin."

When I still showed no sign of recognition, Madame Girard all but scoffed. "You *are* a country girl! Maya's one of the greatest painters in Paris. She's here tonight—you must meet her." She tugged at my hand. "I'll introduce you."

Her ropy arm was surprisingly strong. I shuffled behind her to a table in the front room, where three women were sitting so close their knees touched. My mind fleetingly marked one as petite and one as taller and broader, vague impressions quickly overshadowed by the third woman. She rose as we approached, her limbs unfolding like a crane taking flight. Everything about her was elegant, from the perfect arch of her eyebrows to the curve of her burgundy lips. Her black hair was swept off her face and pomaded into submission, aside from a few rebellious curls that flickered at the back of her neck. She wore a cream silk dress that rippled as she moved, and a man's evening jacket hung over her shoulders.

Madame Girard pushed me forward. "Maya, I've found us a new friend. A fellow artist."

Maya's mouth tilted up at one side. A conspiratorial opening, meant to flatter me.

"Marie Duvall," I said. "Nice to meet you."

Maya leaned forward and kissed me on both cheeks. Surprised by the sudden intimacy, I accepted the kisses but didn't reciprocate.

"Sit down," she ordered me. "*Maman*, bring us some whiskeys. I'm only half-drunk, and I intend to finish the job."

Was Madame Girard her mother? They looked nothing alike. Maya's companions slipped away, obeying an unspoken command. Maya sat next to me, tossing her head like a racehorse in the starting gate.

"Take off your hat. Make yourself comfortable."

Before I could comply, Maya's hands were on the brim, tugging upward. She put my hat on the table and leaned forward.

"I love your hair. It takes nerve to dye it that shade of red."

She reached her hand toward my curls, and I jerked back, terrified she'd nudge the wig off-center. Maya gave me a slow nod, acknowledging she'd moved too quickly.

Madame Girard came back with a tray. The glass she placed in front of me was partly filled with a sludgy liquid that smelled awful.

"I'll water it down, if you like," Maya offered, and I nodded.

She took the decanter Madame Girard offered and sprayed soda until my glass was nearly overflowing. Her fingertips were stained in an abstract pattern of yellow, blue, and green, the only imperfection in her otherwise pristine façade. I took a sip of the whiskey, enduring it more than drinking it. I knew I shouldn't risk getting drunk, just as I knew I shouldn't be wasting time with this strange woman. But I had no desire to move. Such was the power of Maya de Severin.

"You're new in town," she said. "I can tell by your clothes."

I'd known they were ridiculous when I stole them from the theater, but the insult stung nonetheless.

"You're trying out new things. Experimenting. It's what you're supposed to do, when you're young."

The light was too low for me to accurately guess Maya's age. Faint lines sprayed out from the corners of her eyes, but her cheeks and hands were smooth.

"Madame Girard is your mother?" I asked.

"No, no, she's the owner. But we all consider her family." Maya took a languorous sip of her drink. "Have you ever been to a place like this?"

How would Marie answer? She'd want to appear confident, I decided, to cover up her inexperience.

"No," I said, "but I wanted an adventure."

"What a brave little mouse. I promise, none of us kitty-cats bite."

Maya finished her whiskey in two generous swallows. "It doesn't matter where you came from. Who you were, when you lived there. All that matters is who you are now. Or who you want to be."

"I'd like to be an artist, like you."

"Aren't you sweet. Have you seen any of my paintings?"

A woman like Maya might be titillated by bluntness. "I haven't."

Maya's laugh came as a single, abrupt exhale. "How refreshing! I'm so tired of fawning sycophants. Go on. Ask me anything you want."

What she wanted, I guessed, was an excuse to keep talking. And I was all too happy to keep her attention focused away from me. "I want to know everything about you."

"Good thing it's still early."

I could see Maya calculating which way to tell her story before she began. She'd been born in Latvia, she told me, and her complicated family was so rife with changes in fortune that her life sounded like a novel. Or was it just that she'd learned to describe it that way? Throughout her childhood, she'd been shunted off to relatives in Berlin, Warsaw, and Stockholm, never knowing how long she would stay, never feeling that any place was home. Though I was sure the details were embellished for effect, the underlying narrative felt true. This was a woman who'd lived many lives, but only recently found the one she wanted.

Maya kept refilling my glass; I couldn't keep track of how much I'd drunk. With each sip, each encouraging nod, I transformed more fully into Marie. My face felt looser, shifting effortlessly from concern to surprise to glee. My entire body felt transformed, freed—at last!—of Nadia's obsessive self-control. Twirling my hair around my fingers, leaning forward and back, I gave Maya the enthralled audience she craved.

"I was nineteen when I married," she told me. "Baron de Severin was quite a match for a girl like me."

"Why?"

"He was rich, of course. I wouldn't have said yes otherwise. And handsome enough for someone twice my age." She picked up the whiskey bottle again. "A toast, to my husband's bank account."

I knew I should stop. But Marie wouldn't turn down a free drink, would she? After our glasses clinked, I gave Maya a wistful look.

"You didn't love him?" I asked.

"Love is most potent when it is detached from marriage. Come on—I'm tired of sitting. Let's dance."

With bewildering speed, Maya was on her feet and pulling at my arm. My ankles swayed as she led me across the room, so I leaned against her for support. Someone had turned up the gramophone, which was playing an American song—"Sweet Georgia Brown"—and the dance floor was crammed with swaying bodies. I thought of my dancing teacher demonstrating the waltz and felt giggles rising up from my stomach. Maya looked over at me, pleased, and opened her arms. I melted into her, soothed by her sturdiness. She smelled exotic and expensive, a princess from *The Arabian Nights*.

In a contented daze, I watched the couples twirl and shimmy, their faces slack with abandon. Most of them were women, my alcohol-soaked brain dimly noted, and then I belatedly realized even the men were in fact women, dressed in masculine suits. It took me a few moments after that to understand that Maya was swaying from side to side, dancing with me, and what that meant, and how I'd been blind to the nature of this place from the very beginning.

I wriggled awkwardly out of Maya's arms, my reflexes slowed by the whiskey.

"I'm sorry," I mumbled, unable to articulate, even in my mind, what was going on.

Maya gave me a disapproving-governess scowl. "Don't tell me you're going to be sick."

"No. It's only, I didn't know . . . I mean, you're married."

"So what?!" Maya laughed. "If you don't fancy me, be honest."

"I don't fancy women, not in that way."

"Then why in the world did you come here?"

"I followed someone."

"Now you're not making any sense."

Reverting back to governess mode, Maya led me from the dance floor to the entryway, which was mercifully cooler. I was beginning to feel light-headed.

"I can see I was too generous with the whiskey. Why don't I call my car and take you home?"

Woozy with relief, I agreed. Avoiding a Metro or bus ride home would be a blessing. I leaned against the bottom of the staircase as Maya left to talk to Madame Girard. I couldn't hear what they were saying, but madame's disapproving glare burned from across the room.

"My driver will come round the front," Maya told me. She'd retrieved my hat and fit it snugly on my head. "Come on."

Outside, a light breeze smoothed my sticky skin. Maya put her arm through mine, and we stood without speaking, as the sounds of a Montmartre night echoed in the background. A black Renault pulled up in front of us, and the chauffeur climbed out from the driver's seat to open the back door. I recognized him immediately. It was the soldier.

I stepped back, into Maya.

"What are you doing?" she demanded.

"I can't," I stammered. "I'll take a taxi."

"For God's sake, get in."

Maya's hand lashed out like a snake, coiling her fingers around my wrist. Thrown off-balance, I tipped forward as Maya pulled me toward the car. She slid into the back seat first, never loosening her hold on my arm, and I tumbled in beside her.

"Where do you live?" she asked.

I glanced at the driver. He was sitting perfectly still, his head trained forward, but he was close enough to hear every word. I was fairly sure he hadn't recognized me, but would he know the sound of my voice? Directing him to my apartment would give me away, and the only other addresses I could think of offhand were the Soviet embassy and Lee's apartment. Neither seemed like a good idea.

I turned to Maya and pitched my voice high, breathily insistent. "I want to see your paintings."

"Now?"

"Do you have other plans?" Flirty enough to intrigue her.

"Nothing important." She tapped the driver on the shoulder and said, "The studio."

The soldier's skills weren't limited to surveillance, because he swept through the twisting streets at a dizzying speed. Within five minutes, we'd arrived in a neighborhood of workshops and run-down apartments. Not the kind of place I'd pictured a glamorous woman like

Maya. The soldier stopped the car with an abrupt squeal of the brakes. I looked down when he opened the passenger door and away as I stepped out. Behind me, Maya murmured a few short, clipped words that I couldn't distinguish. I didn't turn around until I heard the car drive away. Where was he going? Would Maya summon him later to drive me home?

From a small handbag, Maya pulled out a brass key fit for a medieval castle and inserted it into a set of weathered wooden doors. They creaked as they opened. Maya strode confidently into the darkness as I wavered behind her, then I heard the click of a light switch. A sconce on the wall emitted a dim amber glow.

"This way," Maya called out.

The hallway I entered was paved with broad flagstones, and our heels clattered as we walked. We approached another door, which Maya opened with a second, equally dramatic key. Like a fairy flaunting her powers, she flitted ahead, turning on lamps that gradually illuminated the room we'd entered.

It was enormous. The ceiling soared above me, and the space seemed to expand infinitely ahead. Everywhere, I saw canvases, some leaning against the wall, others piled in stacks on the floor. I counted three easels in my immediate vicinity, each displaying a work in progress. To my right, Maya leaned against a large pine table speckled with colored drops, the surface crowded with paints, brushes, and scraps of paper.

"What do you think?" she asked.

"It's wonderful."

Maya strolled over to a set of canvases beneath a row of windows. The darkness outside was impenetrable, as if we were in the country rather than the middle of Paris. "These aren't my best pieces, of course, just the ones I'm working on. But perhaps you're interested in my process?"

Dumbstruck, I could only nod. Conversation seemed impossible when I was so taken by the images before me, of strong, sinewy women writhing in geometric landscapes. Maya had obviously been influenced by cubism, but her dreamscapes felt bracingly alive, despite the unreal proportions and colors. They were as bold as the woman who'd painted them.

"This is my latest series," Maya explained. "Contrasting the curves of the female body with the angularity of modern design. Collectors always want portraits—they're what I'm known for—but these were done for me."

I tried to imagine one of those pictures hanging in my apartment. It would dominate the entire space.

"Tell me about your work, Marie. Do you paint?"

I remembered the leather case of art supplies Mama used to carry, the interior spattered with colors. What had happened to it?

I shook my head. "I prefer drawing."

Maya handed me a piece of paper and a box of charcoal pencils. "Show me."

I was tired, and a little tipsy, and I still hadn't found out anything about the man who'd driven us here. I shouldn't waste any more time. Still, my fingers flickered toward the pencils, almost automatically. Art had always soothed me, and I felt the tension in my head and body ease as I made the first few strokes. There was no thought involved, only movement. I thickened the lines at the bottom and shaded them out-ward on top: a tree. I drew a branch reaching to the right, then another to the left. Light, quick dashes gave the suggestion of leaves. I exchanged the pencil for a heavier one, to create a sturdy trunk, grounded by roots that clawed the earth.

It had taken only a few minutes, but I'd surrendered to the experi-ence so totally that it took me a moment to realize Maya was leaning over my shoulder. She looked at the drawing, then at me, her expression cool. She struck me as the kind of person who'd always be relentlessly honest, no matter how much she liked you. And I was surprisingly eager for her approval.

"Childish," she declared.

My heart sank.

"I don't mean it as an insult," Maya continued. "There's an innocence to your work, and genuine emotions." She pressed her fingers around mine. "You can't be an artist without feeling."

A thrill shot through me at being acknowledged as one of her own. I wanted to talk to her about technique and materials. Watch her paint a portrait and offer myself up to her tutelage. But that wasn't why I was here.

I giggled and looked downward, seemingly embarrassed. "I have too many feelings, sometimes. My mother used to call me boy-crazy. You saw what a fool I made of myself in front of your driver."

"He's not usually my driver—he works for my husband. My regular chauffeur is sick. You think he's good-looking?"

I nodded.

"René's too serious for a girl like you."

I nodded as she spoke, assessing this new information. The soldier's name was René. He worked for Baron de Severin. So why had he been following me? For all the time Maya had spent talking, she'd told me very little about her husband.

"Will he be coming back?" I asked. "I'm embarrassed by how silly I acted before."

"I dismissed René for the evening. I usually spend the night here when I'm working. You're welcome to stay, if you'd like?"

She sidled up closer, flashing a mischievous smile. Her fingers flickered against my cheek and trailed down my neck. For a minute I was tempted. What would it be like, to be seduced by a woman like Maya de Severin?

"I'm sorry," I murmured, slowly twisting away. I couldn't afford any additional complications, yet I didn't want to leave, either. I wanted to pretend, for just a little while longer, that I was part of Maya's uncon-ventional world.

"You prefer men," Maya said wryly. "It's all right—I have a guest room. Shall we make ourselves comfortable?"

Maya pulled off her shoes, and I did the same, relieved to be rid of their torturous grip. She poured us both glasses of water—"We've got to get you sobered up"—and as we sat at her table, she flipped through art magazines and printed reproductions, educating me on Picasso and Matisse. I kept intending to find out more about her husband, but never found the right opportunity. She shooed me off to bed around two in the morning, when my head and eyelids were drooping with exhaustion. I stripped down to my slip, longing to pull off the scratchy wig. But what if Maya checked on me and saw me without it? I decided to keep it on.

I woke up the next morning dazed and dry-mouthed. After hur-riedly getting dressed, I pulled open the door to the studio. The sun-light surging through the windows made me flinch. Maya was standing across the room, hands on her hips, examining a canvas. Her embroi-dered red robe called to mind a Chinese courtesan, and her hair was tied back with a multicolored scarf, the edges of which trailed along her regal neck.

"You're awake!" she called out. "Good."

As I walked toward her, I noted the details that the previous night's darkness had obscured. The broad-planked wood floor was marked by generations of scuffs and spills. What had appeared charmingly dishev-eled by lamplight was now revealed as simply messy. But the lack of order proved this was a real, working studio, not something created for show.

The left side of the canvas Maya was working on was covered in dark-purple and green color blocks that suggested an ominous urban landscape; the right side was mostly untouched, except for a few mark-ings in pencil.

"What do you think?" Maya asked. "I've been working on this for months, and I'm stuck."

"I told you—I'm not a painter."

"I don't need an expert. I'd like your opinion, that's all. Doesn't mean I'll take your advice."

"It's very good."

Maya sighed with exaggerated annoyance.

I tried again. "It has a definite mood. Darkness. Danger."

Maya placed one palm on the empty stretch of canvas, as if she could imprint her desires onto the surface.

"I want to move beyond form. Create a work that tells a story without using recognizable images. Do you think it's possible?"

"Artists shouldn't be limited by what they think is possible."

Maya gave me a rueful smile and adjusted her scarf. "Tell me, what's the real reason you came to the club last night?"

The abrupt change of subject caught me unprepared, and I could see from Maya's intent expression that it had been a carefully baited trap. *Think like Marie*, I told myself. *Innocent but curious.*

"I overheard some women talking," I said. "They looked interesting, and I wanted to see the place women like that would go."

"Did you know Madame Girard approves each member personally? On the condition we never talk about it in public?"

She had to know I was lying. Better to remain silent than trip myself up with more suspicious stories. I stared back, accepting her unspoken challenge.

"You've got nerve, I'll give you that," Maya said. "Let me guess. You didn't want me driving you home last night because you live in a sad rented room that you didn't want me to see. Maybe you allow the landlord certain favors in exchange for a lower rent? I won't judge you for it."

I bristled, indignant. "I'd rather sleep on the street."

"*Chérie*, we all do what we have to. But it's much less sordid if you have a patron."

What kind of offer was she making? Spending more time with Maya would give me a chance to investigate the mysterious René, but how would I justify this new diversion to Patlov, let alone Alek? I still couldn't rule out that one of them had hired René to follow me in the first place.

"You have real talent," Maya said. "The baron and I are hosting a party on Saturday night, and I'd like you to come. It shouldn't be hard to get an allowance out of my husband, provided you know how to keep the interest of an older man."

Maya wrote down her address on a scrap of paper and handed it to me, then glanced back at her painting. I recognized that look. I'd seen it on Mama countless times, right before she shooed me away so she could get back to work.

"I should go," I said. "Is there a Metro stop nearby?" I had just enough money for the fare.

"At the Gare de l'Est. Turn to the right when you go outside and walk about four blocks. I'll see you Saturday?"

It would mean one more night in the itchy wig, teetering in too-tight heels. Flirting with the husband of a woman who'd all but propositioned me on his behalf.

"I wouldn't miss it for the world," I said.

LONDON

1938

To: Director, SIS

Per our most recent discussion of the case, I have been investigating the location of "Marie Duvall's" death. As Tetchly Road does not lead to or from any obvious points of interest, the obvious conclusion is that "Miss Duvall" went there to meet someone.

My men and I have spent the past week questioning everyone who lives within a three-block radius of the accident. Almost all of them said they did not see or hear anything suspicious on the night in question, and further inquiries into their records revealed no obvious connections to Russia, the British government, or the British military, or any other qualities that would make them targets of the Soviet secret police.

Mrs. George Weatherby confirmed her earlier statement to the police that the woman appeared dead immediately following the incident. However, she also told us she has since remembered seeing a man in a black coat and hat hovering at the edge of the scene (see attached interview transcript). She says the man attempted to push through the crowd to get closer to the victim but disappeared soon after the ambulance arrived. As Mrs. Weatherby has proved herself an otherwise reliable witness, her account supports our suspicion that Miss Duvall's death was not an accident. If she was lured to that location in order to be killed, it is highly likely an accomplice would have been dispatched to confirm her death.

My men and I will continue to investigate other possible witnesses and keep you informed of our progress.

—Roger

PARIS

July 1926

I gave Patlov an edited version of my night with Maya at our next meeting.

"What do you know about Baron de Severin?" I asked. "Why would he want me followed?"

Patlov took a bite of omelet and chewed infuriatingly slowly. From a distance, we might have looked like a father and daughter, enjoying a leisurely meal. But I was close enough to see his eyes sharpen. Beneath the well-fed stomach and indulgent smiles lurked a dangerous man.

"He's rich," Patlov said. "His family has factories of some kind—typical capitalist exploitation. He might be interested in you because of the trade agreement."

"All I do is translate documents."

"Maybe he wants to find out if you're bringing those documents home. See if you'd be susceptible to a bribe so he can get an early look at them. It would give him a competitive advantage."

"I'd like to go to the party, as Marie. I'll find an excuse to talk to him and see what else I can find out."

"As long as you don't waste the whole night dancing." I couldn't tell if he was teasing or warning me. "This business with the baron is a distraction from your mission. Speaking of which . . ."

He took an irritatingly long sip of tea, enjoying my rapt attention.

"That trouble with the Patriot has been sorted out."

"What do you mean?"

"They found out who it was. A deputy commissar for agriculture. He was executed yesterday."

I lifted my cup, to buy time. A trickle of cold liquid dampened my lips. *It's good news,* I told myself. Mikhail and his friends were no longer in danger; they wouldn't risk their lives on an all-but-impossible plan. Still, my relief was tinged with disappointment. The Patriot had given me hope. Made me believe things could change.

I kept my face still as Patlov continued. "Given that you found no evidence of counterrevolution in the league, your work here is finished."

I said the words I knew were coming next. "I'm going back to Moscow."

"It's not for me to decide, but I expect to get those orders soon. In the meantime, make the most of the time you have left. Go to that party, but don't take any unnecessary risks. It would be embarrassing, to say the least, if word got out that a Soviet comrade was hobnobbing with a degenerate like Maya de Severin."

Degenerate. The word lingered in my mind when I arrived at Baron de Severin's imposing mansion a few evenings later. What kind of party was I walking into? My nervousness eased somewhat when a dignified doorman escorted me into a circular entry hall, topped by a cupola fit for a church. Laughter and the hum of a dozen conversations drifted from an adjoining room—sounds that were reassuringly normal.

The doorman looked me over briefly, giving my ensemble his silent approval. I'd spent more than half my remaining francs on a crimson dress, with black embroidery accents at the hem and neckline. My lipstick was a brighter, gaudier shade of red, and I'd ringed my eyes with thick swaths of kohl.

"Who may I announce?" he asked.

I gave him a cheeky grin. "Marie Duvall."

The doorman led me to a large reception hall, where a jazz band was playing in one corner. There were at least a hundred guests, their faces clouded by whorls of cigarette smoke. The room had the proportions of a historic manor—tall windows, a massive fireplace—but its decor was strikingly modern. Black-and-white tiles covered the floor, and mirrored side tables reflected the light from chrome lamps. A painting of an Amazonian woman, immediately recognizable as Maya's work, glared out at the crowd, unimpressed.

The doorman cleared his throat behind a dark-haired man. When he turned around, I realized it wasn't a man at all. It was Maya. She was wearing a tuxedo, but her makeup was aggressively feminine, with exaggerated brows and lips. She kissed me on both cheeks, the grease of her lipstick slick against my skin.

"Marie! How wonderful to see you. I'm tired of talking to the same old people."

I'd decided Marie would be excited, but intimidated. "Is everyone here an artist?"

"They think they are!" Maya laughed. "Hardly any of them make a living at it, of course. That's why they're here. To drink at my expense."

"I'm sure that's not the only reason."

"Aren't you sweet. Come—I want to show you off."

I played my role with coos and eyelash flutters, a country mouse awed by the city's vices. Maya introduced me as one of her most promising new finds, a deft way of complimenting both me and herself. Waiters passed glasses of champagne on silver trays, and I took one whenever it was offered. Marie, I told myself, would drink lavishly, showily. I pretended to be interested in a discussion of nail polish with one intense young woman, then nodded through a lecture on the ways film was ruining traditional theater. I took a sip of champagne, then another. It gave me something to do between murmurs of "I see" and "I had no idea."

Maya, who'd been talking to someone behind me, suddenly grabbed my hand. "Time to meet my husband. He's sulking in the corner, as usual."

The room seemed to have gotten louder, the surrounding faces stretched to more extreme proportions. A taut energy coiled through and around me, the expectation that floods a battalion before battle.

Baron de Severin was sitting in an old-fashioned armchair, the only piece of furniture that looked original to the house. It was a statement of decorative defiance, much like the man himself: middle-aged, dressed in a sober gray suit, his thin lips compressed in a disapproving pout. He didn't stand when Maya introduced me, but he kissed the back of my hand when I extended it. A courtly gesture, done for effect.

"How nice to meet you," I said in my breathiest voice. "It's a lovely party."

"Marie's the one I was telling you about," Maya said. "She has no money, so she's been limited to pencil drawings. I want to see what she can do with a set of paints and some decent canvases."

The baron sucked on his cigarette. "You have an allowance," he said to his wife. "Use it as you see fit."

"I thought you'd be more generous if you knew who I was spending it on."

"I love Maya's work," I gushed, hoping flattery would ease the obvious tension between them. "Your wife is very talented."

"My wife has many talents. Most of them have nothing to do with art."

Maya glared at her husband, a reflexive response to what was apparently a long-running argument. Then she flung an arm around my shoulders and declared, "He's always in a foul mood at first. He'll be much nicer after a few drinks."

Scooting me away, she explained, "Half the people here have already asked him to support their literary review or help them rent a theater. The other half are working up their nerve to do it. He tolerates it because my eccentricities come with certain rewards."

Her breath was so warm I could feel it condensing against my neck. "You're the kind he likes. Just innocent enough. It doesn't take much to please him, and if you do, he might rent you an apartment. Pay for you to mount a show."

Was this how Maya's so-called artist friends supported themselves? I wondered how many women had "pleased" the baron.

"He won't expect much, if that's what you're worried about. He only lasts a few minutes in bed, on those rare occasions his equipment works. He prefers to watch."

I'd never heard a wife talk that way about her husband. "He watches you?" I asked tentatively.

Maya laughed. "As a special reward, when he's done something generous. Like pay for a big party." Her eyes locked on mine, the intensity drawing me closer. "Have I shocked you?"

She already knew the answer.

"Oh, Marie, I keep forgetting how young you are."

"I don't feel young." The protest burst out unexpectedly. From Nadia, not Marie.

"I wish you could see yourself as I do."

A line of sweat prickled along the edge of my wig, and I longed for another glass of champagne, even though I was already light-headed.

"You were raised in a good family," Maya said. "Taught good manners. You've been good all your life. Then something changed—I don't know what, but maybe one day you'll tell me. You didn't want to be a dutiful daughter anymore, wasting her life in a small town. You craved something more."

It was so loud, all around us, but Maya's voice pierced through the shouts and cackles. My protective outer layer was melting, revealing truths I didn't want her to see.

"You're trying so hard to prove yourself. But you're still scared. If you want to be a true artist, you must be free."

"Free to sleep with your husband?"

And inside, silently, *Free to betray my own?*

Maya's laugh was deep and wicked. "I'm not talking about the baron."

She ran one finger along my arm, leaving a trail of sensation. The champagne bubbles had somehow migrated to my bloodstream, clustering and popping, making me reckless. *Why not?* I wondered, gazing into Maya's magnetic eyes. What a relief it would be to surrender control.

"There are plenty of men here who'll loosen your inhibitions. You're welcome to use a bedroom upstairs, if you find someone who strikes your fancy."

I tried not to look embarrassed.

"My friend André swears by celibacy whenever he starts a new sculpture, but I find kisses spark my productivity. You're not meant to be a hermit, *chérie*."

The doorman was hovering, a huddle of guests behind him.

"Go on, enjoy yourself," she ordered me, before turning to her next admirers.

I knew I should go back and make another attempt to draw out the baron, but the prospect wasn't appealing. I couldn't think of a clever way to start a conversation with someone who'd already been so rude. Maybe if I mingled awhile, I'd find out more about him from my fellow partygoers.

A man slid in front of me, wearing a crimson smoking jacket and striped cravat. An actor, Maya had said when she'd introduced us earlier, but I didn't remember his name. He was handsome, in a pouty way that suggested he specialized in drama rather than comedy.

"You look lost." He had the careful intonation of an experienced performer, each syllable precise.

"It's very crowded."

"And you are a beautiful woman who should be dancing."

It was easier to accept his offer than come up with a reason to decline. At least dancing would give me something to do until Maya reclaimed me—or the baron drank himself into a friendlier mood. The actor pulled me into the writhing mass closest to the band, where the horns' harsh wails pulsed against my skull. His fingers tightened around mine, then released, then tightened again. We were planets, swirling in elliptical orbits. I bumped elbows and backsides with my fellow revelers as we moved faster and faster. To my great surprise, I realized I was having fun.

I moved with the music, no longer Marie, no longer Nadia. I laughed at nothing, throwing my head back, my bones rubbery and supple, the armholes of my dress sticky with sweat. The crowd around me was blurry but exhilarated, their heartbeats thumping in time with the jazz. I thought with fleeting wistfulness of Mama. She would have loved all these wild, eccentric people. If we'd left Russia at the beginning of the revolution, we might have ended up in Paris and been invited to parties like this.

I realized, with a start, that Marie was the person I could have been.

The music slowed, and the actor's fingers traced the bumps of my knuckles. He leaned forward, brushing his cheek against mine, provoking an unexpected swirl of lust. And a sudden image of Lee.

I pulled away and shook my head. The actor looked resigned—he'd given it a try, no harm done—and I pushed my way out from the dancers. I took another glass of champagne to fortify myself and saw Maya waving to get my attention. I didn't get a good look at the man she was standing with until after I'd elbowed past a cluster of people. He had a pleasant but ordinary face: brown hair, brown eyes, even features. The kind of person who blends into a crowd.

"Marie, I'd like you to meet René," Maya announced. "He drove us to the studio the other night, remember?"

Would he recognize me up close? Playing coy, I tipped my head so the curls of the wig fell across one cheek.

"Lovely to meet you," I simpered.

"René's a war hero—make him tell you all about it." Maya's words and movements were jerky, slowed by alcohol. "That's why he's my favorite bodyguard. You can't imagine the trouble I attract."

I sipped at my champagne, trying to avoid looking at him directly. His shoes were black leather, freshly polished. No boots tonight.

"Get to know each other. I'll be back in a minute."

Maya nudged me with her shoulder as she left, forcing me to stumble toward René. Talking to him was a risk, but it was also my best chance to learn more about the baron.

"A war hero?" I asked. "Do tell."

"There were no heroes at Verdun."

The military training was still there, in his body and voice. Rigidly self-controlled.

René lowered his mouth to my ear, his words cutting through the din of the party. "I know who you are."

He'd chosen to reveal his hand, though I had no idea why. "Why have you been following me?"

"Not here," he muttered.

He tilted his head toward a service entrance opposite the main doorway, where Maya was holding court. I followed behind him, abandoning Marie's loose sway and walking with brisk determination. As René opened the door, he nearly collided with a waiter holding a tray of canapés. I heard the clatter of a kitchen nearby. René led me down a hallway, then into a darkened room dominated by bookshelves. A library, full of leather-bound books too pristine to have ever been read.

René turned on a desk lamp. The light was faint, waist-high, leaving our faces largely obscured. Had it been a mistake to go off with this man alone, to a place I wouldn't be heard if I screamed? I sipped the last of my champagne, my fingers gripping the glass's stem like a lifeline.

Attempting nonchalance, I asked, "So, who am I?"

"Aleksandr Semelkov's wife."

It was worse than I'd expected. Patlov was the only person in Paris who knew about my husband—or so I'd thought. Had Patlov given me away? Why?

René continued, a judge laying out the evidence. "Anyone who comes to France as part of a Soviet trade delegation gets scrutinized. You're listed on official documents as Nadia Shulkina, but it didn't take much digging to find out that a woman of that name married Aleksandr Semelkov in 1922. It's not exactly a secret in Moscow. The French Security Services suspected you'd been sent to do his dirty work."

"You're with French intelligence."

René's expression didn't change. "We're talking about you, not me."

"I'm a translator. You can ask at the Ministry of Trade—"

"You're there only a few hours a week. I have records of your movements, so there's no point lying." He took a step closer. "Tell me the real reason you came to Paris."

With the single-minded clarity evoked by danger, I knew surprise was my only advantage. I smashed my champagne glass against the desk, then thrust the stem up, against René's neck. The ragged edge pressed into his skin, forming a depression where his pulse throbbed. His quick, shallow breathing assured me that I'd achieved my goal. René was afraid.

"You're strong," I acknowledged. "You might be able to overpower me. But if you move at all, I'll cut your neck. It might kill you; it might not. Maybe you'll only be left with a nasty scar."

A smart soldier knows when it's time for a strategic retreat. René held up his hands in a gesture of surrender. "I worked in intelligence during the war. Since then, I've hired myself out to whoever pays best. Right now, it's the baron."

I slowly withdrew the glass from his neck, my arms clenched, prepared to run. René shifted his weight backward, creating a distance that made me feel safer. We'd become equals, negotiating terms.

"The baron had business interests in Russia, before the revolution," René told me. "He lost a lot of money, and naturally, he's looking for a way to recover that wealth."

"Through the trade agreement?"

"Through whatever means necessary. I have friends in the French security service, and one of them told me a leading Bolshevik's wife had come to Paris under an assumed name. I knew the baron was trying to recoup his Russian investments, so I made him an offer. I'd find out everything I could about you, and he would use that information however he saw fit."

"He wanted to know if I could be bribed. Reveal the terms of the trade agreement so he could profit from it."

René's mouth twitched, the closest he'd come to looking amused. "Those were my instructions. I found out where you lived, who you visited. I discovered you spend most of your time with Russian aristocrats and a British writer. I wondered why."

"And I wondered why the injured soldier who begged on my corner was suddenly following me around Montparnasse. You're not as good a spy as you think you are. I only met Maya because I followed you to Madame Girard's club."

René gave me a brief nod. A point scored in my favor.

"You didn't recognize me that night, did you?" I asked.

"No. But the baron expects me to check up on anyone the baroness befriends. There are no records of a Marie Duvall who fits your description, so I decided to keep an eye on you tonight. It didn't take me long to figure out who you really are."

"And now you've confronted the mysterious Madame Semelkova." I pulled off the wig and ran my fingers through my hair, my scalp twitching with relief. "I'm going back to Moscow soon. Feel free to tell the baron that I can't help him."

"You still haven't told me why the wife of such an important man was sent all the way to Paris to translate some contracts. Did you have your own reasons for coming? A family reunion, perhaps?"

There'd be a tally, somewhere, of all the times I'd visited Mikhail's apartment. All the evenings I'd spent with members of the league.

"Tell your husband the baron is a practical man," René went on. "He's no Communist, but he'd rather work with the Bolshevik government than against it. Especially when both sides can benefit."

I finally understood. The baron could hardly phone Stalin and talk business, so he put forward offers through people like René and me, the insignificant underlings. So many lives had been lost, for seemingly grand causes. But in the end, it all came down to money. Sordid bargains between leaders who said one thing in public and another in private.

I turned away from René; there was nothing left to talk about. I walked clumsily out of the library and back to the party, pushing blindly through the crowd. Bodies were pressed into each other, hands reached out and fingers clasped. I moved through a haze of heat and longing, conversations that were little more than suggestive murmurs. I watched a woman pull two men out of the room, their faces gleaming with anticipation, and I remembered what Maya had said about the bedrooms upstairs: *You're not meant to be a hermit.*

All around me, people were dropping their inhibitions, doing whatever they wanted. Why not me? Just this once?

I told myself it was fate that Lee lived within walking distance. As I left the mansion, I turned toward his apartment, my body making the decision for me. It was only as I got closer that the worries began to surface. Lee could be out. He could be with another woman. He might open the door in chagrined surprise, blocking the opening so I couldn't see who else was there.

Still, I kept going.

When I arrived at Lee's building, I found an obstacle I hadn't counted on: the doors to the central courtyard were closed and locked. I leaned my back against the wall to give my throbbing feet some relief while I decided what to do. I could knock on Madame Gournier's door and ask her to let me in, but it was nearly midnight. She was probably asleep, and what would be my excuse for waking her up? I could hardly claim Lee and I were working at this time of night. Maybe the locked door was a blessing. It had saved me from making a fool of myself.

A heavyset man lumbered across the street directly in front of me, and I instinctively tensed. He wore a bowler hat and businessman's suit, and his face, when he got close enough for me to see it, was unfamiliar. A key ring hung from one finger—he must live here—and he jingled it as he approached.

"May I help you?" he asked sternly.

Fate was offering me a second chance. "I'm here to see Mr. Cooper."

"The Englishman." The man looked me up and down, openly appraising my figure. "Lucky fellow."

From the way he leered, it was clear he thought I was a prostitute. A flush bloomed from my chest to my cheeks as the man unlocked the courtyard door and opened it with a dramatic flourish. I rushed ahead to escape his ogling, my aching feet protesting each step. When I reached Lee's door, I listened for a moment, but the apartment was quiet. He probably wasn't home. If I left right now, he'd never know I'd been here.

And I'd always wonder what might have happened.

I knocked and heard the scrape of a chair, the shuffle of steps. I willed myself upright. Composed.

Lee opened the door cautiously. His suspicious expression quickly shifted to concern.

"Are you all right?"

He was barefoot, wrapped in a dressing gown, and I'd have been uncomfortable at seeing him only half-dressed if I weren't belatedly mortified for myself. Why hadn't I thought to check my reflection in a window? I was wearing a dress fit for a streetwalker, my face plastered with tawdry makeup. I could only imagine what my hair must look like, after hours imprisoned under a wig. No wonder Lee looked worried.

"I went to a party," I said. I couldn't quite summon the nerve to say the next part: *I left the party for you.*

"Hmm. Judging by the looks of you, it was either a very good party or a very bad one."

He looked tired but alert and stood utterly, teasingly still. I stepped forward and kissed him, channeling the thrust of my body into the pressure of my lips, and he pressed back, intent and firm, as if he'd been practicing for exactly this moment. Our feet shifted and touched; his arms curled around my back, and we shuffled inside, catching breaths where we could, falling against each other and the door, slamming it shut with my back.

Those first kisses were scraps of tinder, coaxing a fire to life. My chest pulsed and my hands couldn't stop moving, across Lee's cheeks, his shoulders, his waist. His fingers wound into my hair, holding me still as his lips roamed my neck. I tugged at the edge of his dressing gown and slid my fingertips inside. The warmth of his skin flooded into and through me, racing up my arm. I reached farther, palms grasping, but was left clutching at air when Lee abruptly pulled away. I sagged against the door, panting.

It was hard to decipher the meaning of his pained expression. "Don't," he said, but it was a plea, not an order.

"Why not?"

Lee exhaled a ragged breath that might have been intended as a laugh. "Your husband, for one."

No. I wouldn't allow myself to think about Alek, not with Lee's kisses imprinted on my skin.

"I don't love him," I said. "I was forced to marry him."

It wasn't the exact truth, but close enough. I'd never have risked Vasily's life by turning down Alek's proposal.

"Well, a fellow does appreciate a bit of warning when a lady changes her mind."

Lee was slipping back into his usual role, the charmer who avoided awkwardness with an offer of tea. But I'd just glimpsed another side of him. I had to bring that Lee back.

I reached for his hand. He allowed me to hold it, but didn't return my squeeze.

"I told you I went to a party. It was everything you hear about—decadent, bohemian Paris. Drinking, jazz, men kissing men, women kissing women. Everyone giving in to their desires. And all I could think about was you. How much I wanted *you*."

Lee was silent as I loosened the belt of his dressing gown. When it fell open at the front, I pressed my palms against his bare chest, gliding them from side to side to feel the contours of muscle, the intakes of breath.

Lee's voice seemed to come from far away. "Don't do something you'll regret."

"I'll regret it if I don't."

Lee sank into me, surrendering. I pushed his robe to the floor, claiming his shoulders and back with my hands, pulling him closer. My body tingled with anticipation as my thoughts dissolved into urges: *This*, and then *There*. Lee's touch made me almost desperate with the need to possess him.

"The bedroom," I murmured as I lifted the hem of my dress, giving him permission to pull it up and off. We were equally determined, equally daring. We hurried to his bed, the last of our clothing twisted by wandering fingers.

"Are you sure?" Lee whispered.

His hesitation surprised me. "Of course," I murmured.

"Do you need to take . . . precautions?"

I'd long since memorized the family-planning information Alek had brought me from the Institute of Motherhood. My cycle had just finished; it was a safe time of the month.

"It's all right, don't worry."

Still, he hesitated, rubbing my belly absentmindedly, even as I shifted to nudge his hand lower. He came across as a carefree man-about-town, but he might be less experienced than I'd assumed.

I asked gently, "Is this your first time?"

Lee looked surprised, then offended. "No."

"I wouldn't mind, if it were."

"I know what to do."

His voice was gruff, and I regretted saying anything. My attempt to be kind had only reminded us how much we were still strangers. I started to apologize, but Lee stopped me with a languorous kiss. Pulling back to look at me, he pushed away tendrils of hair and cupped my cheeks with his hands.

"Once we do this, there's no going back," he said softly.

"I don't want to go back."

After that, we didn't need to say anything.

A distant church bell woke me, calling worshippers to Sunday service. I was lying on my side, with Lee curled up behind me. One of his arms was flung across my hip in a gesture of lazy possession, and I gingerly pushed it off. Lee didn't move. The bedroom had a grayish cast, as if everything had been sketched in pencil. Even Lee looked less vibrant, his expression pensive, almost sad. I thought how lovely it would be to kiss him awake. But there was something I had to do first.

I retrieved my slip from the floor and pulled it on. Very slowly, watching Lee the whole time, I pulled open the bottom drawer of his dresser. The wood inched forward without a creak. I saw the same mish-mash of objects I'd searched through before, but no pocket diary.

Moving as silently as I could, I went to the bathroom and washed up. Passing through the front room, I looked at the dining table, where the piles I'd so carefully organized had begun to erode. There was paper in Lee's typewriter, and I walked closer to see what he'd been working on. And that's when I saw the diary, sitting out in the open, taunting me to look inside.

I flipped through the pages, scanning the names. Mine was listed repeatedly, including the day we'd had dinner at Le Dôme. Boris's name was there as well.

"Back at work already?"

I started at the sound of Lee's voice, and the notebook slid from my hand. He was standing in the doorway, watching. My first instinct was to distract him back into the bedroom, a tempting prospect when he looked so charmingly rumpled. My next thought was that this could be the opportunity I'd been looking for. Now that we'd slept together, he might tell me the truth.

I tapped the diary. "I thought this was an address book. I wanted to see how many other women you knew in Paris." Feigning embarrassment, I dropped my head. "I was jealous."

Lee's bare feet padded across the floor as he walked forward. He was looking at me, not the book, and didn't seem upset that I'd opened it.

"It's a list of contacts, for my job."

"I'm one of your contacts?"

"In a way."

Lee reached for his dressing gown, lying on the chair where I'd flung it the night before. It felt like we were moving in reverse, from abandon to caution.

"I haven't wanted to talk about it, since I'm so behind on the Russia book, but I've been making notes for a memoir about Paris. Keeping track of who I meet, for when I write it up later."

"What are you going to say about me?"

"I haven't decided yet."

Lee shifted closer, until one of his knees was pressed against my thigh. The touch grounded me, like the click of a lock. He hadn't stammered or seemed threatened. He sounded like he was telling the truth.

"Would you like coffee?" he asked. "I have a few croissants I bought yesterday . . ."

I nodded. "I should put on some clothes."

My red dress lay in a crumpled heap by the door, looking even more garish by daylight.

"Take this."

Lee wrapped his dressing gown around me, tying the belt and rolling the sleeves above my hands. The fabric retained a hint of his smell, and it felt like his arms were enveloping me, keeping me safe.

"Perfect," he said. "I like you like this, all sleepy-eyed. Cream and sugar?"

We had breakfast together on the sofa as the sunlight caressed us in its glow. When my skin began to feel sticky, I pulled off the dressing gown, fully intending to get dressed and leave. I had plans for lunch with Mikhail, and I knew I should warn Lee this was a one-off encounter, with no future. But when he ran his hand along my back, and I felt his breath along my collarbone, I said nothing. We stumbled back to the bedroom in a whirlwind of kisses, and I told myself this would be the last time. One final reward before I broke things off forever.

When I finally left, protesting that I'd left my cousin waiting long enough, I realized the second time with Lee had only made me hungry for more.

Mikhail was waiting for me outside his building, smoking a cigarette in restless bursts. He looked askance at my rumpled red dress, then grabbed me by the elbow. "We need to talk privately. Away from Mother and the others."

I followed him to the riverfront in silence. Tourists paraded back and forth across the bridge opposite us, like ants retracing the same narrow track. Mikhail's eyes darted around, alert to danger. He spoke quietly, in Russian.

"The Patriot is coming here. To Paris."

"But—he's dead."

With a lurch of my stomach, I belatedly realized my mistake. Patlov was the one who'd told me; Mikhail would wonder how I knew.

Luckily, Mikhail was more interested in continuing his story. "A Party official was executed for treason, but the evidence against him was planted. By who, I don't know. The only thing that matters is that Stalin believes the problem is solved. The real Patriot can continue his work, unsuspected."

Had the other man been an innocent victim? Or involved in a different plot? The web was too tangled for me to unravel.

"We'll be meeting with him in a few weeks. You'll be back in Moscow by then, so we need to find a way to communicate. It will be important to have someone we trust, inside Russia."

Or maybe I wouldn't have to go back to Russia after all. If I told Patlov I'd heard rumors the Patriot was still alive, Alek might let me stay, to find out more. I wouldn't have to tell them the Patriot was coming to France, or that Mikhail was involved. I could even tell Patlov that I'd started copying Lee's diary, so I'd have an excuse to keep seeing him, too. If I was clever enough to dole out the right lies, I could protect both the men I loved.

I might even get to meet the Patriot himself. Was he an army officer, as Mikhail suspected? Only someone with military experience would be bold enough to foment a revolt against the Bolsheviks and make others believe he could win. He'd have to be a natural leader, someone who drew people toward him. And if he came from a well-known family, he'd have no shortage of contacts in the Russian émigré community, as well as access to foreign financing.

I couldn't help wondering—and worrying—that he might be my brother, Vasily.

LONDON

1938

To: Mr. Yevgeny Rostrov, Commissariat of Foreign
Affairs

From: Christopher Howell, Consular Affairs, Embassy
of Great Britain to the Soviet Union

Dear Sir,
I am responding to your request of 3 July to release
the body of a woman identified as Marie Duvall to the
custody of Soviet officials so it may be returned to her
family for burial. I also appreciate the need for discretion, given her identity as the wife of a Communist
Party official. I was not aware that favored wives could
receive special permission for shopping trips abroad,
and I understand the need for assumed names to save
the Party embarrassment.

Though you suggested one of your Soviet embassy
counterparts in London be allowed to examine the
body to confirm the manner of death, we are quite
confident in the conclusion of the Westminster police

that she was killed accidentally, after being hit by a car. Once the cause of death was established, her body was cremated and buried. I am enclosing the cemetery's details, so you may contact them directly regarding possible exhumation.

Please pass on our condolences to her husband, Mr. Semelkov.

PARIS

July 1926

Suddenly, there wasn't enough time. As the Soviet-French trade agreement neared ratification, my translation workload doubled, with documents teetering on my desk in a constantly replenished pile. After I'd told Patlov about Baron de Severin's plan to bribe me, security increased, with Soviet officials double- and triple-checking my work. When I could, I met with Mikhail to find out more about the Patriot's secret visit. Afterward, I sifted through what he'd told me for snippets I could use to keep Patlov interested without harming the Patriot's cause. There wasn't much to share, even if I'd wanted to. I didn't know which day the Patriot was expected, his planned route to France, or the disguise he'd be using along the way. A prominent Russian couldn't just slip out of the country by stealing a costume from a theater.

Amid this churn of activity, the only place I found peace was with Lee. I was as honest as I could be, under the circumstances. I told him I didn't know how much more time I had in Paris. That our affair would have to end eventually. All I could do was savor each night we had together. I was juggling three identities: loyal Soviet comrade, secret conspirator, and woman in love. The last was the only one that felt true.

Lee gave me a key to his building so I could arrive after Madame Gournier closed up for the night. I'd leave before dawn the next day, sleep-deprived and jittery. I barreled through my days on coffee and nerves, always alert, second-guessing everything I said and observed. Had Patlov's smile grown colder? Did Mikhail's increasing solemnness mean he doubted my loyalty?

Lee and I were careful. We rarely went out in public together, and when we did go to a café or restaurant, we never touched. René was no longer begging at the corner in his injured-soldier disguise, but that didn't mean others weren't out there, watching. And I never knew when Alek might make another surprise visit.

When the trade agreement was finally signed, I was invited to translate at the celebratory reception. I was exhausted, nearly asleep on my feet, the voices buzzing around me like flies. I hovered behind a Soviet envoy, murmuring in his ear as his French counterparts made flowery speeches about the revived friendship between their countries. Across the room, I saw Baron de Severin, looking jollier than he had at Maya's party. The deal must have worked to his advantage. Maya wasn't there, which was hardly a surprise. Stuffy occasions like this weren't her style.

Patlov brought me a glass of wine and insisted we toast.

"It's been a pleasure working with you."

I shifted closer and lowered my voice. "There's more to be done. I'm having dinner with two league members soon—I can tell they're close to telling me something important."

"I'm afraid you'll have to cancel your plans. The negotiators are leaving tomorrow, and you'll be taking the night train to Berlin with them."

My stomach lurched. "Why?"

"These decisions are made at a higher level." Patlov gave me a knowing look, and I understood what he meant. Alek was the one recalling me home.

"But tomorrow, it's so soon . . ."

"Well, they're stopping off in Germany for a few days before they go back to Moscow. You could have a few more days in Paris, then join up with them in Berlin, if there are any affairs you need to tend to here?"

Patlov's smile widened. Did he know about Lee?

"You'll want to go shopping, I imagine?" Patlov continued. "Buy some dresses to make your friends at home jealous?"

I gave him the shamefaced nod he seemed to be expecting. "I'd be very grateful."

"Let's see." Patlov drew out the suspense by tapping one finger against his cheek. "What about next Wednesday? That will give you a week."

It wasn't nearly enough. Then again, even a month—a year—would feel too soon. I could tell by Patlov's self-satisfied grin that he considered it a more than generous offer, so there was no point negotiating. The countdown to departure had begun.

When I arrived home, there was a note waiting from Lee.

If you are free, meet me for dinner at Le Dôme.

The place where we had our first real conversation. And not long after, our first kiss. Mentally, I was already in mourning, and the thought of going back felt like a cruel taunt; it would only remind me of everything I'd be giving up. But Lee deserved to know I was leaving, and waiting to tell him wouldn't make it any easier.

I changed into the red dress I'd worn to Maya's party, hoping its brazenness would strengthen my spirits. As I trudged along Boulevard Montparnasse, a rising sense of doom slowed my steps. Should I tell Lee right away? Or enjoy the meal first, delaying the bad news?

I mustered a bright smile when I saw Lee at his usual banquette in the back, reading a newspaper. The mechanical fans overhead did little to dissipate the heat, and I could feel the sweat forming on my chest and face.

"Hello!" Lee stood up as I approached. "I'm so glad you came."

He knew the rules: no kissing, no touching. Anticipation still bristled between us, every time we met.

"I've already eaten, but let's get you something."

He waved his hand, and Henri appeared with characteristic efficiency. Lee ordered a bottle of red wine, then asked me, "Would you like the duck?"

I shook my head. "Salade niçoise."

"Are you well? You look a bit flushed."

"It's this weather. All I want to do is sit in a cold bath."

Lee whispered, "That can be arranged. At my flat."

He gave me what I thought of as his wicked smile, the one he used when we were alone. My impending departure felt like a screen lurking between us, distancing me from his playfulness. If I told him now, in public, I'd be forced to keep myself composed. No crying.

"I've been ordered back to Moscow," I said abruptly. "I'm leaving next Wednesday."

Lee sat back, adjusting his expression accordingly. No longer teasing, no longer happy.

"If I had any choice . . ." I didn't know how to finish. Why say what I wanted, when I'd never get it?

"I'm sorry."

Lee's reserve should have made things easier. Instead, I felt worse, as if he'd already let me go. Henri arrived with the wine and my salad, neither of which I felt like touching. I should have waited to talk about it. Savored Lee's smiles before delivering the blow.

Lee poured wine for both of us, sloshing the liquid nearly to the brim. He took a quick, forceful swallow, the same way he drank his whiskey.

"The thing is, I was going to offer a proposition. It's so hot—as you were saying—and anyone who can afford it leaves Paris in the summer. I thought it would be fun to get away for a spell."

"Get away? Where?"

"Madame Gournier has a cousin who rents rooms in her farm-house, outside Nice. She makes twice as much from tourists as she ever did growing vegetables, now that the Riviera's gotten fashionable. I was going to ask if you'd like to go in August."

He'd meant to be kind by telling me, but the offer only added to my grief. Why tell me about it, when he knew I couldn't accept?

"There might still be time, before you leave." Lee spoke hurriedly, his words following his thoughts. "If we caught the early train tomor-row morning, we'd be there by supper." He began counting on his fingertips. "We could have four or five days."

"Tomorrow morning? It's so soon."

"Why not go while we can?"

One last time with Lee, I told myself. A promise I'd made and bro-ken so often. Lee reached across the table, and I didn't admonish him, or shake my head, or worry about anyone seeing us. I no longer cared. My hand clutched Lee's, and the contact of our palms soothed the wor-ries that darted through me like fireflies. I was exhausted, emotionally and physically. This would give me one last chance at peace, before returning to my life with Alek. A way to delay saying goodbye to Lee. I didn't need to tell Patlov or Mikhail or anyone else. I'd slip away, on my own private mission.

Nothing moved quickly in the village of Aldonne: not the donkey carts bringing produce from the farms, nor the handful of visitors who lin-gered at the town's sole café. There was no clock tower to mark the minutes. After rushing across Paris for months, the unscheduled hours stretched out before me like a mirage in the baking sun. It felt like time had stopped.

The farmhouse where Lee and I stayed was a modest whitewashed building a ten-minute walk from town. Though Lee introduced me as his wife and said we were newly married, our hostess—another Madame Gournier—didn't check my hand for a ring. Making a show of respectability was enough to satisfy her.

She led us up to our room, where a double bed sat under the lower part of a slanted ceiling. The dark wood furniture and limestone walls gave the space a certain seriousness, lightened only by the blue-and-yellow bedding. Madame Gournier gave us directions to the outside privy and said she'd bring supper when we'd gotten settled.

"Rustic living," Lee said, wrapping his arm around my waist. "Do you wish we were staying somewhere more glamorous?"

"It's perfect," I pronounced. Already, I felt soothed by the silence surrounding us. No traffic noises, no sidewalk arguments. No one watching.

Lee stepped aside, to his suitcase. "I brought you a present."

He pulled out a long, flat box of watercolors and a sketchbook, tied together with red ribbon.

"You told me your mother used to paint. I thought you might like to give it a try. The light's supposed to be good in the South, isn't it?"

When you've been starved of love long enough, the smallest gestures seem like grand declarations. My eyes welled up with tears, and I pretended to fiddle with the brushes, so he wouldn't see.

"I'm out of practice," I said. "Don't expect a masterpiece."

"I don't expect anything. You don't even have to show me."

I opened the sketchbook and ran my fingertips over the nubby paper. I resolved not to fret about how little time we had together. I would live each minute in full, grateful for every one.

All those hours together in Lee's apartment, working separately but companionably, had already made us adaptable to each other's rhythms. We started each day with coffee and reading, content in our shared silence. Later, we'd explore the cart paths and fields beyond the farm, where Lee would pick me wildflowers and I'd find shady spots to sit and paint. Lee was one of my favorite subjects. Even sitting still, he projected light.

On our last day, we biked to the beach at Beaulieu-sur-Mer, where Lee rolled up his trousers and tugged at my arm to urge me into the water. He pulled me farther, then farther, until I was wet to the knees. I tossed a handful of water toward his face, jokingly fending him off. Soon, we were splashing like children, a battle that left us both breathless.

"Did you used to do this with your sisters?" I gasped.

Lee stopped and stared at me, surprised. "What do you mean?"

"Play around like this, in the water." I kept smiling, unsure what I'd said to offend him.

"My father never would have allowed it."

Lee's lightheartedness vanished, though he brushed off my questions when I asked what was wrong. He trudged back to the beach and began brushing the sand off his legs.

"Let's go back to that café we passed," he called out. "I'll buy you an ice cream."

I sensed a darkness hovering, Lee desperate to escape its shadow.

Nightfall came quickly in the country, and Aldonne shut down at sunset. Lee and I spent our evenings in the bedroom under the eaves, a place I would have chosen even if we'd been surrounded by restaurants and nightclubs. On that final night, Lee lay with his arm across the pillows, my head leaning into his shoulder. I was already dreading saying goodbye, and knowing I'd hurt him—even unintentionally—would only intensify my regret.

"Today, at the beach." I spoke softly, not looking at him. "I said something that upset you."

"It's not your fault."

"What happened?"

"It's nothing to do with you. You mentioned my sisters, and it reminded me . . . the last time I was at a beach was with my mother."

I listened to the rhythm of our breaths: his quicker than mine, more restless.

"Memories are like that," I said. "They sneak up on you, when you're not prepared."

"It's the last time I remember being happy as a child. Splashing in the water by the Brighton Pier, with Mother."

I knew him well enough by then to wait. Ask too many questions, and he'd retreat behind his shield of friendly banter.

"I told you my father sent me to boarding school. You've no idea how awful it was. I was only eight years old, grieving for my mother, and the very first night, I got caned for crying."

It was easy to picture a younger, more boyish version of Lee. My heart ached for him.

"People say the Communists are antifamily, but you tell me, why do the British think it's civilized to have their children raised by strangers? In a place designed to make them suffer? I'd have gone away to school in time, even if Mother were alive, but she would have looked out for me. She'd never have sent me *there*."

The silence that followed was so long that I assumed he didn't want to tell me any more. I shifted to my side, so I could rest my arm across his chest. He pulled me closer, and I thought of him as a little boy, lying all alone.

"The place Father chose was up in Yorkshire, in the middle of nowhere. Practically a military camp. I was certain I'd die there."

I thought of my lessons at home with Miss Fields. Of Mama traipsing in and kissing my cheek; Papa smiling proudly when he heard about my progress. Their love had surrounded me, invisible yet unquestioned. I'd never appreciated how well I'd been protected during my childhood. Perhaps that had made me strong enough to bear what came after.

I ran my hand along the side of Lee's chest, following the ridges of his ribs. As if I were stitching up past wounds.

"You don't have to talk about it," I said. "But you can, if you want."

He did. In a steady, distant voice, he described the miseries he'd endured. Meager portions of barely edible food. Chipping ice off the bathwater in winter. Marching drills in the rain. The cane used as punishment for an endless list of infractions: speaking too loud, not speaking enough, looking down, looking up, sobbing into your pillow at night. Deprivation twisted most boys into bullies or victims resigned to their suffering. Lee, miraculously, had forged a middle path: he'd dedicated himself to doing everything perfectly right, contorting himself to others' expectations and giving them the answers they wanted to hear.

"I thought of myself as a character I'd created," he said. "Cheery old Lee. The headmaster even stopped punishing me, in time, because I always thanked him afterward. He got no satisfaction from it."

"I understand, now," I said, "why you became a Socialist."

"My old headmaster would be horrified to hear that." His lips flicked into a brief half smile, and I was relieved to see his humor returning. With so little time left, I wanted us to try our best to be happy.

"When you came to my flat, the night of that party." Lee's voice was soft. Confessional. "You asked if it was my first time."

"I didn't mean to offend you . . ."

"I'd gone to a place when I was at university. The sort where you pay for female companionship. But I didn't understand how different it would be, with someone I love."

He said the words so quietly that I wasn't sure I heard them right. He turned to face me and clasped my hands in his. "Marry me."

Shock can take many forms: a racing heart, a roaring in the ears. All I experienced was utter silence, as if the world had stopped to await my answer.

"Don't joke," I whispered.

"I'm not. It's easy to get a divorce in Russia, isn't it? People kept saying so, during my visit. Equal rights for women and all."

"It's not that simple."

Lee's eyes bored into mine. "You don't love your husband."

217

"No."

"You don't want to go back to Moscow."

"No."

Lee brought my hands to his chest, as if the force of his longing could pulse through my skin.

"I've spent years wondering what I'm meant to do. Traveling, writing, meeting all sorts of people, but never anyone who felt as right as you. These last few days have shown me what I want. A simple life, with you. When I wake up and see you there . . ."

Lee scrunched his face in exaggerated irritation, the writer at a loss for words.

"I feel safe."

I understood, because he did the same for me. Like pieces of a puzzle, we filled the gaps in each other.

"We can go anywhere you like," Lee said. "England, France—America, for all I care. Start fresh, together."

Could we? For the first time since I'd received my summons back to Russia, I saw a possible way out. Would Alek agree to a divorce? He certainly wasn't in love with me, and a wife with my aristocratic background was no asset to his career. He might even be relieved if I suggested it; he'd rise higher, faster, with a wife who was connected to Stalin's inner circle.

Then I remembered Alek's face in my apartment, when he goaded me with questions about Lee. Alek might not love me, but he was dangerously jealous. If he found out who I was leaving him for, he wouldn't hesitate to punish Lee, out of spite. He might even force me to watch.

The thought made me sick, and Lee seemed to wilt at my silence.

"It's all right," he said, feigning indifference. "I've put you in a difficult spot."

"It's hard to explain . . ."

"I thought I'd ask, that's all." As if I'd been silly to take his proposal seriously. "Do you fancy a sherry? Madame said we were welcome to the bottle in the kitchen."

I couldn't let him leave, not like this.

"I would if I could. I swear."

"I understand. Some things can't be helped."

I tried to show Lee the depth of my feelings later, as my hands wandered his warm, precious body, and my mouth met his for kisses that were never long enough. I told him I loved him, over and over, and he told me to hush, and I felt the distrust hovering in the spaces between breaths. Did he think I was lying? That I'd willingly choose Alek over him? When Lee finally closed his eyes, surrendering to sleep, my mind was still gripped by the hope of escape. Alek would never let me leave, but what if I simply disappeared? Through Baron de Severin and René, I could make contact with the French intelligence service, which might offer protection in exchange for information on Patlov and the workings of the Soviet embassy. I could run off to England with Lee and start over under yet another name. But wherever I went, I knew I'd never feel safe. Alek had hundreds of spies at his disposal, and he wouldn't rest until they found me. Asking for Lee's help would only doom him, as well.

The next morning, Lee and I politely sipped coffee as we packed. Madame Gournier drove us to the station in her cart, and the train pulled out when the sun was halfway up the horizon. We were the only passengers in our first-class carriage, and I thought we'd take advantage of the privacy to snuggle together. But when I took a seat by the window, Lee sat opposite me, book in hand. I told myself I had no right to be hurt. Not when I was the one who'd rejected him.

While Lee read, I stared out the window, each mile separating me from the peace of the country. The wheels clacked like a metronome, counting down the minutes until I was on another train, headed east. Carrying me back to a life I didn't think I could bear.

I pulled out my sketchbook and flipped through the pages. Grapes on a vineyard trellis. A crooked old tree behind the farmhouse. A stony cliff overlooking the beach. Lee's face, formed from pale strokes of yellow and pink. The pictures already looked like the disjointed remnants of a dream. Vivid, but not real.

"May I have one?" Lee asked. I hadn't realized he'd stopped reading.

I passed him the sketchbook. Taking his time, he examined each page. Finally, he ripped out a picture of the front of the farmhouse. I'd added a few details to make it look more charming than it was, including a creeper of ivy snaking up the front.

"You can take as many as you like," I said.

"This is enough. I'll remember."

We arrived at Gare d'Austerlitz well after dark. The heat was overwhelming, especially combined with the stench of sweat and smoke. Only a few months ago, I'd arrived in Paris sparkling with anticipation. Now, I trudged through the station in silent misery. The contrast couldn't have been more bitter.

Lee hailed a taxi and gave me a pointed look. "Where to?"

"I should go home."

"I don't know your address." He smiled ruefully.

The taxi driver was giving me an impatient stare. Was Lee hoping for an invitation?

"I'm sorry," I mumbled, belatedly realizing the danger I was returning to. Patlov might be at my apartment right now, demanding an explanation for my sudden disappearance. I slid into the back seat of the taxi, and Lee closed the door behind me.

"I'll telephone tomorrow," I told him as he stepped away. I wasn't sure if he'd heard.

My building was silent when I arrived home. Everyone seemed to have turned in for the night, including the Blanchard sisters, whose front door was closed. I walked up the four flights of stairs, each step depleting what was left of my energy. I unlocked my door and opened it slowly, strangely reluctant to enter. I prepared myself to see Patlov perched on the bed, waiting. But the room was empty. After four days closed up, the air was suffocating, and I quickly opened the window. The feeble whiff of humid city air didn't bring much relief.

I turned on the light and saw that the Blanchards had slipped a few envelopes under my door.

A note from Mikhail, dated Saturday: *Please come see me as soon as possible.*

A message from Patlov: *Your shoes are ready at the cobbler's.* That was code, telling me to meet him at the café the morning after I received it. Which I obviously hadn't done.

Another note from Mikhail, sent today: *We need to talk. Very important.*

Two urgent messages from Mikhail could only mean there was news about the Patriot. And the summons from Patlov might have something to do with it. I was already light-headed from the heat; now, I felt queasy. I'd have to come up with a good story for where I'd been, but my brain was too tired to try.

I went to the bathroom on the landing—unoccupied, thank God—and ran the water for a bath. As the tub filled, I washed out my sweaty clothes in the sink. Settling into the cold bathwater was painful at first, until the chill settled into me, providing harsh clarity. I scrubbed the grime off my skin, working through my plan as I worked across my body. When I was done, I pulled on a clean dress, hung my wet clothes on the line outside my window, and walked downstairs to the Blanchards' apartment.

I didn't hear any sounds from inside. It was close to ten o'clock, which could be well past the old women's bedtime.

Céleste answered the door, quickly enough that I knew she hadn't been asleep. She was wearing a white nightgown, and her hair was tucked in a kerchief.

"Marie!" she exclaimed. "I was worried about you. We haven't seen you around."

"I was out of town. Visiting a friend. Would you mind if I used your phone?"

"Of course not. Come in."

Céleste shuffled back and I stepped inside. It wasn't quite as hot as my top-floor apartment, but the atmosphere was still oppressive. The telephone sat on a side table, just inside the doorway. In the faint gloom of a single lamp, I could see Céline in an armchair, her head tipped back against the top, lightly snoring.

"Are you sure I won't be bothering her?" I asked.

Céleste huffed in dismissal. "She sleeps through everything."

It seemed a little odd that she'd continue to stand so close as I asked the operator to connect me, but I could hardly complain. It was late, and she'd been kind to let me in.

Mikhail answered on the second ring, his voice clipped. "Hello?"

"It's me."

"Where have you been?" He was angry, and my shoulders cringed in silent apology.

"I had to go away for a few days."

He took a few heavy breaths, and I braced myself for the next questions: *Why? Where?* Instead, he said urgently, "I have news about our friend."

The Patriot. My heart began to pound.

"He's coming to town. Tomorrow."

"So soon?" I asked, keeping my voice level. Céleste could hear everything I was saying.

"You should meet him. May I bring him by for a visit?"

Was it a request or an order?

"Your apartment's much nicer," I said. "Wouldn't that be more appropriate?"

"The only problem is, it's so crowded."

Of course. Mikhail would want to protect his family from any connection to the Patriot, and a public meeting would be too dangerous. Mikhail knew I lived in a run-down building in an unfashionable neighborhood. A place no one would think to look. If I agreed, it meant I could be there for the meeting. I would finally see the Patriot for myself.

"All right," I said. "What time?"

"Afternoon. I can't say exactly when." Mikhail had told me there was a network of safe houses, each a link in the chain between Russia and France. Every person who helped the Patriot knew only their portion of the plan.

"Tomorrow, then."

I put down the receiver. Céleste was still hovering, and I almost snapped. Couldn't she give me a moment alone to think?

"Is everything all right?" she asked.

Snippiness gave way to shame. Céleste could be irritating, but she'd always been nice to me.

"It's been a busy day," I said, forcing a smile. "I'm sorry if I kept you up."

Céleste wished me a good night, but I was already halfway out the door, preoccupied by what came next. In two days, I'd be on a train to Berlin. Before then, I needed to see Patlov and find out if he knew anything about the Patriot coming to Paris—without giving away what I knew. I'd have to say a final, wrenching goodbye to Lee. And in less than a day, I'd be meeting the Patriot himself. I'd told myself again and again that it couldn't be Vasily, but I couldn't help wondering if Mikhail's involvement was more significant than I'd realized previously. If the Patriot *was* Vasily, he'd put his trust in another Shulkin, wouldn't he?

Back in my apartment, I gulped down a glass of lukewarm water, then opened my suitcase. There was the dress I'd worn to the beach, still gritty with salt at the hem. A nightdress that smelled of lavender and Lee. I allowed myself one last look at the sketchbook. I couldn't bring this evidence of my affair back to Moscow; it would all have to be destroyed. With the solemnness of a ritual, I burned all the pictures in my washbasin, watching them crinkle and crumble as my memories curdled. The happiness captured in those images was an illusion; only this dim room in Paris was real.

That night, I drifted beyond exhaustion into sleeplessness. I tossed and turned, the springs of the old bedframe creaking into my hip bones and shoulders. I longed for the plump mattress at the farmhouse. For Lee's hand on my cheek, to calm my agitated mind. And then, suddenly, I was opening my eyes with a start. Outside, I heard shouts and car horns. The sounds of the city waking up.

It was already hot, the air as thick as soup. My visitors wouldn't be arriving until the afternoon, which meant I had hours ahead to fill. My pulse was already thudding. I'd resigned myself to returning to Moscow and Alek, but the past few months had changed me. For most of my marriage, I'd been afraid, playacting the role of a docile, obedient wife. Now, I knew there were powerful forces working against the Bolsheviks, and I'd allowed myself to imagine what would happen if they were overthrown. Perhaps Russia could finally be the country my uncle Sergei talked about, a place where everyone got a fair share. Mikhail already assumed I'd be spying for him from within the Soviet Union, but I still hadn't decided if it was worth the risk. It all came down to whether I trusted the Patriot with my life.

I kicked off the sheet covering the lower half of my body and sat up. If this was the day that would determine my future, best to get on with it.

I started by cleaning the apartment, not that there was much to scrub. I styled my hair and put on lipstick, determined to look my best. Using the Blanchards' phone, I left a message for Patlov at the embassy, telling him I'd been sick but would meet him "at his favorite place" for breakfast the next morning. With hours of waiting still ahead,

I decided to walk off my restlessness. The whole city seemed to have slowed down: people ambled along the pavement, their conversations subdued. Shopkeepers leaned against counters or slumped in doorways. I headed to the river and stood at the embankment, watching the water. I'd always found its flow soothing, a murmured reassurance. For centuries, the currents of the Seine had followed their destined course. Maybe I, too, would finally find the path I was meant to take.

On the way back to my apartment, I stopped at a café and ordered lemonade and an omelet. Though I'd requested a table in the shade, my face felt flushed, and my legs prickled in my stockings. A middle-aged couple next to me held their newspapers in identical postures. A group of elderly men discussed horse racing over cups of coffee. A would-be writer scribbled dramatically in his notebook. Anyone watching me would have thought I was supremely self-confident, a woman who dared to eat alone in public. None of them could guess the tangle of anticipation, fear, and hope roiling beneath my tranquil surface.

If, if, if. If the Patriot proved he had the support of the army, I might be convinced to join his cause. If the Soviet Union fell, Alek would be imprisoned or exiled—maybe even killed. If Alek was gone, I'd be free to marry Lee.

Not that I was sure he'd want me, when he found out who I really was.

I ambled slowly back to my apartment, trying to avoid staining my dress with sweat. When it was this warm, the Blanchard sisters usually sat outside, or at least opened their front door in search of a breeze. But their door was shut, and the stairwell was silent. The entire building seemed to have come to a stop, waiting alongside me for what would come next. I thought about calling Lee. Almost knocked on the Blanchards' door. But I had no idea what I'd say.

Knowing I still might have hours of waiting, I determined to keep busy. I washed my sheets—still sticky from the night before—and hung them out to dry. I brewed tea and waited for it to cool to room temperature before drinking, a drawn-out process that filled another chunk of time. I tried to sketch, but nothing in my room inspired me, and my imagination refused to budge beyond its walls.

Finally, I heard footsteps on the stairs. I told myself not to get my hopes up; it could be a neighbor coming home. The steps got louder. Closer. Strong and confident—a soldier's walk? The Patriot wouldn't come alone, would he? I'd assumed he'd be with Mikhail, at least. Then again, it might be safer for them to move separately. Easier to make a quick getaway if something went wrong.

I pictured Vasily standing in my doorway. My older brother, come to protect me.

My skin tingled when I heard the knock on my door. I swung it open and saw Alek standing on my threshold.

My husband was the Patriot?

Or was my husband here to catch the Patriot?

I remained silent as my brain tried to sort through what was happening.

"Aren't you going to invite me in?"

The familiarity of his tone—amused, mocking—nudged me into action. I stepped back and Alek stepped forward. He looked around the room. Given the size of the space, it didn't take him long to confirm we were alone.

Make him talk first, I thought. *See how much he knows.*

"It's good to see you," I said. "What brings you to Paris?"

Alek sat at the table and flattened his hands, avoiding my nervous smile. I felt the danger, swirling around us. This was not part of the plan, which meant either Mikhail or I had been deceived.

"Are you hungry?" I asked, slowly shifting toward the door. "I can get some things from the market. Make you something to eat."

Swifter than I'd thought him capable of reacting, Alek shot up from his seat and moved to block me. "Aren't you expecting visitors? The Patriot and your cousin Mikhail?"

Standing this close to him, the object of his chilly stare, I wondered how I could have even fleetingly imagined Alek as the Patriot. He was a Bolshevik to his bones. The only way to save myself—and Mikhail—was to pretend I was still on his side.

"If you scare them away, we'll never find out who else is involved in the plot. Let me talk to them. They trust me."

"And you'll be the savior of the motherland. How heroic. The problem is, you're being awfully secretive. Does Patlov know about this meeting?"

"I'm seeing him tomorrow. I'll tell him everything then."

"I don't know if I believe you."

"You have to leave, before they come," I urged. "Mikhail doesn't know I'm married. You were the one who told me to keep it a secret."

I heard a distant thudding from the stairwell. A man's tread, heavy and steady.

"Please, Alek . . ."

"I want to see you at work. Think of it as your final test."

Alek slid sideways, and I wrenched the door open, hoping there was time to warn the person coming up. All I needed was a few seconds to wave a hand or shake my head. But it all happened too quickly. Mikhail reached the landing, I began to urge him away, and Alek pulled the door open wider, so he was standing directly at my side.

Mikhail, to my horror, came straight toward Alek, grinning happily, his hand outstretched.

"It's a pleasure to meet you," he said brightly, and his expectant smile made me want to weep. He thought Alek was the Patriot, and Alek was playing along.

"Prince Shulkin, is it?" Alek asked.

He was toying with Mikhail, pretending to be impressed. And Mikhail reveled in that reverence. How could I warn him we'd been betrayed?

"I'm not sure how to address you," Mikhail said to Alek. "I don't even know your real name."

"I'd prefer to keep it that way. It's safer."

As Alek gestured toward the table, I hovered by the door, listening for the sound of footsteps. When the real Patriot arrived, we'd outnumber Alek three to one.

"Make us some tea, will you, Miss Shulkina?"

For now, Alek was in charge, and submission was the easiest way to allay his suspicions. I walked dully to the kettle and filled it with water. Took two cups from the shelf and set out the pot. And as I went through my rote motions, Alek chatted personably with Mikhail, extracting information through seemingly friendly questions. Which foreign government officials had promised to finance the Patriot's counterrevolution? Who else knew he was in Paris? What promises had been made to disgruntled Russian émigrés?

"We don't want the Romanovs back in power," Mikhail said. "We've made that clear."

Alek looked puzzled. "I heard Grand Duke Nikolai was involved."

"He likes to exaggerate his importance. He's more talk than action."

"Unlike you and your friends."

The friends who will soon be hunted down by Soviet agents. I felt my heart pounding down the seconds until the real Patriot arrived. Alek looked oddly at ease, and my hopes began to sink. Why hadn't I realized it from the start? Alek wasn't concerned because he knew the Patriot wasn't coming. He was prolonging this conversation for fun, to toy with Mikhail and with me.

If Alek left this room with proof that Mikhail was working against the Soviet Union, it was only a matter of time before my cousin was killed. But what could I do to protect him? Hit Alek over the head with the table lamp? Brandish my dull paring knife? Mikhail and I could overpower Alek if we worked together, but there was no way to explain the danger without Alek overhearing.

"Are you expecting someone else?" Alek abruptly asked me. "You keep looking toward the door."

"I didn't tell anyone else about the meeting," Mikhail said, shooting me a concerned glance. As if I was the one he was worried about.

Alek smirked at me, igniting my anger.

"He's not the Patriot!" I shouted at Mikhail. "He's with the Soviet secret police. You have to leave, now!"

I'd caught Alek by surprise, but it wasn't enough. Mikhail was surprised, too, and confusion kept him from acting during those precious seconds when he could have escaped. He looked at Alek, then me, unsure who to trust. Alek composed himself and stood, positioning himself in front of the door.

"She's right," he said to Mikhail. "My name is Aleksandr Semelkov, and I am not the Patriot. There is no such person."

Mikhail stared blankly at Alek, who gave him a self-satisfied smirk.

"The Patriot was a ploy from the very beginning. A story concocted in my office to draw out potential traitors. There are disgruntled Russians all over Europe, whispering about overthrowing the Soviet government. I was the one who thought of baiting a trap to draw out the vermin."

I heard the words, but it took some time for me to understand their full meaning. Alek had sent me to Paris knowing there was no plot. My real mission—unbeknownst to me—was to earn the trust of Mikhail and the league, so that when I began talking about the Patriot, they'd believe he was real. There must have been other Soviet agents, too, creating a false network of safe houses and secret messages. Concocting evidence of an uprising that had never existed.

Mikhail glanced in my direction, eyes wary, then glanced at the door. Was he sending a signal? I heard his feet shuffle and the rustle of his trousers. I stepped forward, ready to join Mikhail in tackling Alek. Instead, Mikhail straightened his shoulders and gave Alek a dismissive sneer.

"You're lying."

It was the damned Shulkin pride, asserting itself at the worst possible moment. Mikhail couldn't admit to being duped; it was a stain on his honor.

"Nadia's the liar," Alek said. "Did she tell you we're married?"

Mikhail turned to me, and the desolation in his face seared into my skin. In that moment, he seemed to hate me more than Alek. Maybe I deserved it. In Mikhail's eyes, mine was the worse betrayal.

"I've had enough of your games," Mikhail muttered, and I couldn't tell if he meant me or Alek. He turned in a huff, and I thought of Papa, at the dinner table in Priyalko. Acting as if he was in charge, despite the odds against him. The memory made me cry out, even before I saw the knife in Alek's hand. My warning shout sharpened into a scream as the blade sank into Mikhail's stomach, and he collapsed to the floor. I watched the silver transform to red as Alek briskly drew the knife across Mikhail's neck. Rigid with shock, mouth gaping, I didn't even think of running. I had nowhere to go, nowhere that Alek couldn't find me, and his brutality stifled any flicker of resistance. He could kill me, too, without consequences.

As I tried to reconcile the Mikhail I'd known with the lifeless, butchered body before me, Alek briskly dealt with the aftermath. He wiped off the handle of the knife with his handkerchief and tossed it aside. It slid along the floor, leaving a trail of blood behind it. Next, Alek prowled around the apartment, examining my things with an appraising eye. I still hadn't moved. He pulled my suitcase out from under the bed and began tossing in my clothes and toiletries.

"What are you doing?" My voice shook.

"We're leaving. There's a train to Luxembourg in an hour. We'll go from there to Germany."

"Right now?"

Alek pressed the suitcase shut and turned to face me, as calm as if he was instructing his secretary at work. "Do you have other pressing business?"

Panicked, I tried to find an excuse to delay.

"There are two sisters downstairs—they've been very kind, and I'd like to say goodbye."

"The Blanchards?"

How did he know their names?

"Patlov paid them to keep an eye on you," Alek explained. "Another measure of security."

I thought of Céleste, delivering my mail. Céline, asking coyly what I'd be doing that day. Seemingly harmless old women who'd been watching me the whole time.

"They were supposed to report all your visitors, but apparently, you haven't had any."

Thank God I'd never invited Lee over. With a fleeting ache of self-pity, I wondered, *What will he think when I disappear?*

"Patlov," I murmured. "We should see him before we leave."

"He's been recalled to Moscow. It seems his superiors weren't pleased with his performance here. Too much time drinking and spoiling his mistresses and too little time supervising his agents. I've recommended a course of reeducation."

A labor camp? Torture? Patlov would be punished for my lies, and the guilt made me sick.

"Let me tell you what's going to happen next," Alek said. "Those old sisters are going to see you leave the building tonight. Tomorrow morning, they'll come up to your apartment and find it unlocked. They'll discover Mikhail's body and call the police. It won't take long, from that point, for the authorities to determine what happened. The apartment where Mikhail Shulkin was murdered belonged to a woman named Marie Duvall. Her passport picture will be printed in the papers, and a source in the Soviet embassy will inform the police—unofficially—that

Mademoiselle Duvall was the alias of a Russian secret agent. Word will spread, and those idiots in the Russian Cultural League will turn on each other, wondering who knew the truth about you and who didn't. There will be no more conspiracies, because no one will trust each other. And so, resistance to the Soviet Union will wither."

According to René, French intelligence already knew my real name and who I was married to. It wouldn't take them long to judge me capable of murder.

"You can try to run," Alek continued. "Slip away at the train station, or whatever plan you may be considering right now. However, we already have copies of your passport picture, ready to distribute. It will be in every newspaper in the country. As a murder suspect, you'll be the subject of a massive manhunt. It's only a matter of time until you're arrested. Would you really prefer a French prison to our apartment in Moscow?"

I wanted to say yes, just to spite him. But the independence I'd gradually built up in Paris was already crumbling, weakening my muscles and silencing my protests. In that moment, I realized I was no self-sacrificing heroine. I was simply human, clutching at the hope of self-preservation.

"I want to go home," I said, hanging my head. "I won't make trouble."

I took a last look around the room that had once been my refuge. It was defiled by Mikhail's body, a grotesque centerpiece that overshadowed everything around it. I noticed a nightdress hanging on the line outside the window and decided to leave it. A fluttering remnant of the elusive Marie Duvall.

I wondered what Lee would think when he read the papers and saw that the woman he loved was a murderess and a liar. The police would make their way to him sooner or later—what would he tell them? He might try to downplay our relationship, saying only that I'd worked for him, and he barely knew me. Or he might take advantage of the attention to benefit his career. He was a journalist, after all. I could even picture the headline: "My Secret Soviet Mistress."

I didn't think Lee would actually do it. But we never know what someone else is capable of, when their illusions have been shattered.

I took my coat off the hook behind the door. A few steps behind me, Alek lifted my suitcase. I walked out of the apartment, away from Paris, into the wasteland of my future.

LONDON

1938

To: Roger Ballantry, SIS

From: Director, SIS

This morning, I informed the prime minister's office that the Red Mistress investigation is officially closed. I did not attempt to hide my disappointment at your team's lack of results. Five of our best men, working for months, could only confirm that the USSR's top female agent admired the Elgin Marbles at the British Museum. I could not tell the PM why the Red Mistress came to London and if she accomplished what she set out to do. I could not say if she made contact with British citizens working on behalf of the USSR. I could not determine for certain if her death was an accident or murder. Despite harsh questioning, I defended our reputation as best I could.

Privately, I consider this debacle one of the service's greatest failures. In such cases, it is best to undertake a course of housekeeping, so as to be seen as learning from our mistakes. I leave it to you to decide who on your team will serve best as sacrificial lamb.

MOSCOW

1938

Time moved differently in prison, where there were no windows, no clocks, and no hope. Though my best guess was that I'd been arrested a few months ago, there was no way to know for sure. The light in my cell went off and on unpredictably, with no relation to day or night. Sleep came in bits and pieces, never enough to make me feel rested. I might drift off for a few minutes or an hour, but I'd always wake up shivering, overwhelmed by the same desolation: *I'm still here.* Isolated and alone, I had no distractions from my imagination. It's a cruel irony to realize your own mind can create horrors as devious as any torturer's.

It was almost a relief whenever the door screeched open, and a guard hauled me down the hall for another beating. At least then I'd see other people, even if they sneered. During what they called my punishments, there was no space for anguished thoughts. Only survival. *This will end,* I told myself. *It always ends.* I'd limp back to my cell, whimpering but anticipating the relief to come. I always slept well after a beating, despite the pain. A kindness my body granted me, to recover.

I had no idea what was going on outside the prison or even down the hall. Separated from the world and my place in it, I was no longer Nadia Antonovna Semelkova. I was a ragged collection of bones and muscles, a heap of damaged parts. *Resist,* my mind urged at the beginning, before pain and confusion won out. I admitted to everything, even crimes I'd never heard of. They'd already found me guilty—why argue?

There was usually a gap of a few days between sessions; I estimated the time by watching the changing colors of my bruises. When an unfamiliar guard threw open the door to my cell the day after a beating and shouted for me to come out, I drew the obvious conclusion: I was going to be executed. Shot, I hoped, with resigned acceptance. At least it would be quick. I ran my fingers through my hair and straightened my uniform, determined to face my death without flinching. A Shulkin to the end.

The guard's jacket had an iron pin on the collar, an insignia I couldn't decipher. He led me down the hall, past the room where my tormentors went about their business. The few people we passed immediately shifted against the walls to make way. The guard led me through a door and up a staircase. Near starvation had made me weak and slow, and he reached the top when I was less than halfway up. He grimaced down at me, making a show of impatience.

We continued on to a part of the prison I'd never seen, with desks and typewriters and samovars of tea. An office, not an execution yard. Still, my soul was too battered for hope. Most likely, I'd been brought here to sign a written confession. A killing machine as efficient as Stalin's ran on paperwork.

The guard led me into a stark room where two wooden chairs sat on opposite sides of a scuffed desk. I sank into one of the seats, grateful to be off my throbbing feet. The soles had been beaten with pipes the day before, and the echo of each impact still lingered in my muscles.

The guard left, and my mind churned into action, wondering what would come next. A meeting? A new form of torture? After what felt like a very long time—but could have been only minutes—the door opened behind me, and a balding man with round glasses walked in. I recognized him immediately: Comrade Molotov, the chairman of the Council of People's Commissars. One of Stalin's closest confidants. I'd seen him at Party events, though we'd never spoken. What I knew of him had come from Alek, who was jealous of his influence. "That piggish suck-up," he'd say, or "You won't believe what that weasel Molotov has done now." Maybe that's why I was here. Nothing was private in Soviet Moscow, and those insults had wound their way to their target. I was going to pay for my husband's offenses.

Molotov sat across from me and placed a folder on the table. He looked like an accountant going over year-end figures, not a man who'd signed death warrants for former friends. Alek had told me a few of those stories, too.

"Comrade Semelkova. I don't think we've met, but of course I knew your husband."

Past tense. "Alek is dead?"

Molotov nodded, another name ticked off the list. I'd expected the news, but it was jarring to hear it confirmed in such an offhand way.

"My reports tell me you've been cooperative, though not particularly helpful."

"I've told your men everything I know."

Was that the wrong thing to say? If he believed I had no more useful information, it meant I was expendable. "I'm sure there are other things I'll remember, in time. Things Alek told me . . ."

"Comrade Semelkov's confession was quite detailed."

I tried not to think about why. What they must have done to him.

"Your brother has also denounced you."

The betrayal stung, but only for a moment. Vasily had children, and distancing himself was the only way to protect them.

"I've called you in on another matter," Molotov announced. "An opportunity to prove your loyalty, once and for all, in service to the Soviet Union."

The unrelenting hours of darkness and isolation had dulled my mind. I couldn't decide if he was toying with me or making a genuine offer. Molotov leaned forward and placed his elbows on the table. His eyes gleamed through the lenses of his glasses.

"Tell me everything you know about Lee Cooper."

I'd done my best not to think about Lee for the past twelve years. During the long, mostly silent journey back from Paris, I pictured Lee opening a newspaper and seeing my photo. His shock when he found out I was a murderer. That's how he would think of me from then on, all his happy memories corroded by Mikhail's blood. Even if fate brought us together again—and I didn't see how it would—Lee would have no reason to believe I was innocent. I'd lied to him too many times.

Grief for Mikhail caused an even sharper ache. I thought of Mikhail's mother, his sisters, the gallant old men of the Russian Cultural League. Did they think I was capable of killing him? Even if they guessed it was a lie concocted by the Soviets, I'd betrayed their trust. Mikhail would still be alive if it weren't for me.

By the time we crossed the border into Russia, I'd become nearly despondent. A chain of memories and regret kept me tethered to Paris, digging in deeper the farther I traveled. Going back to Moscow was bad enough; I'd never endure it if I was also carrying such suffocating guilt. So, I forced myself to forget. The Nadia I'd been in Paris was dead, as dead as Mikhail. The only way to survive was to never look back.

I had no doubt Alek would punish me. He had proof I'd been keeping secrets from Patlov. That I'd sympathized with Mikhail and his conspirators. With one phone call, Alek could have had me arrested and executed as a traitor. Even if he wasn't prepared to go that far, there were more subtle ways to ensure I suffered. He could have demanded a divorce and made sure I lost my job, which would have meant the end of my housing and food rations. I'd have had to scramble for scraps, a pariah. But when we arrived back at our Moscow apartment—which looked exactly as I'd left it—Alek informed me curtly that I'd been assigned a new job, maintaining archives at the State Library. No more foreign translations; no more exposure to the outside world. Then he said he was tired and went to bed.

For days—weeks—I waited for the hammer to drop, but it never did. We went through the motions of married life: I was quiet and subservient; Alek was distant but polite. We never talked about Paris. I pretended to be grateful, and he pretended I was content. Act a role long enough, and it becomes second nature—close enough to the truth. I moved through my days like a leaf on a river, carried by the current of routines. Keeping to the surface, avoiding the depths. I started sketching again, a welcome distraction when unwanted thoughts tried to batter their way in. Some nights, it took a few shots of vodka to quiet them.

In 1931, Alek was assigned an apartment in the House of Government, a massive modern complex for the Party elite. Technically, it was property of the state, but I did everything I could to make it feel like home, covering the walls with pictures and filling the bookshelves with old favorites. In a corner of the bedroom, I set up a small desk to use as a work space. The new apartment felt like a chance at a new start, and I decided the best way to do that was to have a child.

Motherhood, I thought, would make the future less bleak. It would give me something to look forward to, teach me a new way to love. My physical relations with Alek had never been frequent, but I started making more of an effort, hoping I'd conceive. But I never did. Was it because of my own unacknowledged ambivalence? Or a physical impairment that was never diagnosed? (Alek, convinced the fault wasn't his, refused to see a doctor.) The spiral of disappointment dragged us even further apart. Sex had become associated with failure, and Alek began rebuffing my advances, making me even more withdrawn. In time, we stopped trying altogether, to our mutual relief. I no longer had to pretend to enjoy it, and he was released from a stressful obliga-tion. My grief simmered, then cooled. I assumed Alek had affairs, but I never asked, because I didn't care. Indifference brought its own sort of freedom.

By the mid-1930s, I was living what any Russian would have con-sidered a privileged life. I watched movies in our building's cinema and played cards with other Party wives. I was able to shop at special stores and eat as much as I wanted. But with no true confidants, I was lonely. I made occasional visits to my uncle Sergei and encouraged him to join me in Moscow, but he always refused. Saint Petersburg—as he still called it, in private—was his home, and he didn't have the drive to start over. He continued to write, enjoying his role as an elder statesman of Socialist literature and mentor to younger artists. When he died, sud-denly in his sleep, I couldn't help but think of it as his final kindness to me. There was no lingering illness, no suffering. No matter how much I missed him, I couldn't begrudge him such a peaceful end.

My brother also avoided Moscow, and the physical separation com-pounded our growing emotional distance. Vasily had built a new life two thousand miles away in Tashkent, where he taught at the military academy, married a local woman, and eventually had four children. They seemed happy, in the pictures Vasily sent. But I'd never met my nieces and nephews. I tried not to be hurt by his curt letters, or the fact that he never invited me to visit. I knew Vasily wanted nothing to do with politics, and being known as Aleksandr Semelkov's brother-in-law would bring attention he preferred to avoid. His rejection stung, nonetheless. I'd grown up idolizing my older brother, but I'd spent years protecting him, too. When I was close to starvation, I'd sent food to him in prison; I'd agreed to marry Alek in large part because he'd saved Vasily's life—and because I was afraid what Alek would do to him if I said no. For a time, in Paris, I'd believed Vasily was the sort of hero I'd imagined as a girl: the loyal patriot, charging in to save his country. But

Russia had changed since we were children, and Vasily had a new family. His loyalty lay with them, now.

From Alek, I knew there was trouble in the Party, a constant sense of siege. There were accusations, then trials. Each foiled conspiracy seemed to uncover a new one. When the first prominent Bolsheviks were arrested, I was surprised, but not particularly worried. Evidence was presented against them, and they confessed. Then there were more trials, with less evidence. Charges that made no sense, given what I knew of the men accused. Yet the confessions still came. Stalin's search widened, then doubled back, into his inner circle. Only the most wily and ruthless—men like Molotov—could navigate such shifty tides. Alek was far less adaptable. Self-righteously certain, he thought his years of work on behalf of the Bolsheviks would protect him. He didn't realize that his loyalty to the cause would be measured against his loyalty to Stalin—and found lacking.

They came for us in late February of 1938. Alek had come home exhausted; I was already in bed, close to sleep, but I heard his weary breaths as he shed his clothes. The mattress sighed around us as he lay down. If our marriage had been different, I would have turned over and asked him about his day. He might have laid his arm across my stomach and told me. Instead, I remained silent. When I did fall asleep, it was so deeply that it took me some time to realize a hand was shaking me and tugging on my upper arm.

"Up! Let's go!"

The barking voices were as jarring as the lights, which had all been turned on. Our small bedroom had been overtaken by policemen, all of them shouting. I caught glimpses of Alek protesting, but I was too stunned to speak. Numb and disoriented, I shakily pulled a blouse and skirt over my slip. As voices shouted at me to hurry up, I dithered over which pair of shoes to put on. The old ones with the worn-down soles, so I wouldn't care if they were damaged? Or my best, sturdiest pair, which would hold up better? How could I decide if I didn't know where I was going?

The process was deliberately chaotic, designed to confuse. Alek must have known what was in store—far better than I did—but he was given no chance to warn me. I chose the good shoes, fastened the buckles, and by the time I stood up, Alek had already been taken away. I was dragged out by two men whose meaty fingers dug into my upper arms. Their grip didn't loosen until we were in the back of a black car, where they sat on either side of me, menacingly silent. When we arrived at the prison, they escorted me straight to my cell.

It had been a mistake to wear my good shoes. They were taken away, that very first night, leaving me barefoot. Perhaps they were given to some other Party wife as an unexpected gift. Perhaps she, too, would be wearing them when she was dragged off to a neighboring cell.

As my imprisonment stretched from days to weeks, my world shrank to four gray walls, the past and future obliterated. Now, one of the most powerful men in Russia was sitting across from me, my life quite literally in his hands. If Molotov wanted to know about Lee, I might as well be honest. It took less effort than lying.

"I had an affair with Lee Cooper in Paris. In 1926."

Molotov's gaze remained steady, but his momentary silence made me suspect I'd surprised him.

"Why?" he asked mildly.

The answer that first came to mind—*I fell in love with him*—sounded trite. Those feelings had been dormant for so long that I wasn't sure they'd even been true.

"He was handsome," I finally said. "I liked his smile."

"Did you embark on this affair at the suggestion of your husband?"

I shook my head. "Alek didn't know. At least, I don't think so. He and I never spoke about it."

Molotov jotted a note on one of his papers. It seemed like a performative gesture, an excuse to make me wait.

"Did you ever talk to Mr. Cooper about your husband? Did he know who you were married to?"

"Women don't have affairs so they can talk about their husbands."

Molotov gave me a wisp of a smile. His eyes still glinted coldly, icy crystals behind glass.

"I was very careful never to discuss Alek's work, or even the fact that I was married to a Party official." I remembered Lee's pocket diary, the lists of names and my vague suspicions. "I did wonder if Mr. Cooper was more than just a writer. It's possible the British government was paying him to spy on me."

A long pause. I had nothing to lose by continuing.

"Is it true?" I asked. "Was Mr. Cooper an informer?"

Molotov tipped his head forward. "More than an informer. He was recruited as a British intelligence agent shortly after he visited the Soviet Union in 1922. He was their top man in Paris when you were there. Now, he works for the chief of their Secret Intelligence Service in London."

I was too physically depleted for shock. The hurt spread sluggishly— a dull ache—as I realized Lee had targeted me, from the very beginning. Making clever conversation at the concert, offering me work, flirting just enough to reel me in. And I'd thought I was being so careful! At worst, I suspected he might be reporting on me to a source at the British embassy; I'd never imagined he was running the show himself. He must have known about Alek all along, even on that night he asked to marry me. I'd nearly fallen for that trick—but I hadn't been so careful with the trap just set by Molotov. I'd confessed to an affair with a British spy, a crime that would justify my execution.

"You have not seen or spoken to Mr. Cooper since the summer of 1926?" Molotov asked.

I shook my head, weary. Was he hoping I'd implicate myself even more thoroughly?

"Do you think he would agree to see you, if you asked?"

The question was so absurd that I couldn't hold back my sigh of irritation. "He thinks I'm a murderer."

"That might make him all the more curious to talk to you."

Molotov shifted his papers into a stack and laid his hands on top. A lawyer summing up his case.

"Relations between the Soviet Union and England are in a delicate state. That madman Hitler has all of Europe on edge, and Comrade Stalin wants to keep German ambitions in check. England would be a natural ally for us, to deter Nazi expansion."

"I don't see what that has to do with me."

"The diplomats have been playing their usual games. Dancing around, dropping hints, and accomplishing nothing. The British don't want to cozy up to Communists—not publicly, at least—and Comrade Stalin doesn't know if he can trust them, anyway. What we need is direct communication between Stalin and Churchill, outside the usual diplomatic circles."

Even as Molotov explained further, I couldn't quite believe it. He was sending me to England to deliver a top-secret message from Stalin to Lee. I would travel under my old alias, Marie Duvall, which Molotov implied would keep me in line; after all, Marie was still wanted for murder in France. He assured me I'd have a "protector" at all times, which I understood to mean I'd never be left alone. There was a chance Lee himself might have me arrested for espionage, in which case the Soviet Union would denounce me as a rogue agent and make sure I was silenced—permanently—before I even went on trial. All those dangers were insignificant compared to what I was being offered: a way out of prison, an escape from Russia. Seeing Lee again. My heart leaned across the distance between us, taut with longing. I was thirty-six years old, no longer the young woman he'd known in Paris. I had no idea how he'd react to seeing me again. But I'd risk any humiliation for the chance to explain.

The preparations happened so quickly that they must have been set in motion well before I was pulled from my cell. I went straight from prison to a dental clinic, where I got a cap on the front tooth that had chipped during a beating. I was given a room at the Metropol Hotel—my own apartment had already been assigned to another family—and spent the next week going over the step-by-step plans for my journey. A team of seamstresses designed a new wardrobe, and messengers brought new shoes, a knee-length wool coat, and a tube of red lipstick that brightened my whole face when I tried it on. I looked in the mirror and saw a creature assembled from pieces of the past. My mother's hair and my father's determination. The girl who'd once waltzed in a green dress, and the woman who'd shimmied to jazz in a Parisian mansion. Nadia Antonovna Shulkina Semelkova, looking almost pretty. Almost normal.

On the outside, at least. Inside, I was still empty.

My official escort, Comrade Yanov, was gruff but unthreatening. During our two-day train journey, he acted less like a guard and more like a protective father, watching over a potentially rebellious daughter. We slept in the same compartment and ate all our meals together in the dining car. Our conversations were brief and superficial, both of us aware that it was safer the less we knew. When I stepped off the ferry at Dover, it felt like I'd stepped into an unexpectedly familiar world. The train to London passed by picturesque villages and expansive sheep meadows, the landscape I'd read about in novels for years. The passengers around me spoke in crisp, declarative English, a precise language for a precise people. I remembered the soothing sound of Miss Fields's voice, reading aloud, and wondered if she'd come back here, to her native country. If she ever thought of me.

We checked into a modest hotel in Bayswater, catering to international tourists on a limited budget. Yanov's room was directly across the hall from mine. The next steps had been carefully planned back in Moscow. Lee lived alone in a flat in Chelsea, about three miles away. No wife, no children. According to a report from the Soviet embassy in London, he spent most of his time at his office and dined late, at a private club. He arrived home around ten o'clock most evenings. That's when I would go see him, unannounced. I'd practiced variations of what I'd say countless times, with a pair of Molotov's underlings. But that was a far cry from talking to Lee face-to-face.

That night, Yanov drove me in a car lent by the Soviet embassy. Lee's building was a classic three-story Victorian mansion, with steps leading up to the entrance. Yanov stayed in the car while I stepped out, moving briskly to cover up my fear. I walked up to the front door: six buzzers, with *Cooper* listed at the top. I pushed the button firmly, holding it longer than necessary so my finger wouldn't shake. It was almost ten thirty—had he gone to bed already? Then I heard muffled footsteps. The door opened. And there was Lee, wrapped in a dressing gown, yanking me back to the night I'd surprised him in Paris. The night I'd wanted him so much I could barely breathe.

His lips parted, just a touch, as if he wanted to say something but couldn't. Age had brought the expected changes: his golden hair had dulled and looked thinner against his forehead, and the skin around his mouth and chin had begun to sag. But his eyes were exactly the same: alert and curious. I had a fleeting glimpse of the man I'd once loved, beneath the middle-aged caution that kept him silent.

"May I come in?"

Lee's good manners were second nature, no matter how unsettling the situation.

"Of course."

He led the way up to his flat, only once looking back over his shoulder to confirm I was really there. Once inside, he took my hat and offered me a drink. His sitting room was unpretentiously comfortable, with padded chairs and footstools; a half-completed crossword puzzle sat on the arm of a sofa by the fireplace. A masculine room, but a welcoming one.

Lee pulled out glasses and decanters from a side cabinet.

"Whiskey?" he asked, then quickly shook his head, remembering I didn't like it. "Red wine?"

I nodded. Pouring the drinks provided a distraction for another minute, until we'd both sat down, me on the sofa and Lee in a chair opposite.

"You'd better go first," he said, "as I'm utterly at a loss for words."

Lee's breezy humor was intended to put me at ease, but his legs were stiff, his shoulders tense. I'd prepared myself for all sorts of reactions. Decided what I'd say if he was angry and accusing. Or even— flattering myself—if he tried to rekindle our past romance. What I hadn't expected was the surge of feeling that swelled up when I saw him again. The lies we'd told each other no longer seemed to matter. Love, I realized, could be calm and quiet, a determination to put another person's needs above your own.

"I need to explain what happened in Paris."

"Please do," he said. He raised his glass in a toast, giving me a forced smile. I'd thrilled at his smiles, once, but this one left me cold.

I took a sip of my drink, straightening out my thoughts. The best way to proceed was to be as direct as possible.

"You know I was married. What I couldn't tell you was that my husband was high up in the Political Directorate—the secret police. He sent me to Paris to infiltrate the Russian Cultural League and discover if they were planning a coup against the Soviet Union. My husband believed I could gain their trust because my cousin, Mikhail Shulkin, was part of the group. I thought it would be easy—all I'd have to do was go to a few meetings and collect gossip. Then I started hearing about a man called the Patriot, who was working against the Bolsheviks inside Russia. The more I heard about him, the more I started to believe it was possible. I decided to help Mikhail and his friends. Work against the Soviet Union."

"That took nerve."

"I was young," I said dismissively. "I had no idea what I was getting into."

"Did your husband tell you to . . . befriend me?"

"No. You were a complication."

"I'm not sure if that's a compliment."

Caught off guard by his teasing, I felt a familiar flush work its way up from my chest.

"I enjoyed your company," I said. "You had nothing to do with my mission, and I liked that. When you asked me to work for you, I had to get approval from my handler at the Soviet embassy, and I told him you seemed suspicious, so I'd have an excuse to spend time with you. I never really believed you were a spy."

I waited for him to admit it, and he waited for me to continue. Each of us wary.

"It turns out there was a part of the plan they didn't tell me," I continued. "The Patriot never existed. He was a ruse invented by my husband to draw out potential conspirators. I was told the Patriot would be coming to my apartment for a secret meeting, only my husband Alek came instead. He stabbed Mikhail to death, right in front of me. Then he forced me to go with him back to Moscow. I had no choice."

Lee nodded slowly, as if I was confirming facts he already knew.

"I wanted to call you, or write," I said. "But Alek never left me alone. And once we were back in Russia . . ." I shrugged.

"I never believed you did it."

Relief flooded through me like a cleansing rain.

"I saw photos of your cousin's body," Lee went on. "It was a brutal killing, and whatever else you were guilty of, I knew you weren't cruel."

Whatever else you were guilty of. He still didn't trust me, and rightly so. I wanted to thank him, but he brushed me off with a shake of his head before I could speak.

"Why are you here? Another errand for your husband?"

I realized then that Lee's geniality was as brittle as glass. He took a gulp of his whiskey—too much, too fast.

"Alek is dead."

The stark declaration caught him off guard. "I'm sorry."

I didn't want to talk about Alek, not now. I couldn't explain the mix of relief and regret that welled up whenever I thought of him.

"He was executed, not long ago. An enemy of the state. I was arrested and put in prison. Then I was brought to a meeting with Comrade Molotov—I assume you know who that is?"

Lee gave a brisk nod. Any British spy with an interest in Russia would know that name.

"He told me the Soviet government would like to work with the British to keep Germany in check, but nothing was being accomplished officially. He believes discussions might be more productive through informal channels. He knows your position with British intelligence and that you're good at keeping secrets."

"He thought I'd be more likely to trust you because we had an affair." Lee said the words indifferently, though his eyes were fixed on mine.

"Yes."

Lee let out a sharp laugh, the kind that veers close to mockery. "Go on, then. What's the message?"

I handed him the envelope Yanov had given me earlier that evening.

"There are no names attached, for obvious reasons, but these are the terms Stalin is offering for an alliance with Great Britain. If you could see that this is delivered to the proper person, it could benefit both our countries."

Lee took the paper and laid it on the side table next to him, seemingly disinterested.

"Let's say I pass this on. What then?"

I shrugged. "It's not up to me."

The realization seemed to settle over both of us, simultaneously. We were both pieces in a game that was out of our control.

"When you came up to me at that salon in Paris," I began, tentative, "did you know who I was?"

"Not exactly. I recognized you, from the writers' tour in Moscow, but I thought you were just a translator. It did seem a little odd, us running into each other again, and I thought it wouldn't hurt to find out a little more about you. I offered you the translation work, so I'd have an excuse to see you again. I kept lists of everyone I met when I traveled . . ."

"I know."

"Ah yes, that morning. I caught you looking through my diary."

The memory ripped through me like an electric shock. Me at the dining table, Lee in the doorway. Half-dressed and sleepy-eyed, lit by the morning sun.

Lee seemed immune to such nostalgia. "Well, I looked back through the notes I'd kept when I visited Russia, and I saw the name of the translator who came to the hotel reception. Yulia Kishkina. Yet that very same woman introduced herself to me in Paris as Nadia Shulkina. I was worried you targeted me because you knew I was working for the British government."

"I didn't. I believed you were a Socialist."

"I was, until I came back from Russia. Everything I told you up to that point was true. I was appalled by the poverty I saw in England, and I believed revolution was the only way things would change. I truly believed the Soviet Union would lead us all into a brilliant future. Seeing it in person, however . . ."

Lee took another gulp of his whiskey, draining the glass.

"I saw things that made me doubt. The guides never gave us a minute on our own, and the people I met seemed oddly wooden, as if they'd been told what to say. My father knew a few chaps who'd been in military intelligence during the war, and I got talking to one of them when I was back in England. He said the government was looking for people like me, who'd been to Russia and could help make sense of the situation. My father was so pleased when I told him I'd decided to join the service. I'd finally done something to make him proud."

Lee had told me only half his story: a demanding father; the cruelty of boarding school; his eventual rebellion. He'd left out the next part, the disillusionment and questioning. The fact that he'd never given up on receiving his father's approval.

"I sent a short report to London about you and was told Nadia Shulkina was the wife of a prominent Soviet official. I was encouraged to keep seeing you, to find out if you were up to anything suspicious. I made up the whole story about writing a book so we could spend more time together, but it wasn't only that. I genuinely enjoyed your company."

"I enjoyed yours."

It felt, in a sense, as if Lee and I were starting over. Shyly sharing confidences, unsure how they would be received.

"What happened between us," I said. "I wasn't following orders."

"Neither was I."

He looked down at his glass as he said the words. Then he stood up to refill it.

"We heard rumors about the league. The Patriot as well. From an informant inside the Soviet embassy."

It had to have been Patlov. Playing all sides, making nice with the British in case the Bolsheviks fell. Alek had told me he'd been executed, not long after we returned from Paris.

"The murder of Mikhail Shulkin was all over the French papers," Lee told me as he returned to his seat. "Your picture as well. The mysterious Marie Duvall. It was clear to me that the evidence had been

252

planted—the French police aren't efficient enough to name a suspect so quickly. Still, I was staggered. I didn't know if you were part of the plot or an innocent victim. If you were even alive. You could have been killed by the same person who murdered your cousin. The worst of it was, I didn't think I'd ever know the truth."

There were subtle cracks in his composure. A sadness in his eyes, a sag to his shoulders.

"I was angry, of course. Grieving. Not to mention the fear that I'd ruined my career. How could I explain to my superiors in London that I had no idea what you'd been up to?"

"I'm sorry," I murmured, knowing two words weren't enough to convey the depth of my regret.

"No use moping, I told myself, so I decided to dig deeper into Mikhail Shulkin's murder. I wondered if it might have something to do with your husband, so I took a photo of Mr. Semelkov to the apartment building where you'd been living. Two different people said they'd seen a man who looked like him. I found a conductor who'd been on a train into Paris with him. That was enough to get me a meeting in London with the chief of the SIS. Officially, Mikhail Shulkin's murder remains unsolved, with Miss Duvall as the prime suspect. Unofficially, the British and French intelligence services believe Mr. Shulkin was killed by Aleksandr Semelkov, with the assistance of his wife, Nadia. As far as I know, only a few people at the very top levels of government know the full story. I suppose it was a sort of blackmail, to hold over Mr. Semelkov as he rose higher in the Party."

"The Party's in shambles. I don't know where anyone stands anymore."

"What happens when you go back?"

"Comrade Molotov told me I'd be rewarded for my loyalty." The words rang false even as I said them. More quietly, I added, "I don't know if I believe him."

"Well, then, we'll have to find a way to keep you here. Diplomatic negotiations can drag on for years, can't they?"

A laugh burst out of me unexpectedly, a release from the tension. Soon Lee was laughing as well, and the sound rippled between us, a shared delight.

"Where are you staying?" Lee asked. "Is it safe?"

"Safe enough. I have a minder who follows me around—he's waiting in the car outside. Which reminds me, I should be going. He'll get suspicious if I stay too long."

"He's probably wondering what we've gotten up to."

A joke, nothing more, but an embarrassed flush spread across my cheeks. It was ridiculous to think of us recapturing the fire of our youth. I stood up, eager to leave before I did something foolish.

"I'll make sure the letter gets to the prime minister's office," Lee said. "We should meet again, afterward. Where can I reach you?"

I gave him the name of my hotel, and he scribbled on a corner of his crossword puzzle before tearing it off and giving it to me.

"That's the private number for my office. It's manned twenty-four hours a day. Call any time you need to reach me, and if I'm not there, they'll know where to find me."

"I have a favor to ask. Something personal."

Lee nodded, curious.

"I had an English governess when I was growing up, Miss Fields. She was with us from 1913 to 1914, and my father hired her through an agency in London. I don't know anything else, but is there a way you could find her?"

"I'll have someone look into it."

"Thank you. I'd like to try to see her, if possible, while I'm here."

Lee fetched my hat, and something he'd said earlier nagged at me.

"Why did you ask if I was safe?"

"I don't need to tell you that the Soviets have eyes everywhere, even in London. I imagine they have a full surveillance team watching you."

He was right, of course. Why hadn't it occurred to me that Yanov was just one part of a larger operation? I was no safer in London than I had been in Moscow.

"I'll be careful," I said.

"Good. I don't want to worry about you."

He said it kindly, but with a note of dismissal that confused me. I thought we'd made a few tentative steps toward friendship, but he was clearly ready to be rid of me, opening the door abruptly and standing aside. Poised and distant.

"Thank you," I said, as my fingers fluttered with nervous energy. A handshake, a hug?

Lee only nodded as I stepped outside, and the door closed behind me before I could turn around. Swallowing my humiliation, I hurried down the stairs and out of the building. Yanov was leaning against the car, smoking. He questioned me silently, with raised eyebrows, and I nodded before climbing into the back seat. For some reason, I couldn't stop trembling. Delayed shock, I supposed, at seeing Lee again and finally telling him the truth.

Determined to take advantage of whatever time I had, I convinced Yanov to spend the following morning at the British Museum. We strolled through the grand halls in awed silence, admiring treasures the empire's dogged collectors had sent from around the globe. We had lunch in a small tea shop—decadently greasy bacon sandwiches—and walked through Kensington Gardens, two anonymous tourists amid so many others. I wondered how many of the people we passed had been paid to follow me. When we came back to the hotel in the late afternoon, there was an envelope waiting for me at the front desk. I recognized Lee's handwriting.

Vera Fields Weatherby, 20 Tetchly Road, London W9

If your schedule permits, please join me this evening at nine o'clock at the location of our previous meeting. Drinks will be served, casual dress.

"Mr. Cooper wants to meet again tonight," I told Yanov, ripping up the paper before he could read it. I didn't say anything about Miss Fields. Vera.

I'd always imagined her living in a country town, like one of her Jane Austen heroines. But she was here, in London. I told Yanov I was going upstairs to rest and agreed to meet him in the lobby at seven o'clock for dinner. I only hoped I'd have enough time. I waited thirty nerve-racking minutes in my room, then snuck out into the hall. Yanov's door was closed. Back in the lobby, I asked the front-desk clerk for directions to Miss Fields's house, which was close enough to be worth the risk. I left the hotel by the service entrance, in the back, and flagged down the first cab I saw.

It was the second time in less than a day that I'd appeared without warning on an old friend's doorstep. Unlike Lee, Miss Fields didn't keep her emotions in check. She stared, then gasped, then burst into tears.

"Nadia?" She reached out and grabbed my shoulders. "What are you doing here? Oh, my goodness, come in, come in."

She was wearing a flour-spattered apron over a dark-blue dress, beads of sweat pooling along her hairline. Her body had expanded into matronly curves, but her essence was the same as in my memories: bubbly, quick-moving, warm.

"I was just about to take some loaves out of the oven." She waved her hands, flustered. "Come along to the kitchen."

I followed the woman I still thought of as Miss Fields to the back of the house, where sticky bowls and spoons were scattered across a worktable. She took two pans out of the oven, set them on top with a clatter, and wiped her face with a corner of her apron. Then she turned her attention to me.

"Look at you. After all these years."

I smiled shyly, remembering the way she'd made sure my hair and clothes were suitable before we went off on an outing. "More than twenty years."

"How are your parents? You must tell me all the news."

She didn't know. How would she? She'd been completely cut off from our lives.

"They died, a long time ago."

My heart sank a little, at what I'd have to tell her, but I'd only just started when the front door banged open and a voice called out, "Mother! I've run out of red again, so I'm going to the shop after tea!"

Miss Fields gave me an apologetic look. "My daughter, Sophie." She sounded nervous, though I couldn't understand why. "She's at the Royal College of Art, always buying new paints . . ."

I stopped listening when a striking young woman rushed into the kitchen. She was tall and graceful, with a long neck and dark brown hair. Her posture and carriage were an eerie echo of my mother's. Her eyes, with their melancholy tilt, were Sergei's.

I glanced at Miss Fields and saw my suspicions confirmed. She gave a tiny shake of her head: *Not now.*

Turning to her daughter, she spoke brightly, as if nothing was wrong. "Sophie, this is Miss Nadia Shulkina—we knew each other years ago in Russia. Be a dear and bring us tea in the front room, will you?"

Sophie complied without complaint, though she did watch me, curious, as I followed her mother out of the kitchen. As soon as Miss Fields and I sat down on the sofa, she said bluntly, "Yes. She is Sergei's daughter."

For years, I'd wondered why Miss Fields left so abruptly, worrying it had somehow been my fault. I'd been too young to suspect she was pregnant, let alone that she'd had a secret relationship with my uncle. I understood, at last, why my parents had never explained what happened. In our prerevolutionary life, Miss Fields and Sergei belonged to two different worlds: nobility and the staff. Yet I remembered how Sergei made a point of talking to Miss Fields whenever he visited. He'd said it was to practice his English, but it was obvious, now, that he'd been looking for an excuse to spend time with her. All the books they'd exchanged, their lighthearted teasing—those were the subtle signs of two people falling in love. And our lazy summer days in the country had given them countless opportunities to sneak off alone.

Miss Fields asked tentatively, "Is he . . . ?"

I nodded. "A few years ago. It was peaceful. A heart attack in his sleep."

Miss Fields exhaled; she'd been prepared to hear it. "I was madly in love with him. You know what he was like—he made you feel like the most important person in the world."

I'd been dazzled by my uncle, too. He was clever and handsome and romantic and thoughtful. The revolution had tested him—as it did everyone—and there had been times when I bristled at his meek acceptance of our suffering. It wasn't until I was much older that I'd realized what a gift his steadiness had been. I still believed he was the kindest man I'd ever known.

"I'd have done anything for him." Miss Fields looked down, embarrassed to be revealing so much. "It was a form of madness, really. I've never felt like that, before or since."

I'd felt her attention slipping away from me at Priyalko, and with the selfishness of childhood, I'd been irritated when she ignored me. How many of those times had she been thinking of Sergei? How had she managed to make trivial conversation with him in front of the family, knowing they shared such a secret?

"I realized I was expecting early on," Miss Fields continued. "I'd seen the signs with my mother, when she was carrying my younger sisters. Sergei felt terrible—he was the one who'd told me he knew how to avoid it. We both knew there was nothing to be done. I would have to come back to England and give the baby up for adoption."

"Did my parents know?"

Miss Fields nodded. "Your mother barely spoke to me after Sergei told her, but your father was very helpful. He made the arrangements for my travel and insisted I take my wages through the end of the month. Sergei gave me money, too. And a ring, to remember him by."

I heard Sophie approaching down the hall, and Miss Fields and I sat silently as she put down a tea service and plate covered with cake slices. I made a quick calculation: if Miss Fields had been pregnant in the summer of 1914, she would have had the baby later that year or early in 1915, making Sophie twenty-three years old.

"Go out and get your paint, if you like," Miss Fields told her daughter. "We're catching up on old times."

I started to protest. I'd expected Sophie to join us, and I wanted to keep watching her, fascinated by the gestures that seemed resurrected from my past. But I understood her mother's wish to protect her, by hiding the truth of her birth.

"All right," Sophie said cheerfully. She gave me a perfunctory nod. "Nice to meet you. Won't be long, Mother."

Miss Fields poured the tea, and I took a few bites of cake, marking time as we waited for Sophie to leave. Afterward, Miss Fields released a sigh and said, "Thank you. She doesn't know, obviously."

"You were planning to give her up," I said. "What changed your mind?"

"The war," Miss Fields said. "It began only a week or so after I'd come back to England. I was hardly showing, but I went to a home for unwed mothers, to spare my family the shame. My plan was to let my parents think I was still in Russia. Then, after the baby was born, I'd come home and tell them the job was over. Then the war started. I knew my parents would be worried sick about me, off in a foreign country, and they'd start writing the employment agency if they didn't hear from me. I was reading all the papers—the lists of lads dying—and it began to feel wrong to give the baby up. I loved Sergei so much, and this child was all I had left of him. I realized the war would give me a perfect excuse. I could say I'd been married in Russia, but my husband had been killed in battle. By the time Sophie was born, there were already thousands of war widows in Britain. I didn't stand out."

"Who does Sophie think her father is?"

"She knows his name was Sergei. I told her he was a chauffeur who worked for the same family as me, and that he'd been killed in the war. She's never really asked questions. My mother was suspicious, I think. But my brother was killed at Ypres, about six months after Sophie was born, and the baby saved her, really. You can't help but smile when you're holding a little one. I missed Sergei terribly, and I wanted him to know about Sophie, but I didn't think any mail would get through, with the war on and then the revolution . . ."

Miss Fields shrugged. "I'd met Mr. Weatherby by then. I was helping out at a hospital, and he was brought in, missing half his leg, but he was never bitter about it, not once. We began talking and got married three months later. My mother said I'd be more of a nursemaid than a wife, but I knew he'd be a good father to Sophie. Dependable, too—he's a chartered accountant, and you don't need two legs to do sums, do you? We had two boys of our own, Arthur and Stephen. They'll be home soon, and I'd love you to meet them."

I wanted to stay, nestled into her family as if it were my own. But I couldn't risk it. Yanov could have already knocked on my door at the hotel and discovered I'd gone.

"I'm afraid I haven't time," I said, standing. "I have another engagement . . ."

"But I haven't heard anything about you! Have you moved to London?"

"I'm only visiting, but I'll come again, when I can."

Miss Fields followed me to the door, agitated. "I wish you didn't have to rush. Is there some way I can reach you?"

I gave her a swift, tight hug. "I'll explain later, I promise."

"It's been so lovely to see you. I didn't know how much I'd missed you, until right now."

"I'll be back. Soon."

As far as I could tell, I made it back to the hotel undetected. But how could I know for sure? I heard snores from Yanov's room, but I could have been followed to Miss Fields's house, putting her in danger, too. I lay on my bed, reliving the moment when Sophie entered the kitchen. Elation flooded through me at the thought of her, this stranger I already loved. She was my blood, my family, and in a way, so was Miss Fields. We were bound together by Sophie, and I didn't want to give either of them up. The only life I wanted, I realized with iron certainty, was here in London.

There was nothing tying me back to Russia. Alek was dead, and so was his hold over me. My apartment had been reassigned; my possessions confiscated. The men and women I'd socialized with were being imprisoned and killed. I couldn't even see my own brother without putting his children at risk. No matter what I accomplished in England, there was nothing to prevent Molotov from putting me in jail again. He might even order Yanov to dispose of me quietly, once my work was done.

I couldn't face going back. And there was only one person who might find a way for me to stay.

Lee and I didn't have much time to settle on a plan. At his apartment that evening, we were both keenly aware of Yanov waiting outside, marking off the minutes. Fortunately, Lee was used to working under tight deadlines.

Giving me a new name and identity wasn't enough, he told me. "They have to think you're dead. It's the only way they won't come after you. If it happens in public—something that makes the papers—they're more likely to believe it."

After discussing a few grisly possibilities, we decided on a staged accident. Lee would arrange for the car that would supposedly run me down, as well as the ambulance that would sweep my "body" off to safety. But it would only work in the right location.

"We can't do it on any of the main roads," Lee fretted. "If there's too much traffic, you might really get injured. But it has to happen somewhere with witnesses. People who can tell the police and reporters what happened."

And it would be even better if one of those witnesses was in on the scheme, to make sure it all went smoothly. I was the one who suggested Miss Fields; if it happened in front of her house, she could describe the incident however we wanted. The risks were enormous: if any part of the plan failed, I'd be killed by Soviet agents. But I had nothing to lose. I'd rather take the chance and know I tried.

And so, two nights later, I walked down a side street in Maida Vale, a forged French passport in my pocket. A car sped toward me; I fell to the ground. The neighbors heard the screech of tires; one rushed to my side, while another called for an ambulance. I lay completely still as shouts ricocheted around me. When the ambulance arrived, and I was lifted onto a stretcher, I heard Miss Fields whimper, "Such a shame . . ."

The ambulance doors closed, and the vehicle lurched to a start. A hand jostled my arm, and I opened my eyes to see Lee sitting beside me. I hadn't realized he'd be there. He'd only told me my part of the plan: where to be at what time, the best way to fall.

I pushed myself up with one arm and gazed around. I could barely make out Lee's face, and there was another man next to him, his face obscured by shadows. Lee didn't make introductions.

"We'll be stopping at St. Mary's Hospital. You'll be taken to a private room, where you'll find new clothes. Get changed as quickly as you can."

I nodded, cowed by the knowledge of what we'd put in motion.

"We need a photo for the coroner's report." Lee swiped a thick liquid across my cheek; his fingertips were crimson. "Lie down and play dead."

I followed orders and caught the flare of a flash through my eyelids. As the ambulance slowed, Lee pulled a blanket over my body and face. I lay as still as I could while the doors were opened and I was lifted out, keeping my breaths so slow that my chest didn't move. I heard the din of a busy casualty room, and a deep voice barking out directions. Then the stretcher landed with a jolt on a bed, and Lee whispered, "Back in a minute."

I inched out from under the blanket and found myself closed in on all sides by curtains that hung from the ceiling. Beside me was a chair with a neatly folded pile of clothes. I pulled off my shoes so I wouldn't make a sound when I stepped down. The outfit waiting for me fit the classic British stereotype: tweed skirt, white blouse, and wooly cardigan. I wondered if there was a woman at Lee's office who was in charge of dressing secret agents. Or if Lee had bought the clothes himself.

Though I didn't have a mirror or brush, I did the best I could with my hair, smoothing it down and pushing it back behind my ears. I startled when the curtains opened with a sudden whoosh. It was the other man from the ambulance.

"Mr. Cooper sent me. Let's go."

I stiffened when he put his arm possessively around my shoulders.

"Lean into me," he muttered. "Act sick."

He balled up my other clothes and pressed them into my arms. Then he led me down the hospital corridors, a husband taking charge of his fragile wife. I kept my eyes down, scanning the nurses' shoes and stained linoleum. We walked out a back door, down a narrow set of stairs, then into a black car parked across the street. My escape took less than a minute.

It was only once we were driving away that I began to worry. Lee had said he'd be back; why had I trusted this complete stranger?

"Where's Mr. Cooper?" I asked.

"He had things to tend to. He'll come when he can."

I had a dozen other questions, but the man's frosty manner didn't encourage further conversation.

We drove well out of London, along country lanes that curved and dipped. When we finally pulled into a circular front drive, it was too dark to get a good look at the house, though I could tell it was brick and fairly large. All the lights were off. The driver parked behind a tree to the side, where we wouldn't be seen from the road. He led me from the car to the front door, then ushered me quickly inside. I caught only glimpses of a relatively modest country house, with floral curtains and innocuous framed landscapes, before he hurried me upstairs and down to the end of a hall, where he finally turned on a light. The bedroom we entered was small and musty, with mismatched furniture. A place for the least-favored guests.

"You can sleep here," he said.

I walked in, and he closed the door behind me. Would he be guarding me? Or leaving me alone in the house? I felt utterly lost, drifting between one life and another. Neither one safe.

I pulled off my clothes and lay down beneath the coverlet. I closed my eyes, though I knew it would be impossible to sleep. And yet, when I heard a strange clanking noise and opened my eyes, the room was bright with sunshine and Lee was by the window, tying the curtains back.

"Good morning," he said.

I sat up, then pulled the covers higher to hide my slip. *He's seen you in less than that,* an inner voice teased, making me even more flustered. There was a breakfast tray on the table next to the bed and a pot of tea.

Lee poured me a cup—adding sugar and cream—and I took it with a shy nod. I couldn't help feeling we'd been thrown back in time: Lee offering me tea in the late afternoon, sitting at his messy table in Paris.

Lee pulled up a chair, a more somber, paler version of the man I'd once gazed at across that table.

"It's not the nicest room in the house," he said, "but it's the warmest. Hope you slept well."

"Where are we?" I asked.

Lee took a sip of tea, considering his words. "It belongs to my family."

"You live here?"

"No, no. We spent weekends here, when I was a child. My father let it out when my mother died, but we haven't had any tenants for years. The place needs too much work, and I haven't been able to take it on. Too many other demands on my time."

"I thought the government had places to keep people like me. Safe houses."

"They do. But they wouldn't be safe for you."

Lee leaned back in his chair, exhaustion rippling across his face.

"It would have been easy to make you disappear. All we'd have to do is hide you for a few days, then get you on a ship to Argentina or Cape Town. But if you want to live in England, under a new name, we have to make a very convincing case that Nadia Semelkova is dead. Strong enough that the Russians won't come looking for you. Putting you in a safe house would mean following protocol. Dozens of people would be informed along the way, from secretaries and policemen all the way up to the top of the service. Anyone in that group could betray us—the Russians have sources inside British intelligence, just as we have sources in theirs. The only way this works is if everyone, including the SIS, believes you're dead."

"We've done that, haven't we?"

"The accident was only the first step. What happens next is even more important. There needs to be a paper trail, official documents to back up the story. The police in London have Marie Duvall's passport, so it's likely they've already contacted the French authorities. The French police will confirm there's no Marie Duvall living at the address in the passport, and then look more closely into it and find out she's wanted for murder. They'll alert the French intelligence service, who will inform us that our dead French tourist was in fact a Russian agent.

"The chief and I are the only ones at the service who know the truth. He will demand an investigation into Nadia Semelkova's death, which will generate a series of reports, all genuine, all top secret. What I'm counting on is for someone along the way to leak those reports to the Russians. If they see SIS memos berating everyone for botching things up, it should convince them you're really dead."

"What do you want me to do?"

"Stay here a few days while I sort out your papers. I'll get you new clothes as well. Then we can talk about where you'll go next."

"I was hoping London."

He knew I wanted to be near Sophie and Miss Fields, who'd already proved her loyalty—and her discretion—by playing her part in my supposed death.

"The country might be safer," Lee said.

I pictured Yanov and the rest of Molotov's agents fanning out across the city, tracing my every step, and the uncertainty of my future suddenly overwhelmed me. I had no nightdress or toothbrush, no comb or hairpins, no clean underwear or stockings. I'd reinvented myself before, with Alek. But I was older, now, with no guidance. No one telling me who to be.

Lee stood up. "Once you've dressed and had breakfast, I'll show you around."

Though the house had a faded, neglected air, it had been charming once, with cozy, wallpapered sitting rooms and old-fashioned wide-planked floors. Walking around it seemed to revive Lee. In the kitchen, an older woman with her hair in a kerchief was sweeping the floor, while the man who'd dropped me off last night was reading a newspaper at the table.

"This is Mrs. Sanders from the village. She'll see to your food. You've already met Danny."

Danny gave me a quick nod and turned back to his paper. Neither he nor Lee offered further information.

From the kitchen, Lee led me into the back garden. The mangy rosebushes hadn't been pruned in years, and the flower beds revealed only spots of color amid the weeds. But I could imagine the space as it was meant to be. Just beyond, an overgrown lawn stretched toward a stone fence and curved hills, a rural panorama that seemed dropped from one of Miss Fields's books.

"It's lovely," I said.

"It used to be. Gone a bit wild, I'm afraid."

"I could do some weeding."

"Don't feel obliged."

"I'd like to." Being outside made me feel hopeful, like the dogged little bluebells determined to be seen. "Remember what I told you, in Aldonne?"

I stopped, belatedly embarrassed. We'd said all sorts of things to each other in Aldonne, much of it in bed.

"I like being outside, in the country," I went on hurriedly. "Working in the garden will keep me busy."

"Then you're welcome to do as much as you like." Lee's eyes moved slowly across the garden, as if searching for something. "My mother loved it here. I've been avoiding it, for years, but it would be good to see it brought back."

"Like *The Secret Garden*."

"Pardon?"

"A book Miss Fields and I read together. A long time ago."

It dawned on me, slowly, that we could be talking about ourselves as well. If we were willing to dig and pull, we might be able to tear up the past and plant something new. I could picture myself scrubbing the neglect from this house and sitting in the garden to sketch. It already felt like a place I wanted to live.

Was it because I was here with Lee?

"You said I would be here a few days . . . ," I began, unsure of what to say and what Lee wanted. "Could it be longer?"

Lee smiled, a flash of his old self. "Stay as long as you want. This place could use a good housekeeper."

I smiled back. "You want me to work for you again?"

"I'll pay you a good wage. Better than I did in Paris."

I couldn't tell if he was serious. Hiring me would make sense, according to his plan. It would give me a place to hide out, a world away from the SIS offices and Lee's everyday life.

I braced myself to make the best of it, either way. Then I felt the back of Lee's hand brush against mine. A touch that could mean nothing—or everything.

"I was only joking," he muttered. "You'll stay as my guest. For however long you like."

It was enough to make me step closer. To ease into the conversation I'd been too afraid to start.

"I was sure you'd be married by now," I said.

"I came close, once."

He said it brusquely, discouraging further questions. Selfishly, I wondered who she was. Whether she'd looked like me.

"I called off the engagement. Didn't seem fair to her, given my profession. I could be called away at all hours and never be able to tell her where I was going. I'd have made her miserable."

"I'm sorry," I said, with genuine regret. I could hear the pain in his voice. Sense the shadow of loneliness.

"There was also the matter of not trusting my own judgment." Lee gave me a wry half smile. "I had trouble believing what any woman told me, after my massive lapse of judgment in France."

I could laugh it off. Push these reminiscences firmly into the past and create a new way forward, as old friends. Or I could take a risk. Tell him the truth and see where it led.

"Those days in Aldonne . . . ," I began, tentative.

"The days you forgot to tell me you were a Soviet spy?"

Like a boxer absorbing a hit, I accepted his sarcasm. Getting the poison out was the only way to heal.

"It made me sick, not telling you. But everything I said in private"— *in your arms, whispered against your neck*—"all of that was true."

Lee stared at me, impassive, a judge who needed further evidence to be convinced.

"When you asked me to marry you, I wanted it more than anything. But Alek never would have let me go. And he was so jealous, he'd have come after you, too. Leaving was the only way to keep you safe."

I'd tried so hard to be strong, for so long. I no longer had any defense against the tears that streamed down my face, or the regret that prevented me from saying any more. Lee and I had shared something precious and rare, and even if he agreed to give me a second chance, we were different people, now. It would never be the same.

Lee reached out to brush my cheek, and I leaned into his touch. A lifetime of expectations seemed to gradually dissolve. I'd done my best to protect Mama and Vasily after Papa's death, sacrificing my youth to Alek's demands. I'd reinvented myself as a loyal Communist comrade, unwittingly leading the way to my cousin's murder. I didn't know what I was meant to do next, or who I was supposed to be. I knew only that I wanted to stay here, in this house with its echoes of Priyalko. And I wanted to be with Lee—in whatever way that was possible.

Lee wiped my tears and pulled me close. It felt right, like I'd come home.

18 September, 1938

To: All Staff, SIS

From: The Office of the Director

It is with great regret that I announce the resignation of Mr. Lee Cooper, effective immediately. Mr. Cooper has been a great asset to our service for nearly two decades, serving in various positions in London and overseas. His dedication and persistence were known to many in this office who worked with him, and I know he will be missed.

In order to forestall any rumors, Mr. Cooper has permitted me to inform you of the reason for his departure. His health has been in a state of decline for some years, and the responsibilities of his position have added to the strain. On the advice of his doctor, Mr. Cooper has decided to retire to a quiet life in the country. While he welcomes personal correspondence from his former colleagues, he will no longer have an SIS security clearance and therefore cannot be consulted on any matter pertaining to our work.

His address is below, should you wish to write him directly.

WILTSHIRE, ENGLAND

August 1939

It was a small wedding. Lee and me, repeating our vows at the altar of the village church. Lee's friend Danny, who'd come down from London after finishing one of his mysterious "jobs." All five of the Weatherbys. Vera—as I'd learned to call her—beamed from the front row. Sophie, my sole bridesmaid, stood beside me, looking ethereal in a lavender dress. Her happiness was more restrained than her mother's, but just as genuine.

She still didn't know the truth about her father. Vera had started by confiding in her husband, not long after she'd introduced us. I understood why John Weatherby had appealed to Vera when she was an unwed mother with an uncertain future. He was a decent, steady man, who took the news of his wife's long-ago love affair in stride.

"He said family is family," Vera told me later. "He doesn't mind you spending time with Sophie—you're her cousin, after all. I'll tell her about Sergei, when I'm ready." She paused, hesitant about her next confession. "I still miss him, sometimes."

"Me, too," I said.

In those first weeks after my staged death, I'd begun easing into a new life and name. In what I hoped would be my final act of reinvention, I became Nathalie Dubois, a French widow who'd been hired to get the house in order before Mr. Cooper moved back in. Other than occasional shopping excursions to the village, I kept to myself, conscious of the gossip that trailed me like a shadow. Why had Mr. Cooper brought in a Frenchwoman to spiff up a British country home? Was Mr. Cooper leaving his job voluntarily, or had he been sacked? What exactly had he been doing all those years in London, anyway?

They must have assumed I was his mistress long before we shared the same bedroom. We moved slowly in those matters, too. Long conversations and cautious kisses before we proceeded any further. We both sensed the potential of what might be, hovering between us, but we felt around its edges first, to make sure it would hold. The possibility of love was enticing, but what kept me going were the practical tasks that gave order to my days: cleaning and mending the curtains; polishing scuffed furniture; sorting out the contours of the garden as new plants emerged and old ones were torn out. Mrs. Sanders did the cooking, and she and I coexisted peacefully, developing a mutual respect. Her husband came three days a week to do the heavy work in the garden, and eventually, the two of them put in a good word for me with the villagers. Once I'd proved myself a hard worker, I began to be greeted with nods and polite smiles. But no questions, and I'd never been more grateful for that stoic British reserve.

The house's routines shifted slightly after Lee moved in. At first, I took my midday meal in the kitchen, with Mrs. Sanders, until Lee turned to me one morning in the garden and said, "It's a lovely day—we should eat outside." Without it ever being officially discussed, we began eating together. When he wasn't working in his library with the door closed—crafting the final documents that would end his career—he took up whatever job needed doing, repainting the bedrooms and sorting through boxes of family heirlooms. From time to time, he'd spend an evening at the local pub, where he gradually struck up friendships with the farmers who were our neighbors. At first, they were taken aback to see the master of what they called simply "The Manor" walk into the Four Bells; Lee's father and grandfather would never have set foot inside. But times were changing, even in the conservative countryside, and what we jokingly came to describe as Lee's "stag nights" became another string binding us to our new home.

Winter brought an end to the walks we'd take through the fields after preparing the garden for cold weather. Mrs. Sanders left earlier each day, to get home before dark, and Lee and I were left with more hours alone, by fireplaces that never quite warmed the cavernous downstairs rooms. We found other ways to fight off the chills. We abandoned our separate, icy beds and began sleeping together, burrowing into each other and drifting off with affectionate whispers. Mrs. Sanders must have been suspicious, though she was too loyal to say anything that might be taken as a critique of her employer. Still, she looked relieved rather than surprised when Lee told her we were getting married. She even gave me a hug and said, "I couldn't be happier for you both."

There'd been no dramatic proposal. I simply looked at Lee one day and said, "We should get married."

"It's about time!" He laughed. "I didn't want to ask. You've already turned me down once."

I blushed with remembered shame and started to apologize. Lee stopped me with a squeeze of his hand.

"I'm only teasing. I would have brought it up months ago, only I wanted to make sure you were happy here. That you wanted to stay."

I couldn't blame him for being cautious. How could he be sure I wasn't with him simply because I had nowhere else to go?

"This is my home now," I said. "With you."

I would have married him the next day at the magistrate's office, but given our pasts, things weren't quite so simple. Lee wanted to wait at least a year past the date of Marie Duvall's death, to ensure the whole incident had been forgotten. He'd been going into London for occasional, informal meetings with Roger Ballantry, the SIS director's chief deputy, and so far, there were no indications the Soviets believed Nadia Shulkina was still alive. A minor spy's fatal accident in Britain was irrelevant to Molotov's most urgent concern: stopping Hitler before his army marched into territory dangerously close to Russia. Lee had passed my message from Stalin to the prime minister's office, but as far as we knew, nothing had come of it.

The wedding was delayed still further by the stubborn workings of bureaucracy. I needed papers in my new name to apply for a marriage license, and finding a discreet forger wasn't easy without access to SIS resources. Then there was the matter of finding a day when all the Weatherbys could come. Sophie was taking an art course in Cornwall for most of the summer, and I refused to have the ceremony without her. She was adorably thrilled when I asked her to be my bridesmaid.

We finally settled on the last Saturday in August. I'd initially assumed we'd have a quick civil ceremony, but in time, I began to see the appeal of a church wedding. Standing in an office and signing papers would remind me too much of my marriage to Alek, and I wanted this time to be different. I liked the idea of Lee and me starting our new lives in a place with a sense of history, where so many others had said the same vows. I also guessed—correctly—that a church wedding would make an important statement to our neighbors: we are part of this village, and we intend to stay.

Mrs. Sanders laid out a buffet of desserts back at the house; Vera had come a day early to help me get ready and bake the cake. She was an enthusiastic but haphazard cook, and Lee jokingly asked me if her creation had been inspired by the Leaning Tower of Pisa. But it tasted delicious, and the sun came out in the late afternoon, and Vera's husband took photos in the garden, and I smiled until my cheeks ached.

A telegram arrived soon after we ate, a concise congratulations from Roger Ballantry.

"He's buttering me up," Lee muttered, so only I would hear.

A few days before, Molotov had signed a nonaggression pact with Ribbentrop, Hitler's minister of foreign affairs. After unsuccessfully courting other countries to stand against Hitler, Stalin had done an about-face and allied with his former enemy. It felt like a sudden, giant step toward the war everyone said was inevitable.

"Roger asked if I'd be interested in coming back aboard," Lee continued. "My expertise with the Russians could be useful."

I wanted to shake my head and say no. I'd finally escaped that den of lies and didn't want Lee to go back in. But it would be different, if we were at war. Lee would feel bound to serve his country, in whatever way he was needed. Maybe there was a way I could help, too. But I didn't want to think about it on my wedding day.

Later, when Arthur and Stephen Weatherby were playing croquet on the lawn with Lee and the vicar, and Sophie was helping Mrs. Sanders clean up in the kitchen, Vera pulled me aside. She visited so often that we'd dubbed one of the bedrooms "The Weatherbys'," and that's where she took me, telling me she'd brought a present.

"You didn't have to," I protested. "The cake was enough."

"I'd be giving it to you anyway, wedding or not."

I stood by the window as she went to the dresser on the other side of the room. I could hear the whoops of the Weatherby boys and their father's shouted encouragement to Lee: "Show my lads how it's done!" Would Lee and I have children? I hoped it wasn't too late, though I couldn't shake off my ingrained impulse to expect the worst. Lee would be a wonderful father. But I also knew I was enough to make him happy. He'd told me so many times, I'd come to believe it.

Vera pulled a flat, rectangular box from one of the drawers.

"I packed this away years ago. Had it framed, for the occasion."

She opened the box, and I saw a flash of silver. The object, when she handed it over, was unexpectedly heavy, weighted down by a layer of glass and metal. It was a photograph of a group of people, standing in front of a house. As my eyes strayed from face to face, the names came to me as whispers from the past. Mama. Papa. Vasily. Sergei. Our housekeeper, Elena, and her husband, Yuri. Me, in a white dress trimmed with lace, standing in front of Miss Fields.

"You remember how your mother was always pushing the family to pose for pictures," Vera said. "I stole this one, the day I left."

I recognized the front steps of our summer house. The weather-beaten chairs on the porch in the background. I remembered Mama corralling us all into place, excited to try out her new timer. How she fussed from behind the lens, then rushed over for the shot. She'd taken hundreds of photos that year. This was the only one that hadn't been lost.

I didn't mind crying in front of Vera. I knew she'd be pleased, to see how much her gift moved me. She teased me sometimes about being too reserved—"It's all right to have fun, now and then!"—but with her encouragement and Lee's, I was learning to be softer. No longer seeing my emotions as a weakness.

"I want us to talk to Sophie, together," Vera said. "It's time she knew about Sergei, and I'd like her to hear about him from you."

My first impulse was to tell Vera it should be a private conversation between mother and daughter. Sophie might be ashamed or hurt; she could get angry. Then I realized that's exactly why Vera wanted me there, as a buffer.

"Let's go find her," I said. "Take a walk together."

We were family, after all. Sophie was my cousin. Had things gone differently, Vera would have been my aunt. After so many losses, I'd cling to whoever I had left.

I clutched the picture to my chest. Vera had given me more than a present; she'd returned a piece of my past. From now on, I could look at the faces of the people I'd loved. I could see their faces from a time when they were happy. Smiling and expectant, radiant in the afternoon sun.

AUTHOR'S NOTE

Write what you know" is a well-known literary cliché. For *Red Mistress*, I followed the advice of novelist and writing teacher Colum McCann: "Write toward what you want to know." I'd always been curious about the Russian Revolution, wondering how such a vast country could be transformed so completely, in such a short amount of time. After reading a stack of Russian history books, I decided I was brave enough—or crazy enough—to attempt a story set during that turbulent period.

While Nadia and her family are fictional characters, their experiences are based in fact. After the Bolsheviks took power in October 1917, members of the Russian nobility had their property confiscated and were denied food rations; some were attacked in their homes and killed. *Former People: The Final Days of the Russian Aristocracy*, by Douglas Smith, was a particularly helpful resource, tracking the devastation suffered by two extended families. When I fulfilled a longtime history-nerd goal and did further research at the Library of Congress in Washington, DC, I read memoirs written by Russians who'd escaped to Europe in the years immediately after the revolution. They described the day-to-day realities of survival, whether it was going barefoot all summer to avoid wearing out your only pair of shoes or trading with a black-market "bagman." In the words of one such writer: "For a ham, people take off their suits, coats, and hats on the spot. A sheet secures three days of life, a towel brings half a pound of bread, and even the glass from a picture frame can be exchanged."

I was inspired by the resilience of some young aristocrats who did their best to adapt. Some, like Nadia, took pride in being good workers. Others, like Vasily, fought against the Communists during the Civil War, but were later recruited by the Red Army, which had a shortage of trained officers. Tragically, no matter how much they tried to prove themselves, many were later executed during Stalin's purges of the 1930s—simply because of the family they'd been born into.

The Italics Are Mine, a memoir by the Russian writer Nina Berberova, was helpful in describing the Russian émigré experience in 1920s Paris. *Flappers: Six Women of a Dangerous Generation*, by Judith Mackrell, introduced me to Tamara de Lempicka, a provocative Russian painter who was the inspiration for Maya de Severin. While Maya's story is fictional, my descriptions of her paintings are based on works by de Lempicka. *Memoirs of Montparnasse*, by the Canadian writer John Glassco, was a chance discovery at my local library that vividly described a world of artistic and sexual experimentation. Let's just say that some of the stereotypes about 1920s Paris are true.

Figuring out how spies of that era operated was more challenging. From reading the official history of the British Secret Intelligence Service (SIS), I learned that SIS documents were routinely destroyed during that time period; there was no thought of saving them for posterity (or future historical-fiction writers). However, the Patriot plot in *Red Mistress* was inspired by a true story. After the Russian Revolution, the major powers of Western Europe were understandably concerned. Would Communism spread throughout the continent, as Lenin vowed it would? Meanwhile, the new Soviet government in Moscow worried about all those formerly noble Russians who'd emigrated. Were they planning a counterrevolution, funded by their new Western friends? To find out, they set a trap. The Soviet government created a fake group called the Trust, which was supposedly working to overthrow the Communists, and lured Russian émigrés and foreign governments into supporting it. The British operative Sidney Reilly (later known as the "Ace of Spies") was lured to the Soviet Union with the promise that he'd meet one of the Trust's representatives. Instead, he was captured and killed.

There are hundreds of accounts of the Russian Revolution, and I haven't come close to reading them all. But if you're looking for a readable starter book that explains how it happened, I highly recommend *The Russian Revolution: A New History*, by Sean McMeekin. One of the most important things I learned while writing *Red Mistress* is that the Russian Revolution wasn't a single uprising—it was a series of events, each of which had multiple potential outcomes. The Bolsheviks were a relatively fringe movement, until they took advantage of political squabbling to seize power. They created the Soviet Union through ruthlessness, not persuasion. While Alek is not based on any one real person, I gave him the qualities that Vladimir Lenin and other leading Bolsheviks shared: an unswerving belief in his own righteousness and indifference to the suffering his movement caused.

ACKNOWLEDGMENTS

Thanks, eternal gratitude, and hugs to the people who supported me along the way:

My husband, Bob, for keeping the household running when the book took over and I ignored everyone. Thanks for letting me sleep in.

Clara, James, and Alan for being quiet on those mornings I was sleeping in and for making me laugh on the days when I really needed to. Extra thanks to Clara for helping me work through some tricky plot points and for naming Lee (among others).

My parents, Mike and Judy Canning, for surrounding me with books while I was growing up.

My sister, Rachel, who somehow manages to be sympathetic when I complain, "Writing is *hard*!"

My brother-in-law, Simon Motamed, the ultimate Fun Uncle. Someday I'll find a way to put you on the payroll as my PR and social-media manager.

Danielle Egan-Miller, my agent, for helping me find a way forward from a not-so-promising beginning.

My editors, Erin Calligan Mooney, Jenna Free, and Jodi Warshaw, for their positive vibes and encouragement throughout the editing process.

My fellow Lake Union authors, for being the ultimate sounding board for all things writing- and publishing-related. I'm grateful to have you as my virtual water-cooler buddies.

Rachel Gottlieb, for the Russian advice.

There are many friends who supported me in ways big and small as I was writing *Red Mistress*, and I'm afraid I'll leave someone out if I try to list them all. (I'll thank you in person!) I dedicated this book to Mike Bailey, who sparked my interest in early-Soviet-era Russia. He and Mary Jean Babic were the first people I talked to about *Red Mistress*, back when it was just a vague idea we jokingly referred to as "Sexy Bolshevik." Mike and Mary Jean, thanks for making me believe I could do this.

ABOUT THE AUTHOR

Photo © 2019 Rebecca Gould Photography

Elizabeth Blackwell is the author of *On a Cold Dark Sea*, *In the Shadow of Lakecrest*, and *While Beauty Slept*. A graduate of Northwestern University and the Columbia University Graduate School of Journalism, she lives outside Chicago with her family and piles of books she is absolutely, positively going to read someday. For more information about the author, visit www.elizabethblackwellbooks.com.